A Fistful
of
Marigolds

Joyce Worsfold

Fishcake Publications

<u>A Fistful of Marigolds</u>

Published by Fishcakes Publications
71 Royds Avenue, Linthwaite, Huddersfield, HD7 5SA

www.fishcakepublications.com

ISBN 978-1-909015-21-0
Kindle Edition

© Joyce Worsfold 2014

About the Author

Joyce Worsfold

Joyce Worsfold was a teacher for 25 years and absolutely loved it.
Since retirement she paints, writes and gardens, has qualified as a
reader in the Church of England and has been known to enjoy the
occasional afternoon tea with lots of lovely friends. She is married to
David and has 3 talented children who are far too old to have ages
mentioned here, and 3 amazing grown up grandchildren.

"Grateful thanks to everyone who has supported, helped and
encouraged me on this writing journey. Special thanks to Sue Clark
and Val Turner for reading, Martin Rothery at Fishcake Publications
for editing, to all at Holmfirth Writers Group, the Association of
Christian Writers, and the National Association of Writers Groups for
just being there whenever I needed them.

Thanks also to all my lovely friends at St John's, Lepton and to all the
dedicated, caring teachers I have had the honour to work with.

Last, but certainly not least, my family to whom I owe everything."

Contents

September 1973

Just my luck, the first day back and playground duty! Today of all days, when the past grabs me by the throat, pummels my face and threatens suffocation.

I fasten up my heavy-duty duffel coat and peer into the mirror. I look as if I've seen a ghost; pale as paper with freckles imprinted like scars, my hair like torn beech leaves, lifeless and blown into a heap. I lift my chin and square my shoulders.

I will *not* be beaten; underneath this fragile exterior is a springy strength. I just have to search for it!

The wind is howling around the playground, funneling through the hotchpotch of buildings, and acres of sodden grass on bleak playing fields. Children career around madly; coats fastened like cloaks that billow behind them like the sails of ships. Empty crisp packets swoop and swerve, browning apple cores roll and revolve.

'Miss, Simon's got loads of little balloons and he's giving them away but he won't give me any.'

'Yes Miss and Wayne's in the toilets and you can get gallons in 'em and he's using 'em as water bombs.' This is from a tiny mite whose hair is dripping, her shoes pool around her. *What on earth is going on*?

I hurry to the boy's toilets, with a caterpillar of the curious following close behind. Everywhere I look children are blowing into white latex. I had not realized they could be blown so big! There are long distended ones filled with water, some splattered against fat cheeks, others fitted around chubby hands. A few hang limply from noses and Darren Dunford has them hanging like snot from every finger. Thankfully none of them appear to be fitted to the appendages they were designed for!

Condoms, condoms everywhere! Where on earth have they all come from? Has some child raided his parents' prolific hoard? Have they been nicked from the chemist? I stand amazed as I notice little foil packets bowling around the playground, hundreds of little packages all bearing the legend 'Durex'. I bend down and begin to scoop up as many as I can,

'Come on children, let's see who can pick up the most packets, quickly now!' Always keen for a challenge they begin to chase the skittering wrappers. I gaze around in search of someone sensible and spy Linda.

'Oh Linda, love, go into school, please and get Mr Bullivant, then you can ring the bell.' I'm standing, intent on stuffing as many packets as I can find into a cardboard box, retrieved from the litter bin, when a deep voice startles.

'Hello, hello, hello, what's going on 'ere then? Mm, very interesting, is that a week's supply or what?' I gaze up into the face of Mike, our community constable, and feel my face redden.

'It's, well...the children they...' I start to giggle and find I can't stop.

Don Bullivant, Deputy Head, appears in the wake of Linda and I try to explain. Don is an open-faced cheerful, man with smoky eyes that twinkle behind brass spectacles. He smooths his white hair, gazes into the carton and says, 'Well! You have been busy,' then, gazing around the playground quips, 'It's a mighty fine science lesson you've been conducting Miss Johnson, though a trifle advanced I feel for infants.'

Mike grins wickedly. 'Aye, and if it catches on around here, you could all be redundant.'

Don offers to see the children back into school saying, 'I'll leave it to you to explain to *her majesty*, it should be an interesting conversation.'

I walk down the corridor suddenly quite sober. What will I say? Will the Head even know what they are? Do I call them condoms or...I knock nervously and wait for the flashing green light, 'ENTER' it says. I clutch the carton close to my chest.

"Ah. Kathy, shouldn't you be with your class?' My heart thumps ferociously. She sits like royalty, impeccably groomed in dark-green crimplene. Her greying hair tightly permed. She peers over her spectacles and waits.

'There has been an incident, er well several incidents in the playground, Miss Denton and I...well...'

She takes off her spectacles and waves them about, 'Well you'd better bring them in, dear!'

'No, no! It's not a fight or anything it's just that, well, the children have been...'

She puts the spectacles on again but they slip sideways. I press my lips tightly together so I don't laugh. I clear my throat. 'The children have all been playing w...with...Durex!'

She gazes at me in horror, brown eyes wide with shock, 'Durex!

You mean the paint! They've been throwing paint?'

'No, no, no, that's Dulux. No, Durex are...' I hesitate, then search the box for a dry one and hold it up bravely, 'condoms!' She looks puzzled, and then it seems as if splotches of memory quiver. The silence lengthens. She licks her lips. She taps absently on the desk and adjusts the pristine blotter.

'Do you know where the children acquired these...things?'

'No, Miss Denton, I don't.' Silence again. Then I have a brain wave, 'But the Community Constable is in school and he is aware of...the situation.'

'Oh, right, well can you point him in the direction of Mr. Bullivant and together they can deal with...things. Now you must go back to your classroom, my dear.'

'Yes, I'll just,' I look round wildly for somewhere to put the box of offending rubbish. She pushes the waste paper basket with her foot,

'Oh just pop them in here dear, Mrs Biggins will see to it later.'

I am sure that she will! But someone had better explain to her first or heaven knows what gossip will be circling the estate by this evening.

I return to my classroom where Don is telling the children about his recent holiday on the Isle of Wight. I inform him of Miss Heaton's wishes and he beats a hasty retreat. The rest of the day passes quietly, for once.

Getting to know You

Sometimes the memories overwhelm unexpectedly; fight them, push them away. My brain feels glued up, sticky. Take deep breaths! *Breathe*! I look around my living room. Peace. *Breathe!* The pale green carpet and white painted furniture lit by the afternoon sun. *Breathe!* My books, my music, all arranged for my delight.

It's in the past. It's okay. I can cope. As long as I never talk about it, I can keep it hidden in the cellar of my soul. There's too much emphasis nowadays on talking. Where does talking get you? No! There will be no weeping in corners, no blame, this way no one else will be hurt. I swallow, there's a stone in my chest.

'There's too much to do to waste time in sniveling,' I say out loud. I reach for the pile of exercise books on the coffee table. Now, what news do my seven year olds have for me today?

Their spelling is really something else! Linda has written, 'The man in the toishop raped up the doll and put it in a box.' I can feel my face crack into a smile.

That's right, kids, bring it on!

Robert has written about me, 'My teacherr wears black shinny shoes and black tits, she has orange hair and a spot on her chin.'

I glance down at my black nylon clad legs and vow to go for American tan next time!

A brief knock is followed by a voice, a deep, dark-chocolate voice. It's Mike, 'Hello there!' He lumbers in, a mountain of a man with flushed face and lopsided grin. I feel his lips brush my hair, as he bends awkwardly towards me. He smells of peppermint and woodsmoke. I clear my throat, stand up and offer tea.

'Don't mind if I do.' He hands me a creased paper bag. 'Paradise slices, I know you like them."

'Thanks that's…brilliant!'

'Eh! What's wrong? Have you been crying? Are you OK?' He holds my elbows lightly and leans towards me. His eyes are like reflected sky.

'Just a bit of a cold,' I sniff. 'What have you been doing, lighting bonfires?'

"Putting them out more like, you know what the kids around here are like for pre-empting bonfire night.'

'But that's months away!'

'Aye well, some of 'em 'ave been chumping since Easter. Caught three of your seven year olds in the woods this morning, dragging half a tree, their sticky hands clutching axes and a rusty old saw.'

'Axes?' It's a wonder any of them make it to their teens, talk about safety first! 'Well I suppose it'll keep them off the rubbish tip for a while. Lord knows what they pick up there.'

'Aye well, we all know what they picked up last, condom seconds! What next I wonder.' We both laugh and I relax. I warm the teapot and put in two bags, he likes it strong. He slides his arms around my waist and my stomach churns.

'And how's my girl, then?' I feel a wave of irritation. 'Have you thought any more about coming away with me at half term?'

I bite my lip, concentrating hard on cutting my paradise slice into tiny, neat portions. The marzipan oozes, it's rich with raisins and cherries, my mouth waters.

'I don't know, Mike. I like you, you're a lovely bloke, but I'm not ready for a serious relationship. After all, we've only been out a couple of times!' His eyes are masked.

'Single rooms, of course!' he says. I can't help laughing,

'I don't think that would work, knowing you!' A wave of irritation crosses his face, then a big smile that does not quite reach his eyes.

'Are you casting aspersions?'

'No, I'm stating facts. But Mike, let's take it slowly, please.' Disappointment covers him. He drinks his tea.

'OK, no sweat! Look I was wondering, the church is having a medieval banquet at half term and I've been asked to go as Henry VIII, guest of honour and all that. Being Community Constable has its perks you know.'

'Mm, typecasting, more like!' I pat his spreading girth.

'Well, will you come as one of my wives?'

'Not an enthralling prospect, how does the rhyme go? *Divorced, beheaded, died, divorced, beheaded, survived.*'

'Ah, I see what you mean.' He rubs his chin.

'Maybe I'd better be Katherine Parr, at least she survived.'

'Oh, I don't know, she might have been a bit boring.'

'Mm, well, I think I'll stick with boring. Yes, it sounds like fun, I'd like to come.'

His radio begins to bleep. He answers, and then clumsily leaps to his feet.

'Sorry, got to go. Fire on Bismark Terrace.'

He plants a kiss on my cheek and is gone, leaving me sick with apprehension. I search wildly in my memory; 'Who, in my class, lives in Bismark Terrace?'

Bismark Terrace

'*What time is it, our Ali? I'm starving. How much longer is me mam going to be?*' Robert jumped onto the sofa and threw a cushion across the room. '*Can we 'ave some chips? I'll go to 't chippy. Me belly thinks me throat's cut.*'

Ali sat cross-legged and continued to stare at the television, winding her hair around her finger.

'*Ali! We're hungry. Can we 'ave some chips?*'

'*No we can't 'ave chips, we've got no money, stupid. You've already had bread and jam.*'

The twins, Jade and Ruby, were making a doll's house from a cardboard box. It had a lounge, a kitchen and two bedrooms. Jade was cutting flowers from a catalogue that they had found on the door mat and Ruby was sticking them on the bedroom walls, using a flour and water paste that she'd made herself. As she snipped, her tongue curled around like a pink snake in search of prey.

'*It's going to be a palace, is this, a right bloody palace,*' said Ruby.

'*Yes and it's going to 'ave a state of the ark kitchen, state of the ark!*' Jade said proudly.

'*Art, state of the art,*' Ali corrected but no-one seemed to hear.

'*Yes, it'll even 'ave a fridge!*'

'*Wish we 'ad a fridge,*' moaned Robert.

'*Yes, that'd be good then we could 'ave ice-cream and make our own lollies,*' said Jade.

'*I'd make rhubarb ones cos I like rhubarb and I've never 'ad a rhubarb lolly, 'ave you had a rhubarb lolly our Ali?*' Ali stood and struck a model girl pose,

'*Never, in all my twelve years but, very soon, when I am an air hostess, I will have lollies made from…champagne. So there!*'

Amber was leaning against the sofa, sucking her thumb. She released it and cuddled her knees, her blue eyes staring, vacantly, ahead. Ali noticed her flushed face and worried that she was going to get another chest infection.

'*Amber, are you feeling all right?*' No reaction. Ali raised her voice, '*Amber are you feeling poorly?*'

The thumb went back into her mouth and she shook her head, her blonde curls trembling. '*Just hungry,*' she said.

Ali looked at the clock, her mum must have gone straight to the pub. She sighed and went into the kitchen. There were two large potatoes sprouting prolifically in the vegetable rack. The chip pan was on the cooker. She stood on tiptoe and peered in. It smelled funny, but there was plenty of fat with a lot of black bits floating about.

She lit the gas ring and was just about to start peeling potatoes when she heard a scream from the other room. She ran to investigate, slamming the door behind her. Jade was howling and clutching the side of her face. Ruby was standing, with an expression of surprised horror, holding at least six inches of her sister's black hair and the scissors.

Ali felt the anger rise up in her like a hot flood and she flew across the room, her face contorted hands like claws. She grabbed Ruby's arms and ran her nails down the flesh, tearing and scratching. Blood bubbled and flowed.

'You stupid, stupid, bitch. You silly fucking cow, I'm going to fucking kill you!'

She hit out in a frenzy, thumping, slapping, nipping, scratching.

Suddenly, there was a sound of retching and a frightened moan. She turned; Amber was by the kitchen door, bending double as she vomited her face as white as lard. Robbie ran over to her and patted her on the back.

'All right, all right. You'll be all right. Don't cry.' Suddenly he jumped. 'Bloody hell!' he shrieked, 'This door's red hot!'

Ali was there in an instant, though she felt like someone in a slow motion film. She was walking through treacle, her brain melting, and eyes stinging. She put her hand out to grasp the door knob but Robbie thrust her to one side.

'Don't open the door!' he screamed. His breath was coming in gasps now. He must try to remember. The fireman who'd come to school, what had he said? Keep the doors closed. Have an escape plan. He looked towards the windows. Uncle Kev had boarded them up last week, because they couldn't afford to replace the broken ones.

'The hall,' he commanded, 'we'll have to get out through the front door.'

He ran, dragging Amber with him. The hall was tiny, only six feet square. There was a tall wooden door with an oval leaded window at the top. There was no key.

Ruby and Jade began to cry. Ali, who perhaps of all of them knew the seriousness of their predicament, began to scream in terror. Robert looked around helplessly.

'The axe, pass me the axe.' Amber didn't need telling twice. With all the force with which he was capable Robbie hacked at the door with the sharp tool. The wood began to give way; a hole was beginning to form.

The roar of the flames was closer. Black smoke was spewing under the living room door. It puffed up through the stair treads. They viewed one another through a suffocating fog. Robert pushed his younger sisters through the jagged hole. He turned back for Ali.

'The cat!' She pushed open the living room door, just a crack and was enveloped in a wall of flame.

'Ali!' screamed Robert. Then there was nothing, nothing but blackness and choking and pain.

Waiting

The staff room is strangely quiet. People are just sitting, hands clasped around coffee cups for comfort. Everything is grey and bleak. A thick mist that drips its own misery has followed heavy rain.

'Any news?' I ask, my voice a tinny triangle of sound.

'Ali is in intensive care. Severe burns to the arms and trunk, apparently she was trying to rescue the cat.' Janet rubs her face with her hands and blows through them, a deep, shuddering sigh.

'And Robbie?'

'Still unconscious, smoke damage, apparently...you know he has asthma?'

I nod and press my lips together. I must not cry.

The bell rings and we all begin to gather up our belongings. How do we act normally on a day like this?

*

My class is beside themselves.

'Miss, Robbie has been burnt to death!' shouts Wayne as he bursts through the door.

'He hasn't!' says Linda.

'He has then; I saw them pulling him out. His face were all black and his 'ands were all red. Burnt to the bone, me mam says.'

Linda begins to cry. I summon up all my strength.

'And STOP! That is quite enough. Stand behind your chairs.' They shuffle into place.

'Good morning everyone.'

'Good *mor*ning, Miss *John*son, Good *mor*ning everybody,' they chant.

'Well done, you do look smart. Now, quietly, without scraping your chairs, sit down.' With great concentration they do as I ask.

'Lovely, you are getting good at this. Right, we'll have the register. Jonathan Andrews... '

Later, I sit them quietly on the mat and we talk about the dangers of fire and they express their worries and fears and we talk about the cleverness of doctors and nurses. Many want to write about what they saw and heard last night, so I abandon my lesson plans and we go slowly, one step at a time, for we're all emotionally shattered.

At break I am relieved to see Mike in the staffroom, but my heart turns over when I realise that he might have brought bad news.

He smiles at me, 'It's all right, Kathy, just here to give you an update. I've come from the hospital. Apparently Robbie has regained consciousness and is as chirpy as ever, except for a deep raspy voice. He was really proud, though, that he had remembered all that the fire safety bloke told them last week'

'Thank God that he did,' says Steve. 'And what time did the mother poll home?'

'Let's just say she was in time to miss the main performance, but, give her, her due, she's in a right state now!'

'And so she should be,' barks Sandra, 'she wants locking up! She's not fit to be a mother!'

I sit drinking my coffee; I just don't have the energy to join in the general witch hunt. I've always had the feeling that Robbie's mum means well, but is just totally inadequate. Pregnant with the twins when just sixteen and with four others over the next four years, she seems to live in a permanent daze.

And who wouldn't? I think, *how on earth does she cope?*

I venture to communicate this to Barbara who has just sat down.

'Rubbish! What planet are you on, Kathy? Yes she's had six kids in six years but they're all to different bloody dads! She's the estate bike and needs no sympathy from anyone. She should be forcibly sterilized. Poor little blighters, how do you think they felt last night, all alone in that God-forsaken hole and not knowing when they'd be fed or if they'd live or die? We haven't all had the benefit of your salubrious childhood, you know. Some of us know what it's like to fight for every morsel; so don't go on at me about poor Mrs Boon. As far as I'm concerned she can jump in the canal tomorrow!'

I feel my hands begin to shake, I am totally unprepared for this vitriolic outburst and the tears that have been threatening all morning are welling up fast. My chest feels like it is being ripped. My thoughts are jagged shards, threatening to tear me apart. *What does she know about my childhood? How dare she shout at me like that?*

Unbidden, my thoughts slidder back twenty years, a deep, dark hole threatens. I pull myself to my feet, spilling coffee as I lurch and make blindly for the door, just as the bell rings for the end of break. I go to collect my class from the playground.

Julie

'Julie is a loony, a loony, a loony
Julie is a loony
Who talks a load of crap.'
The child slumped away from the group. Their words burned into her ears and she pressed her frozen hands against them to block out the hurt. Her brain searched frantically for an answer, a way of getting back at them and then the answer came.
She turned, legs apart, hands placed on non-existent hips,
'Schicks and shones can bweak my bones
But worbs can never huwt me!'
The gang of oppressors shrieked with laughter. Her speech impediment made nonsense of any rejoinder. In sheer frustration she let out a string of expletives
Some of the girls tittered nervously but for the majority the amusement was only increased. They continued their taunting…
'Who's a smelly stick insect?'
'Yer mother's a slag and yer dad's a prick.'
Julie screamed with rage and lunged at them. Like a wild animal she bit, scratched, kicked and punched.
'Julie Thorne! Stop it! This minute, stop it at once. Go stand by the wall! The rest of you get into line. Now! This instant!' The class shuffled hesitantly into line at Miss Rayworth's command. Wayne muttered, 'Heil Hitler!' but only under his breath. You didn't mess with Miss Rayworth. The force of Julie's outburst shocked some children; others were ashamed, only too aware of their own contribution to it. They filed into school obediently. Thirty- two 'butter wouldn't melt' seven year olds, ready to continue their day.
Julie turned, surreptitiously to view her handiwork. Carl had a bleeding nose, Janine's face was badly scratched and stupid Vicki Harmon was carrying locks of her own blonde hair! A derisory smile curled Julie's lips.
'Serves em wight, the bastards,' she muttered, 'serves 'em bwoody wight!'
Inside she was shaking, inside she was screaming and sobbing, but her face was calm, insolent and smiling. She had learned from an early age to weep in secret.

Miss Rayworth read the riot act, raised voice, angry face, and jabbing finger. Julie had heard it all before. She waited patiently.

'NOW, DO YOU UNDERSTAND?' shouted the teacher.

'Yes Miss, sowwy Miss,' and then hung her head to denote contrition.

'Well, run along then, you'll be late for your lesson and, Julie, don't forget, I want to see you in my room at playtime!'

Julie was glad about playtime. She hated everything about school, but most of all she hated playtime. At least today, she might get some peace.

*

I watch as Julie takes her place, yanking her chair and bumping Wayne on the shin. Julie is such a problem, but then again, aren't they all?

Somehow I have to raise her self-esteem, but how? I've tried all the usual things; making her a monitor, awarding stickers, lots of praise, but nothing seems to penetrate that hard little shell. I rack my brain for the umpteenth time but no answer comes. Julie's sister, Marie, is everything that Julie is not; curly blonde hair, blue eyes and dimples. She is bright and quick witted too. Of course they do have different fathers, on this estate that's common. It is rumoured that Julie's mother is on the game, so she could have been fathered by one of many. That might explain her mother's total lack of affection. I slam down a pile of books to vent my frustration and am met by startled stares. *How on earth can I help? What can anyone do? Why do I bother? Why do I care?* I think. But I do care and it hurts like hell. I'm busy working with Steven when I look up suddenly. Julie is totally absorbed with something in her hand. I stand carefully to get a better view. She's holding a bunch of marigolds. She touches one tenderly and ruffles its shaggy petals. She lifts the bunch to her nose and sniffs ecstatically. Her face is soft and luminescent; a lump catches in my throat. I move to the cupboard and take out a vase of shiny cobalt blue and move to Julie's side.

'Julie,' I whisper, 'would you like to give your flowers a drink of water; they're looking a bit thirsty.' She gives me a lopsided grin, her eyes veering in opposite directions.

'Yes, can I? Now?' She seems hardly to believe her luck.

'Of course, I think they'll look very pretty in this blue vase. You might like to put them on the windowsill facing your table, then you'll be able to see them all the time.' She nods happily and sets about her task, all the while beaming and shining.

Julie spent part of the lunch break outside the staffroom door with extra work to do. She worked in a desultory fashion, jabbing at the dirty page with her pencil.

'I 'ate 'em, I 'ate em all!' she muttered. 'Bloody kids, fucking teachers, me mam.'

Yes, most of all her mam and the 'orrible secret.

*

At lunchtime I pop out to get some sweets to use as prizes at the end of the week.

The children work hard for merit points but on Fridays love these to be translated into penny chews or liquorice sticks. I smile as I think of them on a Friday afternoon at *golden time*, when I read out all the notes that I've written to myself and placed in my golden box. There they sit, with straight backs and puffed out chests, arms folded, waiting with big eyes, for their own names to be mentioned. Bribery and corruption it may be, but in an area of such deprivation that little bit extra is a treat for these children.

As I pass the greengrocer's shop a magnificent pink azalea catches my attention. Large and bushy with green, glossy leaves and a mass of fat pink buds it's certainly a wonderful specimen. How I love these plants that seem to go on and on, when they are constantly fed and deadheaded, I wonder if I should treat myself. It would certainly look well in my sparsely furnished living room and would brighten up those grey winter days. I look in my purse, yes, there is just enough. I'll have to make do with pasta again tonight but it will be worth it. I carry my prize back to school in triumph and place it carefully on the corner of my desk. It shines out, an oasis of beauty in that shabby room. I am well pleased.

Later, while helping Adam with a writing problem, I look across at Julie and am startled by a look of pure joy. She is staring, as fixedly as her squint will allow, at the azalea. The unexpected beauty of her face takes my breath away. At afternoon break; as the others make for the cloakroom and the freedom of the playground, Julie lingers at my desk, still looking. I watch from the door as she edges towards it, sniffing, eyes closed. With butterfly fingers she touches the silky petals of a single bloom. I walk quietly towards her and her eyes meet mine with such a heartrending smile, the happiest look I have ever seen on her grey, pinched face.

'It's awight, Miss, ain't it? It's bootifuw!' I bend to touch the plant.

'It certainly is. I fell in love with it as soon as I saw it in the greengrocers. Do you like plants? Have you got plants in your garden?' Even as I ask the question I know how stupid it is. All the houses on the estate have gardens, yes, but most are full of child high weeds and dog excreta. Mini scrap yards. Dustbin overflows.

'I got these fwom the park,' she nods towards the marigolds, 'I never seed any before.' She says it in a matter-of-fact sort of voice and I am stunned. Of course she's seen a plant before, hasn't she? She cuddles the azalea and the vase of marigolds as she might hold teddy bears, allowing the tight buds and shaggy orange petals to rub against her thin cheek. My heart clenches.

Julie asks, 'Do they have names, Miss? Like us kids do?'

'They do indeed.' I point to the plant, 'This is an azalea.' She repeats the word slowly. 'And *these* are marigolds.' She laughs revealing some blackened teeth.

'Mawwygolds. Is that a wedding fwower?'

'A wedding flower?'

'Yes, when people mawwy that's a wedding and they have gold wings.'

'Oh I see, wedding rings!'

'Yes,' she nods rapidly, 'so mawwygold like wedding rings.'

'You're quite right Julie; I'll have to remember that if I ever get married.'

*

Slowly, life begins to get easier with Julie. She stays in the classroom most break times. She is the plant monitor, the nurse of all greenery, the advisor of all 'would be gardeners'. She trots around importantly with the measuring jug and learns how to feed and water each of her treasures. I add to them each week, my living room still starkly bereft of plants and my purse definitely slimmer.

Julie, who cannot pronounce her own name properly and is struggling with red book one, can painstakingly sound out azalea, gloxinia, stephanotis and of course, marigolds. True, her speech impediment translates them strangely, so what? She knows the ideal conditions for each of these green children and as they blossom and grow in strength, so does she. The other children grow to respect her knowledge and expertise and occasionally they present her with a new treasure;

'Eh Julie! Me grandma's got this plant, but it's sickening for summat. I told 'er that you'd get it reet. Ere you are, she says you can keep it,' announces Wayne magnanimously and he is only one of many who are growing to value Julie's important part in this community.

A Date with Mike

'So how long have you and Mike been going together?' asks the woman on my left at the dining table. I try to answer without my eyes appearing glued to her huge breasts, which peer above her shimmering top like doughy cottage loaves set out on display. Mike appears to have the same problem but he has to lean forward to get a good view.

'Er...sorry, I didn't catch what you said?'

'I said, have you two been together long?'

'Well, we're not actually together, I mean, well we've just had a few dates.'

She cackles with laughter,

'A few dates! Well, for Mike that's definitely being together, why, you're practically engaged!' She blows smoke all around and my eyes begin to smart. Mike is red faced and loud and has consumed several pints. It looks like I'm driving! Phil, who is sitting opposite, keeps staring at me glassily and I wish I were a million miles away. The waitress slams down a glutinous mass that she claims is Black Forest Gateau and Mike pours half a jug of cream on his then says, 'Does anyone else want cream?' *Fat chance*, I think, and break my dessert apart with little relish.

Now it's time for the dancing. Mike drags me onto the floor and pulls me tightly to him. We shuffle around and he sings loudly in my ear. 'Save the last dance for me' he roars tunelessly, the palms of his hands sliding up and down my spine like uncoordinated pistons. Why on earth did I ever believe he was attractive? The record finishes and I manage to get him back to our seat before he starts on 'The Birdie Dance'.

'Ohhh I like thish one! Wiv a liddle bit of thish and a liddle bit of that,' he croons, leering drunkenly. I prop him against the Dralon covered banquette and turn to talk to my friend, Meg, who works at the Police Station as a telephonist.

'Looks like you're going to need a bit of help later,' she says, nodding in Mike's direction. 'He's not a bad lad, you know, he just can't hold his drink.'

'Evening Miss Johnson, are you 'avin a good time?' I stare blankly and the man smiles, 'I'm Sally Arnold's dad, she loves being in your class, she says that you're quite mad and do loads of interesting things.'

'Oh well, thank you for that, she's a lovely little girl you must be very proud of her.'

'Oh I am that, I allus tell her she's my little princess. It took us ages, yer know, before Liz fell on with her, we'd just about given up.' He begins to laugh loudly and then he adds, 'Aye we'd never no need of them little balloons you 'ad such a job with the other week, by all accounts.'

I feel my face redden as he turns to go back to go to his wife. Would I ever live that incident down? Meg begins to giggle and suddenly I feel more cheerful. Poor Meg, she's had a rotten time lately. Steve, her husband of fifteen years, died suddenly six months ago. They had been inseparable and being childless had lived only for one another. They shared the same ridiculous sense of humour, adored their old black Labrador, Lulu, and two fat cats, Bonnie and Clyde. They'd spent nearly every weekend touring the Yorkshire dales in a battered old caravan and amazingly all the animals had gone too. They'd walked the Three Peaks and the Pennine Way, picnicked by the rushing white waters of the Strid at Bolton Abbey and made love amongst the wild heather on Baildon Moor.

'You can't beat it, you know, out in the open air with the curlews calling and the sun beating down on you. Quickest way to orgasm I know, talk about peaks and valleys!' and she laughed, but her voice was like torn cloth. Suddenly this whole lifestyle was gone.

'We were climbing Skiddaw when it happened, up in the lakes. A beautiful day it was, sky as blue as a kingfisher's wing, the lake like a jewel far below and fat sheep pilfering our sandwiches. There we were laughing and joking and suddenly his face goes all funny like and he clutches at his chest and that was it, there was nothing I could do!'

She'd broken down then, when she was telling me and I'd felt so helpless, I'd just held her and felt my own throat closing up and my own chest tearing. I gaze at her now and feel such a rush of affection. There are new lines of pain that have etched into her skin, but she has beautiful clear green eyes and in spite of the flecks of grey in her conker brown hair, it's still thick and shiny. She is a slim, active fifty year old who sometimes, in the dark hours before dawn, weeps into her pillow and wonders if her life is over. But tonight her wide, engaging smile reaches eyes which glitter with mischief, and she is determined to live...lavishly.

'Come on pardner,' she says now, grabbing my arm and pulling me onto the floor, 'let's twist!' and we dance until we're breathless. Some time later, during the Beatles 'Yellow Submarine' I glance towards Mike and just at that moment the music stops, and my erstwhile escort emits a very loud snore.

*

'Miss Johnson! Miss Johnson! Do you know what?' Sally Arnold comes flying across the playground like an infant gazelle. Huge brown eyes shining, long plaits flying, face flushed with excitement.

'What don't I know?'

Its me mam, Miss, she's 'avin a baby a real live one and it'll be 'ere in six months, they take nine months to cook but she's 'ad three months already because she just wanted to be sure like 'afore she told us, well she didn't tell us really because I guessed. Isn't it wonderful Miss?'

'It certainly is. Would you like a brother or a sister?'

'Well, a sister really, cos brothers are not much use, cos Debbie's got one and they allus want you to be the one that gets killed when you're playing. You know, when you play cowboys and things its allus the girls that get the boring, dying type bits. So I'd like a sister best.'

*

Sally was born maternal. Even at three years old she mothered her infant cousins. When they wriggled and squawked their way into the world she was ready and waiting to cuddle and croon but as soon as they grew and became playmates her arms felt empty and nothing filled the ache in Sally for something to love and care for.

'Mam, can we 'ave a baby?'

'No, we've got enough babies with you.'

'Oh, Mam!'

'Go and play! Babies? As if I don't 'ave enough problems.'

'Well, can we 'ave a kitten then, or a budgie?'

'Or a baby budgie,' Dad chortled laying down his newspaper, then added, 'no, no pets and that's final. Now leave yer mother alone.'

Bill looked across at his wife, Liz, with concern. He knew how such questions hassled her, how she longed more than anything else for another child. His heart ached and a nerve twitched by his temple. She was looking out of the window, twisting strands of her hair with one hand and tapping the side of her leg with the other. He slid his arms around her and drew her close

19

'*Don't fret, lass, it'll 'appen one day, you'll see,' he murmured,' never give up.'*

So Sally went on yearning. Last Christmas when she'd lovingly stroked the china doll, representing the infant Jesus in the crib, her friend Pauline had whispered her secret, '*My mam's 'aving one of them.'*

Sally stared openmouthed, '*A JESUS?'*

Pauline nodded sagely. '*Well, not exactly, just an ordinary one.'*

'*Who told her, was it an angel?'*

Pauline scratched her head thoughtfully, '*Don't think so, reckon it were the clinic.'*

'*The clinic?'*

'*Yes, over't road from school, that's where they tell you you're 'aving them. They mostly don't bother with angels nowadays.'*

Sally assimilated this information and turned it over in her mind. If only she could get her mam to the clinic. By the summer holidays Pauline's mam was very fat, like a big, squashy balloon. Pauline said that was because the baby was inside her.

'*But how did it get there?'*

'*Don't know, must 'ave been at the clinic.'*

Their friend Vicki laughed scornfully, '*They don't do that at the clinic, stupid. Yer dad puts it there.'*

Two awed faces turned towards her. Vicky was a Catholic, they knew about everything.

'*Really! How?'*

'*I don't know exactly,' said Vicky, biting her lower lip, 'but I know that he plants a seed when they're in bed.'*

Sally thought hard. '*What if they have single beds?'*

'*Well they don't, do they? I expect that's why they 'ave double ones in case they want to plant seeds.'*

Pauline clasped her face with both hands and whispered gleefully, '*Yes, but on our holidays they 'ad to sleep in single beds. Just imagine if my mam found seeds on the floor and said, "Eh, did you forget we was on holiday?"'*

They chuckled and Pauline's voice was barely audible when she stated, '*My cousin told me that they...the men....plant the seeds with their willies!'*

'*Aaah! Yuk!' This from the others in unison, their faces lit with horror.*

'No! There must be some other way. My mum and dad wouldn't do that!' cried a shocked Sally. The others nodded in agreement. It certainly was a mystery but eventually they came to the conclusion that it must be something to do with bellybuttons. They didn't seem to serve any other purpose.

One night after watching Blue Peter, Sally was curled up in the large armchair immersed in Charlie and the Chocolate Factory. The comfortable buzz of her parents' conversation washed over her head. That is until the word clinic penetrated her brain.

'Clinic, what clinic? Mam, why 'ave you been to the clinic?'

Mam and dad smiled shyly at one another and then dad nodded.

Mam cleared her throat, 'Well, you know that you're always asking for a baby brother or sister? Well, we're going to have one.'

'Yippee!' The book flew across the room and Sally threw herself into her mother's arms. 'A baby, oh a baby! Aw Mam, will it be a girl? I'd like a girl, ah Mam!'

Her mother smiled. 'It depends on what they've got left,' she replied softly.

Harvest Festival

'I'm gonna bring some oranges and apples to the harvest festival and my mam's going to put them in a basket with purple paper, she say's it will look dead good,' announces Christopher after registration.

'Well! That's nothing,' says Wayne, 'I'm gonna bring a box of beer.'

'You can't bring beer to a harvest, it's all gonna go into church. You can't take beer to church.'

'Can then, they 'ave wine every week, my grandma told me, she's been a lot, about six times, so there!'

'Right children, let's have everyone on the carpet and we can talk properly about the harvest festival,' I command. 'Now who can tell me *why* we are having a harvest festival?'

'Don't you know, Miss. It's because Miss Heaton says so.'

'And the vicar!' added Steven. 'It were his idea, I think.'

'Well, at this time of year all the food that has been growing right through the summer has been gathered in from the fields. Let's think together about all the things that we like to eat and where they have come from. Sally, what do you like to eat?'

'All sorts, Miss'

'Yes, but right now if you were to choose something, what would you have?'

'Er…ice-cream.'

'Good, and where do we get ice-cream from?'

'Mr Whippy!' chorus the children and Wayne goes on to explain further, 'He's got a van Miss and he drives round the streets and he makes this kind of tinkling music noise.'

I sigh. It's going to be a long day. These city children don't have a clue where their food is sourced. There's a lot of work to be done. I decide to pop to the shops at lunchtime and see what I can find. At Robinson's, the greengrocers, I manage to source red cabbage, cauliflower, potatoes and parsnips. Then I find some carrots, still with ferny tops and bearing a smidgeon of soil about the roots. That should give them a clue. Mr Robinson also has a small-sized herring with marmalade eyes and shiny metallic scales. They'll love that.

As I enter the tiny supermarket on the shopping parade I am surprised to see young Linda carrying a very large shopping bag and a wire basket. I am just about to greet her when my heart sinks. Linda is obviously consulting a long list; she's a good little reader. I watch in amazement as she reaches up for a tin of peaches, but somehow it never makes it to the wire basket. The same happens with two tins of pineapples and a tin of cream. Sugar, however, is placed in the basket, as is margarine. Linda continues her shop with solemn dignity. It appears that daily essentials are placed in the basket but luxuries go straight in the bag. I stand quite still, heart beating fast, brain whirling. Is Linda really shoplifting? Surely not, after all she is only seven! She strolls along, her eyes darting back and forth. Her grubby little hands enclose a large chocolate bar and although I watch very carefully, I don't actually see it go into the bag. She's obviously very skilled. A box of eggs is put in the basket, but tins of salmon, tuna and ham are not. The bag is sinking lower and lower, almost trailing the floor with all its weight. Just another few feet and she will be at the checkout. My mouth is dry. What should I do? Should I tell the woman at the till? I look at her, a small darting woman with a severe expression and cold, dark eyes. She glares at Linda,

'Come on. Come on. I haven't all day. Where's your purse? That will be three pounds, seventy five pence.' Linda places the bag carefully on the floor but it still makes an audible clank. The woman does not appear to notice. The child carefully opens a zip on the back of the bag and takes out the money. I move into place behind her and for the first time, Linda appears to see me.

'Hello Linda, are you shopping for your mum?' She stares with large, terror filled eyes. She looks away quickly and nods, her gaze intent on the floor tiles. Hurriedly, she throws her purchases into a plastic carrier bag. Then, holding one bag in each hand, she clatters towards the open door. I complete my own purchases and follow at a slow and measured pace.

Linda is rattling down the road at a rate of knots, her tiny arms obviously having difficulty with the weight she carries. I walk towards school with a secret, ruinous burden and a heart that aches for this child I've grown to love.

*

After registration, with the children all seated on the mat, I continue the lesson about harvest. They are all eager as they wait to see what's in my bag. I lift out the large red cabbage and hold it tenderly in both hands holding it towards them as a gift. A square of sunlight reflects from the window, catches it and suddenly it has a ruby glimmer and is burnished, shining and magical.

Julie squints up and surveys it thoughtfully. 'It ain't a plant, Miss, cos it's not in the soil.'

'Well, it's not a plant now, but it was a little while ago.'

Julie looks around at all her plants and smiles gently, 'It wook wike a cabbage but it's the wong colour.'

'Well done, Julie, you are quite right. It is a cabbage, and just like flowers have different colours, so do cabbages. Now who can tell me which family cabbages belong to?' There is a puzzled silence. Then Jonathan, that master of wit, replies 'Well it's not the royal family that's for sure.' He giggles happily, poking Trevor in the ribs at the same time. A bit of playful punching takes place. I marvel at the way Jonathan's face twinkles and shines as his wire spectacles reflect sunlight and mischief in equal measure.

'I wonder what else is in my bag.' Immediately there is silence as the children wait and I reveal a cauliflower. When all the items are lined up like soldiers on parade they finally manage to work out that they were all part of the vegetable family. Thank goodness for that! Then there follows a happy afternoon, while we observe the vegetables carefully, cutting them up and marveling at the way they are formed, and then making meticulous pencil sketches. Some children even manage paintings; carefully mixing the right shades of powder paint to resemble thin watercolours and using the very best paper that is kept especially for important occasions.

The silver herring with the marmalade eyes is a great success and to my surprise Trevor asks, 'Miss, me and Jamie 'ave been talking, like, and we don't want to draw. We'd like to make one of them there college fings with silver paper and stuff.'

'A collage, oh what a good idea. That will be lovely!'

Jamie is nodding happily and a smile polishes his thin, pallid features. I watch happily as they become engrossed in the fulfilment of their plan. Jamie speaks very little but seems delighted to have a new friend and glues and sticks industriously.

When all the children have gone home, I mount the pictures carefully on black sugar paper and then on beige. I name and title them with my special felt-tip pen. As I pin them onto an orange background, my friend Karen comes in to borrow the staple gun.

'Wow! They've made a good job of them. Look how Julie's got all the folds of that cabbage spot on. She's a funny little thing isn't she, you can never make out where she is looking and I can't understand a word of what she says!'

'Oh she's coming on leaps and bounds and her diction is so much better.'

'Rubbish, it's just you that's got used to her. Anyway, it's a lovely drawing; she never did anything like that when she was with Sandra.' I want to say that that was probably because she'd been too scared, but I think better of it. Karen continues to admire the art work.

'Wayne's is a bit bold isn't it, was the cabbage really so purple?'

'Oh definitely, a future Turner prizewinner that one, I'm sure.'

'Now this is interesting,' she picks up the metallic looking collage. 'Animal, vegetable or mineral?' she asks with a grin.

'Erm, it's a fish, but prepare to be amazed, it's a Trevor and Jamie masterpiece!'

'Now I *do* believe you're performing miracles, I've never seen Jamie take his thumb out of his mouth longer than five seconds. Wow! Look at Linda's, such attention to detail and all those beautiful shades of pink, I always found her such a shy little thing, wouldn't say "boo" to a goose, maybe there's hope for her yet.'

'She's certainly got hidden depths. Oh Karen, I don't know what to do. I saw her shoplifting at lunchtime. I didn't know whether to tell the woman at the checkout or not, but it was that fierce looking woman with the beady black eyes and the hairy chin, so I chickened out.'

'Did she take much?'

'Mainly tins as far as I could see. I suppose they would be luxury items in that family.' Karen gazed into space for a moment, her eyes sad and kind of haunted.

'Maybe, it's best to do nothing then, at least we know she's going to get some good meals, bless her.' She squeezes my arm and goes back to her room.

*

The next day is one of those lovely autumn days where the sky is very blue, the air crisp, and the trees just on the turn. As I walk towards the estate I revel in it all. I pass houses clothed in Virginia creeper, all scarlet and burgundy. There is a waving crowd of pink Japanese anemones in one garden and flashes of orange and scarlet dahlias stand to attention as if awaiting inspection. I find myself wishing that Julie could be with me. How she would love all these amazing jewels and how I would delight in showing them to her. As I enter the estate the flowering stops abruptly, like I'm in a foreign land. There is graffiti on walls and pavements, piles of rubbish, redundant cars, televisions and dog mess. My spirits sink as I walk towards school.

In the classroom, however, there is brightness and order. I view the walls with satisfaction. Children's drawings and paintings carefully mounted and neatly arranged. Books we have constructed bound together and hung at the eye level of a child so that they can be read with pride. There are labels about classroom rules and an inviting book corner with bright floor cushions. My spirits rise and I make my way to the playground to welcome my charges.

'Miss, look at this,' Wayne hoists a huge marrow onto his shoulder, 'me granddad grew it on his allotment and you know how it got that big, he kept on giving it horse shit!'

'Yuk, don't bring it near me,' yells Linda. 'Anyway I've got more'n you for't harvest, I've got loads and loads!'

As the children gather on the carpet we examine our treasures. Sally has brought some beautiful red apples; each one wrapped in pink tissue and rubbed up to a shine. We weigh and measure Wayne's marrow, it's certainly a whopper, as long as Jamie's arm and nearly as fat as a football. Then Linda places her bag, in the middle of the circle, with a great thump.

'That sounds heavy,' says Wayne, 'what yer got in there, a sack of coal?' Linda's face beams and her soft brown eyes shine with pride.

'Wait 'til yer see what I've got. There's a tin of salmon-'

'Wow, it's red salmon, we ave that at me gran's when we go for a special Sunday tea!' says Christopher.

'-then there's tuna,' Linda stacks this carefully on top of the salmon, 'some luncheon meat, *and* pineapples *and* peaches.' The tower is beginning to grow 'and...' she pauses, and then adds triumphantly, 'a big tin of cream!' There is a gasp of excitement and then the whole tower comes toppling down and there are squeals and giggles all round. For a moment I cannot speak for the lump in my throat. Poor, sweet Linda. What else would she do to gain approbation from her peers and, I suppose, from me?

'Well, that's really exciting, lots of things for our harvest festival; I can't wait to see them all in church. Well done children, you've all tried very, very hard!'

Linda smiles at me, 'I remember what you said, Miss, about the tins being auctioned so as to get money for all them poor, 'ungry kids in Bangle Desh so I made sure I got tins. I like helping the 'ungry don't you?'

The Medieval Banquet

The Saturday before Harvest festival is the day of the Medieval Banquet and my date with Mike, or should I say King Henry? Meg has been asked by her cousin, who is a regular worshiper at St Michael's, to be a serving wench, so she and I spend the morning at the fancy dress shop in Leeds, where we try on a variety of Tudor inspired costumes. Eventually she decides upon a low cut blue gown in a coarse linen effect material. It certainly shows off her plentiful assets to perfection.

'Blood and sand! I look like Nell Gwynn, only with two great melons,' she says, twisting and turning before the mirror. 'It's to be hoped I don't have to bow low before your king Henry, or your head will be on the chopping block and no mistake.'

I look in the mirror at my small chest and sigh. The salesgirl comes towards me carrying a mound of rich, russet velvet and my heart lifts. Oh it's beautiful. I step into it eagerly and she zips me up.

'Perfect, absolutely perfect, it goes beautifully with your lovely nut brown hair. Now just try the headdress, it goes like this…' She pins it into place and I stare into the mirror. Gosh!

'Oh Kathy, you look a picture,' breathes Meg. 'That colour's perfect for autumn. You'll be the belle of the ball!'

'Well, I'm supposed to be, you ninny, I am the Queen!'

*

When we arrive the church hall looks breathtaking. The sills of the high gothic windows are festooned with garlands and candlesticks are placed all along their lengths, each holding fat wax candles. In the centre stands a Maypole, its red, white and blue ribbons coil and flutter around it. Each long trestle table is covered in bright red cloth and there are more candles. There are posies of flowers pushed through the centres of lace doilies and placed in jam jars. Each table bears a beautiful bowl teeming with apples, oranges and fat blue grapes. The stage, at one end of the room, is festooned with bunting and bales of hay are scattered upon it to add to the harvest effect. People are beginning to arrive and look splendid in all their Tudor finery, satins and velvets, contrast with rough cloth and furs. I head for the vestry, where I am to wait with Mike, until the trumpets sound and we follow the procession to our thrones. The vicar, Reverend Thomas Bell, greets us warmly.

'Hello Mike, how are you Lad? Still pounding the beat and making our parish a safer place. Good to see you.' He shakes his hand vigorously, pats his shoulder, then turns and smiles at me. 'Kathy, love, I don't think I've had chance to speak to you lately, I do hope you're still enjoying the job. How long is it now, about three years?'

'That's right. I enjoy it very much, the children are lovely.'

'And you are looking very lovely yourself, Kathy, you make a beautiful Queen.' He grins mischievously, 'And which one *are* you?'

'I thought, Katherine Parr, all the others met such an untimely end.' His laugh reminds me of hot chocolate and marshmallows, there is such softness about him.

'Nay lass, you're far too young and beautiful. To my mind you're more like sweet Jane, I hope you don't mind me saying so.'

'Thank you, and you are a perfect monk.' He is a cherubic, square faced man with wispy silver hair and a face that smiles even when he doesn't. He has such laughing eyes and a mass of fine lines that are the residue of a lifetime of good humour. I feel a surge of affection for him. There is a knock on the door, indicating that it's time to go. He smooths down his brown habit, smiles into my eyes and says, 'I think this calls for prayer.' He places his hands on our shoulders and begins. 'Dear God, thank you so much for all your abundant gifts that we celebrate this weekend. Bless these two young people, Lord. We thank you for all that they do in this parish and all the love that they share with others. Amen.'

He squeezes my shoulder lightly, and Mike and I follow him out into the corridor where we take up our places in the procession. The trumpeters are obviously father and son, both having the same red hair and copper coin eyes. They are not in tune and I suppress a smile at this dissolute fanfare. Mike walks ponderously, his padded stomach leading the way and his muscled legs looking incongruous in stretch, scarlet tights. Even so, he makes a fine King Henry, red faced and bejeweled with a loud, hearty laugh and a convincing red beard. We march together to the rather hesitant Trumpet Voluntary and fall about laughing as we reach our thrones, two upright chairs bedecked in cloth of gold.

'Your Majesties! My Lords, Ladies and Gentlemen, let the festivities begin!' shouts an important looking man in a gold and red tunic. Music begins to play, and several young men enter, all dressed in green and white with bells around their ankles on ribbon bands. They dance and waft white handkerchiefs in an effeminate fashion, occasionally catching members of the audience on the head. They hoot with laughter as they dance and prance and we all clap in rhythm. I recognise nobody, and suddenly realise that there is a whole population in Becklefield whose lives I am not privy to, people who live honest, and decent lives, who care about their children and enjoy simple pleasures. I suddenly feel a twinge of guilt for lumping everyone together and being judgmental. Mike beams at me, 'Eh! They're a rum lot, these church folks.' Not a drop of alcohol to be had and they're as merry as hell. Don't know where they get it from.'

'I don't know either, but whatever it is, it works,' I say, lifting my goblet for another refill of what appears to be some kind of fruit punch. Non-alcoholic it may be but it's absolutely delicious. I savour the sparkling mixture, the tang of strawberries, the bite of lemon and something else that I can't quite place. The dancing ends and a troop of big-bosomed wenches bounce in, carrying large wooden boards stacked high with bread. Meg appears before us and curtsies, I am tempted to cover my eyes, but the King has no such scruples. Her face creases in a familiar grin and she winks cheekily. The bread is warm and crunchy; the yeasty scent conjures up my appetite. I break open a roll and touch the soft white within, then reach for the butter. Meg returns with steaming bowls of vegetable soup. It is homemade, or perhaps I should say church made, and thick with lentils and root vegetables with just a taste of herbs. Music plays from a tape machine, all madrigals and harpsichords and there is the sound of laughter and animated chatter. I feel at home, as if I belong.

'I could murder a pint and a Chinese,' Mike whispers, 'I wonder how long we have to stay.' I don't reply. I just savour the rich, comforting soup.

After the starter, a group of younger men and women entertain us with a maypole dance. It is hilarious, ribbons are mixed up or dropped and people turn the wrong way and bump or trip or simply just fall about laughing. Then it's time for the main course. The wenches arrive again, carrying large wooden trays filled with sizzling golden chicken breasts and plates of salad stuff. We use our wooden soup bowls again and eat with our fingers. I glance around the room; there must be about two hundred people present. I turn to the Vicar who sits next to me, 'Do all these people come to church?'

'At some time or another, I would say, yes. Some come Sunday morning and others in the evening. But we also have mid-week services too. Generally people come when they can. It's certainly not only about Sunday. The beauty of big events like this is that all the different groups get a chance to meet one another.'

'Wow, I'm impressed. But it must be awfully hard work for you.'

'Oh I don't go to everything; there are lots of people equally capable of organising things. We're getting a new curate just before Christmas, that will certainly lighten the load; we're all looking forward to meeting him. Actually a number of our people are going to a preparation course for advent. It struck me that it might be something that would interest you.'

'Oh, I don't know...'

'Don't worry, you don't have to answer now, I'll pop round sometime with the information and you can give it some thought. You might find it useful in school.'

The trumpets sound yet again and a rather large lady appears and begins to play the harpsichord. She plays 'Greensleeves' reputed to have been written by Henry VIII and a beautiful, blonde-haired maiden begins to dance, and I cannot help but notice that the 'King' is more than a little enthralled.

After we have helped ourselves to fresh fruit, an assortment of dried fruit and some delicious fudge, the auction is announced. A craggy-faced young man, wearing the costume of the king's fool, leaps lightly onto the stage. He is a rainbow feast to the eye wearing possibly every colour of the spectrum and an assortment of jangly bells. All the tinned goods are piled up behind him and he begins, not with jokes as I expect, but with a short but meaningful explanation about the present situation in Bangladesh where famine is rife.

'It is estimated that there have been over a million deaths so far. Only two years since the liberation war and these people are dying of starvation or from cholera and malaria. From April to July there has been heavy rainfall, which has resulted in devastating floods along the Bahmaputra river. Many lives have been lost. Many homes have been destroyed and the rice crops, decimated. Now you might say, well what is that to us, we're thousands of miles away, what difference can we make? Well, we have experience of this, haven't we? Not of floods and starvation, but of helping people in the past. We know that God will use every penny that we send.

So, let's send as much as we possibly can. Now who will bid for three tins of succulent pineapples? Do I hear £10...£12, well done sir, £15, any more for any more?' He bangs down his gavel, 'Going! Going! Gone! To the man standing by the hatch with the beautiful wench.' I turn to see who it is, oh my! The beautiful wench is Meg and boy, is she looking radiant. I stare at her companion as he goes toward the stage to collect his booty. He is tall, well made, with a lovely beaming smile and a dimple in his chin. His silvery hair shines in the light from the stage and as he walks back towards Meg, his eyes never leave her face. Now there's a turn up for the books!

More fruit is being auctioned now and people are paying incredible prices. Linda's little stash had certainly borne fruit. Was it *ill-gotten gains*, I wonder, or a *shower of blessings*?

It's no surprise, when later that night, Meg phones.

'Hi, it's me.'

'Hello me.'

'Erm, I was wondering if you would like to go to church with me in the morning?'

I pretend ignorance, 'To church! Whatever for?'

She giggles, 'Well, it's the Harvest Festival, and well, I thought that you'd like to go.'

'But we've never been before.'

More giggles, then a dirty laugh. 'You know very well why I want to go. I'll do the same for you one day.'

'Not likely, I don't fancy anyone at church.'

'But there might be someone you haven't seen yet.'

'Nah, they're probably all old fogeys like you!'

'Cheeky! Please Kathy; I can't face walking through those big doors on my own.'

'OK, pick me up at quarter to ten. Will I have to wear a hat? I haven't been to church since I was fourteen, well apart from weddings and funerals. I haven't got a clue what you do or anything.'

'Well, John says that it's quite informal and very friendly.'

'Mm-mm, did he now, sounds like he did a good P.R. job on you!'

*

Somewhat bleary eyed, I'm ready when Meg arrives driving her little green Mini. But there is nothing tired looking about her, she positively shines. I'm amazed, when we pull into the car park, at the number of cars there.

'Good grief! Do all these people go to church?'

We enter the building to a buzz of conversation, peals of laughter and the smell of fresh coffee. We are greeted like long lost friends and choose seats near the back. So do most of the congregation because all the front rows are empty. The hymns are lively, the 'talk' stimulating, short and to the point. This is not how I imagine church to be! When worship finishes a pleasant, rose-cheeked woman invites us to stay for coffee. She settles us at a table and returns with steaming cups and chocolate biscuits.

'Here you are girls, get that down thee. Have you come far?'

Meg grins happily, 'We both live on Mugglefield Road, we're neighbours and came to the medieval banquet last night. I'm Meg and this is my friend, Kathy.'

'Very pleased to meet you love; I'm Edna, Edna Sheffield. I've been coming here since I were a lass and now I'm eighty five, yer know, eighty five years and I still feel like a lass of sixteen, well apart from my legs that is.' I'm aware that Meg is staring inanely somewhere to the right of Edna's shoulder and cannot suppress a grin. Edna turns to see what has distracted us.

'Oh aye! I wondered how long it'd be until thee came over, old John Cromer. Well I must be getting on; I'll leave thee in his capable hands, the old rogue. My son's picking me up, we're off gallivanting.' She gives each of us a warm smile and a dramatic wink and rolls ponderously away. John rubs his hands and sits in the vacant seat, beaming and twinkling, then leans across and gives Meg a hug.

'I couldn't believe it when you walked in, I was that chuffed. How are you lass? And this, well this must be Kathy. Eeh, you were a right royal queen last night and no mistake, you looked a picture.'

'Thank you, kind sir!' He looks right into my eyes and there is such an openness about him, such a simple, direct manner that I feel as if we are old friends. He turns back to Meg and suddenly the bond between the two is awe inspiring. I slip away, muttering something about seeing the Vicar. He is standing by the door, waves when he sees me, then hobbles forward.

'So good to see you, lass. It gives me a real boost to have you here. Did you enjoy last night?'

'Oh I did and this morning. The church looks stunning, all those beautiful flower arrangements and the fruit and veg, the corn stooks and that huge loaf of bread. Wherever I looked, I was filled with thankfulness. It's like being in the countryside.'

'Well, that's just it, isn't it? Wherever we are we are dependent on the land to supply our needs. So often, nowadays, people forget that.' I nod my agreement and suddenly make a decision.

'You mentioned last night, something about a conference.'

'Oh yes, the Advent course. It's at half term, that's why I thought of you. It's in a beautiful country house in Derbyshire, surrounded by stunning countryside. It's so peaceful there and the teaching is first rate. I'll get you a leaflet.' He heads off towards the notice board and I wonder what I've let myself in for.

Meg comes towards me grinning like a Cheshire cat.

'John and I are nipping off for a spot of lunch somewhere but we'll drop you off first.'

'There's no need, it's a lovely day, I think I'll go for a walk.'

'OK, I'll pop round and see you later.' She squeezes my arm and then tip-taps away in her best stiletto heels.

The vicar smiles, hands me a leaflet and then waves to John as he opens the door for my friend.

'Now isn't that something to be pleased about,' he nods towards them. 'John is a wonderful fellow, salt of the earth; I haven't seen him so happy since Doreen died. He worshiped the ground that woman walked on. She died of cancer eighteen months ago and he's scarcely smiled since. Oh I 'm glad he's found someone.' I feel a niggle of fear.

'But they've only just met.'

'I know, love, but sometimes, you can just tell.'

I bite my lip, and feel tears threatening and I can't for the life of me understand why.

'It never seems to happen like that for me.'

He takes my hands in both of his; they are warm like a hot water bottle on a snowy night. 'It will, my love, you just have to look in the right places.'

The Hero Returns

Robert arrives back at school the week before half term. The children gather around him excitedly.

'Hi Robbie, is it true you put out the flames with yer bare hands?'

'No he didn't, he had an axe!'

'Yes and yer nearly died in't ambulance and they had to narcissus you, didn't they?' This latter statement from Wayne,

'Don't be daft,' said Julie, 'a narcissus is a fwower, everyone knows that.'

'All right! All right! Sit down children, please. Come and sit nicely on the carpet and when we've had the register we can welcome Robert back properly.'

After registration Robbie comes to the front and stands by my chair.

'Is there anything that you would like to share with us, Robert?'

'Well it were really hot and the smoke was horrible. It made your eyes burn and your throat hurt and I was scared our Ali was going to die, but she didn't.'

'We're so glad that you're all right, Robbie. Is Alison better now?'

'Well, where her skin got burnt they've had to put new skin on and it looks a bit better now and it doesn't hurt as much. She went back for't cat you see, but it died anyway.' There are several gasps from the children and I think it best to draw the discussion to a close.

'Well you were very brave, Robert, and it was good that you remembered everything that the fireman told us when he came to school. Have you got any advice to give us about stopping fires from happening?'

'Yes, *don't make chips*! The fireman said chip pans are lethal. There's too much fat you see and it gets really, really hot and then it explodes and sets fire to everything.'

'Thank you, Robbie. I'm sure that we'll all remember that and never go near the cooker when our parents are not there to look after us. Now, has anyone else got anything to share?' There is a forest of hands waving and thrusting. I choose Julie because she is sitting quietly, one finger of her left hand on her lips and her right hand still in the air. I notice a newspaper wrapped parcel on her knee.

'Julie, what have you got to show us?' She comes towards me

beaming, stands proudly in front of the class, unwraps her treasure and holds it up triumphantly. Some of the girls on the front row scream and even two of the boys look worried and inch backwards on their bottoms. I try to hide a smile.

'What on earth is it, Julie? It looks a bit like a spider.'

'Yes a dead one,' shouts Wayne.

'It's not a spider,' teases Julie. As she grins she displays the empty darkness where once lurked two baby teeth, 'do you want another guess?' she giggles happily.

'Is it a frossil?' asks Robert. Julie looks puzzled and unsure. I shake my head.

'No it's not a …fwossil,' she replies shaking her head determinedly. I intervene.

'No it's not a fossil, those are bits of animals or plants from a long, long time ago that we sometimes find in rocks and stones. Shall we give them a clue, Julie?' Her squinty eyes sparkle, bless her; she is never happier than when passing on her growing knowledge of plants.

'It gwows!'

'Oh, no,' says Wayne, 'not another bloody plant!'

'Wayne, language!'

'Sorry Miss.'

Christopher has his hand up and waving even though he looks puzzled. I give him a nod.

'Yes, but what does it grow into?'

Julie can scarcely contain her excitement. 'It gwows into a dahwia. The shoots come out of here,' she says pointing at the top of the corm, 'and these tail things go down into the soil. And then they gwow up and up and up,' she stretches her arm high, 'and then the bootifuw fwowers gwow all different cowours. I saw some in the park and the man there he gived me this. It called a c...c...corm.'

She pronounces this last word slowly and carefully and my heart swells with affection for her. Her eyes might squint in two different directions and her hair might stick out at angles and be thin and sparse, but oh the joy on her face when she talks about flowers. What a miracle it was when I bought that first azalea.

*

Sharing time over, our lessons continue and later we go into the hall for a musical recital. We cluster around the piano and Mr Robson, a tall, bald-headed man with thick-lensed spectacles, explains how a piano works. When he takes the back off our ancient instrument and reveals how the different keys strike, there are gasps of amazement. He plays tunes that are very low and heavy,

'What does that sound like?' he asks.

'Elephants!' they shout. He plays the tinkly high notes next and some of the girls shout, 'Fairies!' and the boys scowl, pull faces and make derogatory remarks.

After he has explained about black notes, white notes and sharps and flats he proceeds to play for us, interspersing short excerpts from the classics with Beatles hits, a selection from Abba and television commercials. It is lovely to see their smiles when they first recognise a piece, some of them move in time to the music and others conduct with their fingers.

Nobody appears bored, just lost in the music. When Mr Robson finishes, I ask Steven to give a vote of thanks. He looks very pleased to have been asked, stands tall and pulls down his sweater,

'Mr Robson, we'd just like to spress our thanks for the good time what we have had. You must be a very strong fella to open a piano like that and I liked to see all them brass things what striked. But, best of all I liked the DA DA DA, DAAAAA, it were great that 5th Beethoven thingy, it just reminded me of the Wheel-tappers and Shunters Club on the telly. So…Thank you. Come on you lot give him a clap then.'

We all clap enthusiastically, and I marvel once more at the amazing ways in which a child's mind can work. Steven is certainly on form today.

After lunch we have an R.E. lesson and I have prepared the story of the young Jesus getting lost on the way home from Jerusalem.

'Have any of you ever been lost?' I ask. As usual a forest of hands wave in the air. 'Robbie, tell us about your experience. He stands proudly, then aware that his nose is running rubs his sleeve across the offending orifice. I bite my tongue. No, forget it this time; it's more important that he speaks. I make a mental note to have a quiet word later.

'Well it were like this, we was in town, right. That one where you go on the bus, it's called, Leeds. We was in this right big shop and me mam was buying some clothes and we kept asking for things so she said, "Go away! Go wait for me by the escalator," so we went, but we didn't know what one was, so we went.'

'Went where?' I asked confused.

'Back 'ome on't bus. We didn't know what to do, see, so we waited and waited and nobody came and we couldn't find no escalator, so we went.'

'That must have been very difficult,' I say. 'How did you feel?'

'Well we felt really pis...' Robbie pauses, thinks about it and replies, 'fed up. We didn't want to go in the first place but me mam was worried about the social coming.'

'I see, so being lost is a bit scary, would you say?'

'Yes, 'specially if you don't know what an escalator is.'

Linda is waiting patiently with her hand up so I choose her next. She is quite a shy little thing and doesn't often volunteer to stand before the class. She holds the bottom of her cardigan nervously and winds it round her hands.

'I got lost at the seaside. We went on the club trip. Some people went on a pub crawl and round the arcades. My mum and dad took us on the beach. It was dead good. I was building sandcastles and I went to the sea for some water to put in the moat. Then I saw a starfish, I've never seen one before so I picked it up and put it in my bucket and I kept on seeing things like that so I kept on walking and picking them up. When my bucket was full I turned round to go back to my mum and dad but I couldn't see them anywhere.'

'Oh dear, how did you feel then?'

'I felt really, really scared and I looked and looked but there were loads of them deckchair thingies with people sitting on them and none of them was my mum and dad.'

'Did you 'ave any food?' asked Wayne.

'No, I didn't.'

'Oh 'eck, you could 'ave starved to death!'

'What happened next? How did you find your family?' I ask, trying to bring the children back on track.

'Well, I started to cry and this lady came and said "are you lost?" and I said "yes." So she got hold of my hand and took me to this telephone box and she rang for the police and this police car came and...guess what?' The children stare, all agog.

'My mum and dad were *in* it!' The children shake their heads, amazed. 'They had been looking for me and they were dead scared because they thought I'd drownded, but I hadn't but another girl had and she was wearing the same swimming costume as *me*!' Linda's eyes were like saucers.

'My goodness, that must have been terrible.'

'It was. I don't know if she got her costume in Woolworth's but I did.'

I began to feel that the lesson was slipping away from me so I started the story, confident that the children all understood about getting lost.

'This story is about a time when Jesus got lost. When he was twelve years old Jesus went with his family to Jerusalem. It was a long way and they had to walk because they didn't have cars and buses in those days...' And so I continue.

When I get to the part where Mary and Joseph realise that Jesus is missing I give it all I've got.

'They searched and they searched, but they couldn't find him anywhere. I expect that they felt like Linda's mum and dad did and were worried that something awful had happened to him. Perhaps he had fallen and hurt himself; perhaps he was lost in the desert, hungry and thirsty.'

'Maybe someone had pinched him. You know, 'Stranger Danger' like you told us about. Maybe a bad man had taken him off!' This is from Christopher, who looks at life very seriously.

'Well, Mary began to shout, "Jesus! Jesus!" But there was no answer. Then all the people began searching and shouting. Can you help me, let's all shout for him.'

'Jesus! Jesus!' we shout dramatically and then pause to listen. Everyone is quiet and then Steven interjects excitedly.

'I know what 'appens, I've guessed. I expect he was stuck on a cross somewhere and couldn't get down.'

So much for Religious Education! I continue as If I've not heard, but the biblical ending does seem to be rather an anti-climax.

During the afternoon I decide to respond to Steven's new found love for Beethoven's Fifth symphony. I give them each sheets of 'best' drawing paper and some brand new sets of felt-tipped pens. There is much excitement at having such lovely tools. Equipment is scarce so our stock cupboard is carefully controlled (I had to steal these during hymn practise).

'Now children, this morning when our visitor, Mr. Hobson, came he played for us all kinds of beautiful music. Some of you particularly liked a piece by a man called Beethoven, his Fifth Symphony, so I'm going to play some of it for you in a minute.'

'Oh cool!' interrupts Steven. 'That's the Da Da DA, DAAA one isn't it. Oh I like that, it's like when yer watching the telly and the baddy's just about to come on and it goes Da Da Da, Daa! It's ace.'

'Well, when we hear that little bit it's like a pattern and that pattern gets repeated over and over again. In music we have a special name for those patterns; they are called 'motifs'. When you listen very carefully, you can hear lots of other motifs and it all joins together to make a beautiful piece of music. Steven, if you were to draw that pattern that you just sang to us, what would it look like? Do you think that you could draw it on the blackboard for us?'

'I'll 'ave a go, Miss.' Steven comes out to the blackboard and draws three short horizontal lines and one long one.

'Well done, Steven. That's a really good try. Would anyone else do it in a different way?' Up goes Robbie's hand and he ambles out to the board.

'I think it sounds kind of rough and jagged, so I'd do it like this.' He proceeds to draw what looks like a small mountain range with the slopes getting progressively taller.'

'That's lovely; I can tell that you're really thinking about this. We all see and hear things in different ways. So I would like you to listen very, very, carefully to the music and choose a different colour for each different pattern. Every time you hear the same pattern I want you to draw it in exactly the same way and with the same colour, like this.' I demonstrate on the blackboard, check that everyone has understood, answer some questions and begin. It is heaven! No one talks; there is just the sound of scratching felt-tips and glorious music. Sunshine floods the classroom and I walk around whispering praises to each of the children from my vast vocabulary of such words; 'super, great, magnificent, what beautiful colours, what good use of imagination, that is brilliant, that's really interesting, I love the way you are doing that' and so on.

Five minutes before the end of the lesson we gather the work together and then share what each has done. They have produced some startling pieces and I encourage the children to make positive comments. I hold up Julie's bold and colourful creation but don't mention the name of the artist.

'Just look at this one, isn't it beautiful.'

'Yea, 'ave yer noticed how every pattern is like a bit of a flower. I bet it's Julie's picture,' remarks Wayne. Julie blushes prettily, lowers her head shyly and smiles.

'It is, it weminded me of a garden, all differwent colours.'

Linda has used thick, black pen for the main motifs and pale colours for the other patterns. It is very striking, if a little disturbing. When I hold it up, the children see this too. Christopher remarks, 'That's really good but sort of scary. Why is it scary, Linda?' She is quiet for a moment, rolling her hands together and then chewing on her fingernails. Then she says softly, 'It reminds me of the bad things.'

'What kind of bad things, Linda?' I ask. She pushes her thumb into her mouth and shakes her head rapidly from side to side.

'She means monsters and stuff,' says Wayne. I decide to leave it for now but I'm puzzled that Jamie, who is sitting next to Linda, has his face covered by his hands and is also shaking his head.

After we have admired the work of all the children it's time to go home. The children lift their chairs onto their tables and stand straight, hands by their sides.

'Good afternoon, children. I hope you have a lovely holiday.'

'Good after*noon* Miss John*son,* Good after*noon* every*body*.'

I stand at the door ready to watch them walk up the corridor. My colleague Karen is on cloakroom duty, she gives me the thumbs up sign meaning, I suppose, half-term holiday at last. I grin and then feel someone patting my arm. Steven is looking up at me with eyes of such a singing blue, his blonde hair rumpled and a smudge of red felt-tip pen down one cheek. His grey school jumper is spattered with gravy and his school bag bursts open to reveal all manner of stones, conkers, screwed up comics and a spilling of P.E. kit.

'Thanks, Miss,' he says. I'm puzzled.

'What for, Steven?'

'For today, Miss. It wasn't half good. I love that Beethoven, Miss. He must 'ave a reet good band. See you after the holidays.'

'Bye Steven,' I say, feeling slightly dazed.

The Conference

I awake on the first day of the holiday, my limbs ache, my head is heavy and I feel overwhelmingly tired. That's the thing about school holidays I always seem to be ill as soon as the adrenaline cuts out. Then I remember, today is the day I go to the conference and I am really looking forward to a change of scene.

*

It is time. Light cascades from the main hall. Chatter drones and fizzles, my heart thumps. I push the door. The place is packed. My spirits dangle on a thread somewhere around my feet. Trust me to be late! I know not one person. I look to my right, lots of well turned out, confident people neatly sitting. I look to my left and a smile envelops me. His hand pats the empty seat beside him. Confused and stumbling I hurry over and take my place. Everything else fades. The meeting, my reason for being there. All the focus of the past weeks.

All I can think of are his abnormally long legs spread casually into the aisle, his dusky blue jacket which has been hoisted from the seat and crumpled on his knee. I try to concentrate on the speaker. My companion laughs as does everyone else. I must concentrate. I have waited for this time. He turns as if to share the joke, his face rugged and alive with light. I note the ruffled blonde hair and the eyes. No, it can't be right to say I *noted* the eyes, rather that I am swept into them. Can you drown in someone's eyes? I find myself smiling back, going deeper into the blue, rinsing myself in his laughter. I must turn away. I must concentrate.

There is stillness about him that I find rare in a man. His large, square fingered hands lie comfortably on the crumpled ball of his jacket, his immense feet placid on polished floor. His arms are so long that the sleeves of his jumper are too short, revealing golden hairs on tanned skin. He leans towards me, bending his head to mine.

'I'm Peter, Peter Bield, by the way.' Again that smile.

I stutter, 'A...And I'm Kathy.'

My hand is suddenly enveloped in his. So big, so warm. Mine just nestles there, like a dormouse.

The talk is excellent, amusing, inspiring, challenging and when we retire to the bar there is much to discuss, but all I want to know about is Peter. I think how to frame my first question but he gets there first.

'So Kathy, tell me about you.' That's unusual; all the other men I know just want to talk about themselves. Trouble is, I can't think of anything to say. He grins at me, his eyes crinkle at the corners and there's mischief in them.

'Tell me about your favourite foods.'

'Oh, ice-cream and Yorkshire pudding.'

'What a combination!'

'I don't mean together!' and suddenly I am telling him about school and about Julie, and Robbie and Linda and the estate and all its problems.

'It sounds like you love your job as much as I love mine.'

'What do you do?'

I was ordained in the summer and start as a curate just before Christmas. I should have started in September but I've been in hospital for a few months. I was involved in a car crash, a couple of joy riders on the wrong side of the road. Smashed up my leg pretty badly, I'm still having physio but getting there.'

'It sounds horrible, is it very painful?'

'It's getting better. So, where do you come from? Where is this den of iniquity where you teach?'

I explain about Becklefield and he's suddenly very quiet.

He stands abruptly, 'Let me get you another drink, lager again?'

'Please.' He lopes off taking enormous strides with just a slight limp and I see him laughing with a group at the bar. When he returns he shakes his head and starts to laugh.

'What's so funny?'

'Life, I suppose. Would you believe it, in just a few weeks I start work as curate of St Michael's...in Becklefield'

'You're joking!'

'I certainly am not. I'm just amazed that out of all the hundreds of people here I've found you.'

'Well, I'm glad that you did.' Then I flush with embarrassment.

'So am I, very definitely, so am I!'

*

As I lie in my narrow bed that night I marvel at what has happened, at this amazing connection between us. Meeting him was like an electric shock, a spark of recognition. I smile in the darkness until my jaw aches.

*

I awake, aflame with energy and go for a walk around the grounds before breakfast.

I rustle through leaves, marvel at colour, texture and shape. The sky is a startling blue; I can almost taste the fecund earth. I return to the conference centre with a throbbing heart and rosy face.

The dining room is set with long tables covered with crisp cream cloths and people mill around, looking for friends, or like me, wondering what to do next. I seat myself facing the door so that I can see when he comes in. I feel suddenly anxious. What if I imagined our connection last night? What will I do if he just walks past? Suddenly I can't bear the thought of him sitting elsewhere. My heart thumps. My mouth feels dry. People come and sit on either side of me. We smile and exchange greetings and all the time I want to say, 'No! Don't sit there; I'm saving it for someone.' Then, all at once, he's here. He sits opposite me and again that huge smile and those eyes, drenching me with blue. I cannot look away, I reach for my breakfast roll, and my heart rises like bread dough.

'Morning, did you sleep well?' he asks and suddenly we are chattering easily, like old friends. After breakfast I am booked into an art workshop and he into music but we have a free afternoon. We arrange to meet after lunch to walk by the river.

I spend the morning learning printing techniques, my hands covered in sticky red and green paint as I try to produce unusual place mats and Christmas cards. I'm enjoying the freedom to poddle about and create and imagine doing something similar with the children at school. Then after I've cleaned up it's time for chapel and worship. Not being a church-goer, I don't know what to expect.

People walk in carrying a variety of things they have created. There are collages, paintings, roughly carved objects, flower arrangements and so much more. These are all placed reverently on a long low table at the front of the chapel. The worship leader begins a rousing chorus and the building erupts with a joyful noise. It is like nothing I have ever experienced before. I join in with delight.

*

The afternoon is crisp and shiny. We stroll, hand in hand as the river gushes alongside us. I feel tiny beside him, I don't even reach his shoulder but when he looks down at me, his face creases with affection and I feel safe, safer than I have felt since...the 'awful time'.

Peter suggests a boat and helps me as I wobble into my seat. He takes the oars confidently. His arms are exquisite. I lean back and trail my hand in the river and feel it throb against my skin. We brush against the fingers of yellowing willows and I inhale the scent of water. I gaze at Peter, his earlobes look edible, his blond hair dipped in sunlight. The oars dabble in and out of the water, softly drizzling fat droplets back onto the smooth surface. I can't remember ever being so happy. We decide to give afternoon tea at the centre a miss and opt for a riverside I. The garden glows with dahlias and chrysanths in red and gold, coffee and amber. Beech trees are clothed in coppery leaves and as we sit, one falls and lands upon my head. He reaches forward and gently plucks it from my hair, looks at it and places it carefully in his shirt pocket.

I laugh, 'What are you doing with that?'

'It's exactly the colour of your hair. It will remind me.' My heart quickens.

Later we delve into our crumbly scones and spread them thickly with raspberry jam and cream and give ourselves up to the enjoyment of taste and texture. The ducks huddle beneath the picnic table waiting for the crumbs to come.

As we walk back to the conference centre autumn envelops us. Rosehips hang like baubles lit with a ruby glow and the hawthorn is like a pointillist painting with dots of vibrant red amongst the green and brown. I notice a fat slug slithering, a glutinous trail following behind. 'That's me,' I think, 'that's how I was before I came here, sluggishly moving through life carrying with me a great trail of sorrow'. I sigh and Peter pulls me close,

'What's wrong, sunshine? You sound so sad.'

'I'm not, not any more. I was just thinking that's all.'

He turns to face me, his hands gently touching my shoulders. He gazes down at me. 'You have such a lovely smile,' he says, 'but I just get the feeling that inside is a pain that you're trying to push away. I'm right, aren't I? Do you want to talk about it?' I shake my head rapidly, *No talking, there's too much talking. It's best just to forget.* My thoughts are juddering and crunching. I shiver and he draws me close.

'Come on, I'll race you back to the house!' He starts to run but he doesn't let go of my hand.

*

The week passes far too quickly. It's like we are locked in a parallel world. There are more workshops and talks, I meet people from all walks of life and from many countries, people all bound together by faith. I have never experienced that before. In the evenings there are concerts and hilarious sketches and stand-up comics and poets and singing and dancing. The ceilidh on the last night is fantastic, everyone holding hands and counting out the steps with the caller and getting things hopelessly wrong and collapsing in giggles. Then twirling and making bridges with arms and dancing through and clapping. I am out of breath and sweating and Peter suggests we go for a walk. We amble to the lake, suddenly shy with one another. We have been together for almost a whole week and we have never even kissed and I am longing for his lips on mine. I place my head on his chest and can hear his heartbeat. He strokes my hair, tenderly tucking a wayward strand behind my ear.

'Kathy, I've loved being with you this week. Would you understand if I say I think I love you? I want to be with you all the time but, if we weren't going to live in the same place, it would probably be easier.'

'I know, but we'll still be able to meet, won't we?'

'Of course, but we'll have to take it steady. I'm just beginning a new life, I have to make a good job of it, it's what I feel called to do. I mustn't be too distracted, too involved. Oh Kathy, do you understand?'

I am beginning to.

Dear Santa

The run up to Christmas has begun. The children are already making Christmas lists, no problem at all getting them to write a letter to Santa Claus. Robbie has got big ideas.

'He's gonna bring me a train set, one of them reet big ones with loads o' rails that you fit together and engines and carriages and everything.' Wayne is not impressed.

'I've already got one o' them. Me dad made little stations and trees and things. It's in the loft. It looks *dead* good. Darren's dad comes to play sometimes. He brings his own engine, it's the Flying Scotsman.'

'Don't be daft, engines don't fly!'

'No it's...'

'Wayne! Get on with your writing please. People cannot concentrate.' He sighs loudly, but returns to the job in hand.

Robbie seems to have few ill effects from the fire. I watch him. Thankfully he doesn't seem particularly traumatized but his asthma is much worse. I have his inhaler in my desk drawer.

I doubt very much his dream of a train set will become a reality. That's the trouble with the Santa myth. It makes anything seem possible, but I know that many of these children will be disappointed. I walk around the class, checking their work and helping with spellings. Oh dear, Linda is another one destined for a let down.

'Dear Santa, please can you get me a doll that wees its nappy and cries and a pram to push it around in. A pink wun wud be gud. Fanks.'

Since her dad left to live with Wayne's mum there doesn't seem to have been much in the way of treats, in fact Wayne is showered with gifts and Linda just seems to have been forgotten. Poor kid! Unless of course her mother is also a shoplifter.

'Miss! Miss! Jamie is asleep!' and there he is, his head on his arms, whey faced and shabbily clad. I bend towards him and catch the sharp smell of urine and unwashed clothes. His forehead is hot and damp; he doesn't stir at my touch so I decide to leave him for a while.

Julie squints at him and shakes her head. 'He had an 'ard night,' she remarks.

Puzzled I ask, 'What was he doing, Julie?'

She presses her lips together and shakes her head. 'It were 'ard that's all.'

In the hall for P.E. Jamie is awake but still looks shattered. I drop him off at the staffroom and leave him with Mrs Lambing, one of our nursery nurses. She'll make sure he's looked after.

The children chatter like starlings as they pull on shorts and t-shirts and music and movement begins. Earlier in the week we had watched a snippet on television of the world figure skating champions, Lyudmila Pakhomova and Alexander Gorshkov.

The children were mesmerized as we saw the ease with which they skated, the graceful movements of arms and legs, the dizzying twirls as they danced, completely at one with the music. I put the music cassette in the player.

Now it is our turn, without skates, on the polished floor. I watch them coil and spin, gyrate and swivel. Sally and Linda dance together, encircling one another their faces like silver. I had half expected giggles and groans from the boys but they are taking it so seriously, Steven gives himself up to the music, swaying and twisting, lifting his arms gracefully and balancing on one leg whilst he lifts the other leg from the ground. Oh wow! They're really into this. Robbie, is wheeling and whirling and has a feline grace that I've never seen in him before. He sweeps the ground with the tips of his fingers and then lifts both hands high exultantly. He seems to have forgotten where he is. He moves around the hall in a trance. He expresses the music with every movement. I am amazed. Then, all at once, there is a puddle around him. He stops, coughing and confused. He has wet himself. He looks at me in terror, his beautiful face cracked, tears leap in his eyes. Quickly I cover him with my jacket and ease him out of the hall whispering;

'It's OK don't worry, just go find Mrs Lambing in the staffroom, she'll sort you, off you go!'

He hurries off along the corridor, with a clumsy wide-legged gait as his P.E. shorts hang with the weight of his own pee.

Later, when the children have gone for lunch I search out Jamie. He is sitting on Mrs Lambing's knee wrapped in a blanket.

'He's got a right temperature on him, poor mite, he keeps shivering. Summats not right and that's for sure. Miss Heaton's been trying to get his dad but he's not answering the phone. She says will yer tek 'im 'ome?' She brushes Jamie's hair away from his eyes and smiles tenderly. I feel a wave of affection for this large lady with soft brown eyes and several chins. She usually radiates joy but now, her lower lip trembles and her eyes are liquid sorrow.

I help Jamie out to the car, still wrapped in his blanket and drive a few hundred yards to Bismark Terrace. I am surprised to see that the windows of Robbie's house are still boarded up. Jamie lives just three doors away. I leave the blanket in the car and hold his hand; he grips mine tightly and trembles. As I reach to knock on the faded blue door it swings open. I gasp.

Jamie's dad is balanced on a kitchen chair and one of his legs is in a plaster cast. He is intent on securing a tumble of gold and silver foil to the wire of the central light fitting. The room is hung with cascades of glitter. There are yards and yards of fairy lights twinkling on every side. In the corner of the room stands a huge Christmas tree which drips multicolored baubles reflecting light. Brightly wrapped presents are piled beneath it.

'My goodness, it looks like fairy land,' I say and then, taking Jamie's hand lead him into his home. Is it my imagination or is he pulling back?

'Come on Jamie, look at what your dad has being doing and with a poorly leg too. Isn't he clever?' There is no reply. His skin looks as dry as parchment, his eyes two empty windows. I turn to his father who has climbed down from his eyrie.

'Hello Mr Coggs, I'm Jamie's teacher, Miss Johnson. He's not at all well so we thought it best to bring him home.' I reach out my hand to shake his, it is limp and clammy. He stares at me with cold metallic eyes; he is wearing a long flapping anorak and pushes back his lank, greasy hair. I feel the intense cold within the house. There appears to be no form of heating.

'You'd better go up to bed then, if tha's poorly. Go on, up yer go. I'll see to thee later.'

Jamie walks slowly across the floor, head bowed, and shoulders slumped.

'Bye Jamie,' I call, 'hope you feel better soon.' He turns to look at me and my heart sinks at his blemished, frightened face.

Unwelcome Visitor

'So, my love, only ten more days until I start at St Michael's. I can't wait to see you again.'

'Me too,' I breathe, 'I miss you so much. Take care.'

'And you, I'll ring again tomorrow.'

I replace the telephone receiver. The warmth of his voice seeps through me. Only ten more days, I can't wait. Peter's induction will take place on the first Wednesday of advent. Meg and John and lots of other church folk have been cleaning and polishing and generally preparing the building for this special occasion. There is to be a huge feast after the service and all are contributing. Meg has been busy coordinating the list of sweets and savouries. I see her shadow against the glass of the front door and open before she knocks.

'No prize for guessing who that was,' she laughs indicating the telephone.

'It could be anyone.'

'Could be, but no-one else puts a look like that on your face.' I catch sight of myself in the hall mirror. She's definitely right. I grin inanely.

'Now, I've had promised six dozen scones, ten Victoria sandwich cakes, five dozen cupcakes, two dozen almond slices and two dozen coconut slices and...'

'My goodness, how many are we feeding?'

'Well, they reckon about three hundred. Do you think we'll have enough cakes?'

'I haven't got a clue.'

'Never mind, I'll ask Mrs Midgley, she knows everything.'

'Doesn't she just.'

'Anyway, what I really want to know is, have you met his parents yet?'

'No, we don't want to do anything too formal because, well, it's early days yet. So, when they arrive on Tuesday night, a group of us are just going out together for a meal and Peter was wondering if you and John would like to come too. I *was* going to come over later, to invite you.'

'Sounds good to me, I'll mention it when we meet on Saturday. We're going to the flicks to see Murder on the Orient Express.'

'Oh is that the one with Albert Finney and Sean Connery?'

'Yes, and Ingrid Bergman, I like her, she's brilliant,' Meg laughed happily. 'I can't tell you how good it is to be dating again. I feel like a new woman.'

'And you look like one,' I add, noting her radiance. How good it is to see my friend happy once more. We share a couple of glasses of red wine and some black forest gateau and then she goes back home to her lists.

Later in the evening I receive another visitor.

'Oh, hello Mike, I wasn't expecting you.'

'No I bet you weren't.'

'What's that supposed to mean?' He shrugs and his eyes lock on to mine.

There is an unspeakable stillness. I try again.

'Look, I thought we agreed; we are just friends. Why are you so angry?'

'Why do you think?'

'I don't know. I told you right from the beginning, how I feel. I like you but that's all.'

'So that's it then! I'm supposed to go, just like that!'

'Friends don't need to go anywhere,' I snap back angrily.

'We're not just friends. I fancy you like mad, you know that.'

'Yes, me and a dozen others. Come off it, Mike, there is nothing special between us and there never has been.' We are standing in the hall. He suddenly moves closer, pushing me against the wall.

'Oh come on! Stop playing hard to get.'

'Mike, no!' I catch the smell of beer on his breath. He puts his arms around me pressing his body close and kisses me deeply, his tongue is snaking in my mouth and his hand lingers around my waist. I try to struggle out of his grasp but this seems to excite him even more. His hands are moving slowly, sensuously over my body. Terror floods through me and unbidden, desire. He is pulling at my skirt.

'No, I said no!'

'You like it, you know you do.'

'No, I don't.' His hand cups my breast.

'Come on, we deserve some fun. Stop pretending. I want you, you know I want you.'

I struggle in an attempt to free myself and manage to knee him in the groin.

'You bitch!' He lets go and bends double in pain.

'Get out of my house, you bastard. Get out!'

He glares at me, his eyes darkening and stands with his back to the door.

'No way, you've been dangling me on a string long enough. Well, now it's pay back time.'

He lurches towards me, he has obviously drunk more than I realized. He pins me against the wall.

'No!' His mouth is on mine again, his hands probing. *Help me! Help me!*

My head is buzzing, think! Think! Suddenly there is a fierce rapping on the glass door. He jumps away from me. The door bursts open and Meg stands there. She glares at him.

'I think you had better go! Now! Scram! Before I call your bloody inspector.' Then to me, 'Are you okay he didn't...' I shake my head, tears of shame scalding my face. He stares at me in fury, eyes full of hate, and then lurches down the path.

'Randy bastard! He just can't hold his drink and all his brains are in his boxers. Are you all right, love? Do you want me to stay awhile?' I nod my head and stumble to the sofa. I sit and thrust my head between my knees, dizziness overwhelms me.

Meg sits alongside, her hand on my shoulder.

'It's all right, love, he's gone now and I don't think he'll be back. Come on, we'll have a nice cup of tea. I'll go and make it.'

As she rattles around the kitchen the old familiar shaking begins and I know that once more I have seen the dark of things, the gloom that broods. Somehow, I know this is not the end.

Plans and Performances

Agnes Heaton prepares to lead our staff meeting. In spite of the fact that she has just dealt with two irate mothers fighting in the playground while hoards of children circled like birds of prey over a carcass. She is calm and unruffled.

'Now, I just want to run through with you all, the plans for Christmas. First, the film show, I have booked the cinema projector and the large screen for the second Friday in December, so it might be a good idea to have the parties that day as well.'

'O God! Not the parties,' whispers Steve. 'I haven't got over last year yet.' There are grins all round as we each remember the drunken Santa Claus lurching down the corridor ringing a bell and singing, 'Jingle bells, Batman smells, Robin's had it away.' And a red faced Miss Heaton running after him calling, 'Santa! Santa! I've made you a nice cup of black coffee. Santa!'

She glares at Steve and he wipes the smirk from his face. By the end of the meeting we have arranged parties, film shows, the carol service and the staff pantomime. This is a tradition in our school as many of our children have never been to the theatre. We practise often until late at night, it's the best team building exercise I know. This year it's Snow White and the Seven Dwarfs. Don volunteers to be Snow White; I can't wait to see him in costume. Ron is the wicked Queen and the rest of us are the dwarfs, which is a bit painful as we have to practice walking on our knees. Clara Biggins, our cleaner, offers to help Mrs Lambing with the costumes. Sandra has written the script and it's a corker. The children will love it.

It's late when I arrive home and I still have marking and preparation to do, but, I wouldn't swap my job for anything. Must get on, the mayor is visiting tomorrow.

*

'Miss, it's true isn't it? There's a bear coming today, a bear with a chain. I can't wait to see it,' says Robbie.

'I know,' adds Wayne excitedly, 'some of 'em are twelve foot tall!'

Oh no! They're going to be *so* disappointed. I explain about the mayor.

'Well if that's all he does why does he need a chain?' asks Wayne grumpily.

'Our dog's on a chain,' says Linda. 'It's to stop 'im getting out of the yard.'

'Well I can see't sense in that, but what does a mayor wear one for?' asks Robbie.

I explain that it is a tradition for mayors to wear chains, 'It's like a badge of office,' I conclude.

Wayne argues, 'He could just wear a badge then!'

'Aye, one with he's name on,' pipes up Julie

'Look at that!' exclaims Wayne suddenly, gazing out of the window. 'That's a real posh car, and there's a chauffeur in it, wearing a uniform and everything.'

The children crowd at the window and wave excitedly.

'Look, look, there's the Queen!' exclaims Sally as the Lady Mayoress steps from the car. 'Oh don't she look lovely Miss, you can allus tell it's the Queen cos she's got all them lovely hats.'

'Let me see,' shouts Robbie. 'But she's only got *one* on.'

'She don't wear them all at once you ninny, just one at a time. I expect all the rest are on top of the wardrobe in 'at boxes.'

I suddenly feel very tired and it's only ten o'clock. Roll on playtime. I definitely need a very strong coffee.

*

The days pass quickly in a haze of Christmas preparations. Our child-produced cards and calendars adorn the walls and glitter and glue adhere to every surface. Santa comes to school next week but my own particular Santa arrives on Tuesday and I'm just like a child, full to the brim with excitement. Every evening his phone calls have been like a nightcap easing me into deep and dreamless sleep, very rare for me. In addition there have been long, loving letters every word of which I have savoured. Now I'm to see him, touch him, my fingers tingle and burn.

I glance around my living room with satisfaction. Two dark blue glass vases are filled with freesias, their perfume fills the room. A white sheepskin rug lies before the fire and blue and yellow cushions are spread invitingly on the cream sofa. I can hardly wait.

*

Suddenly he's here, eyes like a sunlit sea and I am in them and floating.

'Hello Titch,' he grins and folds me inside his fleecy jacket. I feel the warmth of him. I put my arms inside and around his waist and

54

snuggle.

'Hello you! Oh it's so good to see you.' I catch the scent of lemons and spice and hear his heart beat like a celebratory drum and there is no need for words, just kisses. It's a while before he talks.

'I met with Tom, the vicar, this morning. He's a lovely bloke, isn't he?'

'He is, I warmed to him the moment we met. He's so honest and sincere I feel as though I could trust him with anything. It was he that suggested I go to the conference.'

'I know, he told me. I went down on my knees and thanked him for that.'

'You didn't, you idiot.' I pick up a cushion and throw it at him.

'Why, you ungrateful wench, here I am your curate, come to call and offer you solace and all I get is disrespect. Come here,' and suddenly I am in his arms again melting into him. He is my soul mate.

We never do get round to making coffee. Our time alone passes so quickly.

'Gosh, is that the time? I must fly, got to pick Mum and Dad up at the station at half past four. So, just let me check, we meet at the Hare and Hounds at seven, okay? How are you getting there?'

'I'm traveling with Meg and John.'

'Oh yes, met John this afternoon, he's seems a smashing bloke'

'Well, Meg seems to think so.'

'See you later, sweetheart.' We share another long kiss. And then I close the door pressing my back against it and rubbing my tingling lips with my finger.

*

I soak in a lavender-scented bath and dream. I have a new dress made of soft lime-green wool, olive-green stiletto heel shoes and a matching bag and belt. When I'm dressed and ready I ponder about jewellery. My grandma's pearls are too heavy and nothing else looks right either, never mind I'll go without. Later, as I pass the front door I notice a small package on the doormat. There is a card which I open first. A picture of a long line of cows bears the words; 'I love you 'til the cows come home.' Signed Peter xxx. The box is swathed in Sellotape necessitating the use of scissors and inside there's a note, 'I knew you'd get in eventually!' I open the box and there, lying on red velvet is a gold locket, something I've always wanted. I stand before the mirror and fasten it around my throat. It's a long time since I've felt the power of love.

*

Meg looks stunning in a royal blue sheath dress and John obviously thinks so too.

He helps me into the back seat of his Cortina and off we go. The Hare and Hounds is a pleasant pub in the nearby village of Beneton. Peter and his parents have already arrived, as have Reverend Tom and his wife, Alice. Introductions are made, 'Mum, Dad, I'd like you to meet my friend Kathy who is a teacher at the local school, Kathy this is Mum, also known as Hannah, and my dad, Harry.' Hannah takes my hand in hers and smiles warmly; 'Lovely to meet you at last, Kathy, Peter has talked so much about you.' She is the epitome of elegance, tall, white hair swept up into a bun, startling pale blue eyes and the softest skin that fractures into lively wrinkles whenever she smiles.

'I love your dress, Kathy, what a beautiful colour; you look a picture, my love.'

'Thank you, I've been looking forward to meeting you so much.'

She hugs me warmly and I catch the scent of violets and experience again that feeling of safety and peace. There is something so solid about Peter's family. His dad gives me a bear hug and whispers, 'Good to meet you, lass, good to meet you.'

During dinner we chat about Yorkshire in general and the North York Moors in particular. I mention my love of Hutton-le-Hole, Rosedale and Kirkbymoorside and the glory of the moors in August when the purple of the heather is truly stunning.

'I wish that the children in my class could see it, some of them have never been to the countryside.'

'Perhaps you'll be able to bring them one day,' says Peter's mum. 'Now I want you to tell me all about Becklefield.'

The dinner passes very pleasantly. Reverend Tom has lots of stories to tell of his long ministry and Peter's dad, Harry teases his wife affectionately.

'You know,' he says at one point, 'marriage is a partnership where no matter how hard a man tries, his wife is still the better half. Aren't you my, love?'

'Aye and sometimes it's more than half,' she quips amid much laughter

Meg tells the story of when I had my phone fitted.

'I rang her pretending to be the phone service and asked if she could possibly measure the wire between the input point and the telephone as we were several yards short, and what did you say, Kathy?' she asked laughingly.

I said, 'There is rather a lot. Wait one moment please and I measured it with a ruler!' Peter smiles into my eyes affectionately.

John asks about Peter's time at agricultural college and about working on the farm.

'I bet you worked long hours when you were dairying.'

'I certainly did, but lambing was worse. Sometimes I'd go for a week without a good night's sleep but it was a great life. You know, you feel really close to God in the dead of night with a new life in your arms. It's very special.'

John smiled softly and said, 'Aye well it'll be a bit different here in Becklefield. Some of these children don't know the difference between a sheep and a cow and probably wouldn't know what a lamb was.'

I smile at this and add, 'Yes but they do know where babies come from. Some think they are really clued up on the facts of life.'

And then Reverend Tom tells the tale of the condoms.

*

I remember all this the next day as I tell my class part of the Christmas story.

'And there were three wise men,' I begin, showing them the beautiful illustration in the story book, 'who spent a lot of time studying the stars. One night they noticed a really special star in the dark sky. It was bigger and brighter than all the others. "This star means that a special King has been born. We must follow it and try to find the new king," said Melchior and that it was they did.'

Wayne was listening very carefully, 'Miss, if they were men, why were they wearing dresses?'

Before I had chance to reply Robert said, 'Some men do, I heard it on the telly. They're called Trans... Transylvania.'

I decide to carry on with the story, quickly.

'So they climbed onto their camels and began to ride through the darkness, following the star.'

'Some people do change sex,' interrupted Wayne, 'there was this programme about a tennis player.'

'Wayne! So they followed the star all through the night and every night until one still, quiet evening it came to rest over a house where the baby Jesus was with his mum and his dad.'

Sally's hand flew into the air and waved like a flag. 'Miss, miss, my mum's 'avin a baby and it won't be long now. Her belly's getting really big and the baby moves inside her. I feeled it with my hand. Aaw it were lovely Miss and do you know what? It grew from a tiny seed and-' At last, the bell begins to ring.

'Right, children. Stand. Well done, now walk very quietly to the door. Jamie you're standing nicely you can be the leader. Wayne you can be like a sheepdog and help everyone from the back.' Phew! I need coffee!

After break the children are working through their maths work cards and I am hearing some children read. Outside the air is crisp and light with a thick frost upon the ground. Inside it's a different matter. The air is thick and heavy and the windows are stuck fast, caked with years of paint. The smell of unwashed clothes, rancid fat and urine is even stronger than usual.

Christopher is reading about Deb the Rat and I ease off my shoes and wiggle my toes under the desk. He reads like a Dalek, jerky and monotonous.

'The-mouse-is-in-the-shoe-house, oh miss, that's right funny that is.'

I look at him puzzled. 'What's funny, Christopher?'

'The mouse, Miss, it's in the book in a shoe *and* it's under the desk in *your* shoe.' I look down quickly, just in time to see a small grey mouse leaving one shoe and scrabbling into the other.

'Aaaaah-' I manage to stop the scream before it leaves my mouth and quickly place my feet on the rungs of the chair.

'Miss, there's a mouse!' shouts Robbie. Not another one surely?

'Oh Miss! There's another!' screams Sally leaping onto her chair.

I stare in disbelief. There are mice scurrying everywhere. I start to shake. They didn't prepare me for this at college.

'Aand STOP!' I shout, believing in my heart that the children will obey.' (They did teach us that.)

There is an almost silence, just a few little squeals and nervous giggles. I notice that Sally is crying. I lower my voice to a deep, calm whisper.

'Now, this is what we are going to do. Ready, sit on your desks. Good. Now fold your arms. Well done. Now in a minute we are going to sing to the mice. Wayne, will you go to find Mr. Bullivant, please. Tell him what has happened and ask him to come to our classroom, okay?'

'Yes, Miss Johnson.'

'Right, off you go. Now let's see how many mice songs we know. Do you remember this one?

> *'Six little mice sat down to spin,*
> *Puss passed by and he looked in...'*

When Don arrives some time later we are singing;

> *'A mouse lived in a windmill in old Amsterdam*
> *A windmill with a mouse in and he wasn't grousing'*

Don opened the door and with his characteristic chuckle, joined in the song,

> *'He sang every morning how lucky I am*
> *Living in a windmill in old Amsterdam.'*

After a quick consultation I walk down the corridor and stand by the library door whilst Don sends the class to walk quietly towards me. We go in, silent as mice and close the door.

*

As I enter the staffroom at lunchtime I am greeted by a chorus of;

> *'I saw a mouse where?*
> *There on a chair?*
> *Where on the chair,*
> *Right there!'*

My experience is the talk of the school and the cause of much hilarity.

'Eh, Kathy.'

'What?'

'What are crisp, like milk and go "eek, eek, eek" when you eat them?'

'Go on.'

'Mice Krispies!'

'Thank you Don, I'll remember that.' I take a bite of my cheese sandwich.

'Oh, Kathy.'

'Yes?'

'What is a mouse's favourite record?'

'I don't know Steve, but I have a feeling you are going to tell me.'

'Please cheese me!' And so it goes on. I have a feeling that I will always be associated with mice, oh and of course, condoms.

When I've eaten, Don suggests that we go back to the classroom to see if the traps he has set have been successful.

We peer through the glass at the top of the door and stand open-mouthed at what we see. There are several traps scattered around the room, each one loaded with Kit-Kat from the staff tuck shop. By the nearest one there are two mice each trying to access the chocolate without being caught. Tiny little mice, reaching out minute little hands to capture chocolate crumbs. It looks like something out of a child's cartoon programme.

'I don't believe it,' bellows Don, 'I just don't believe it.'

My class and I spend the rest of the day in the library.

New Beginnings

Coloured light floods out across the darkened street and through the open doors comes the foot-tapping clamour of drums and guitars. I am glad I've walked through the estate as there are cars parked as far as the eye can see. Reverend Tom stands at the door, his face scrubbed and rosy, his white hair shining. He beams as I enter and whispers, 'We've saved you a seat at the front next to Peter's mum and dad.'

I feel honored. I hope that Harry and Hannah don't mind. Hannah's beaming smile of welcome chases away all my fears. 'Come on love, snuggle up, isn't it cold outside, I was dreading coming in here but they seem to have a good heating system, better than our church anyway and doesn't everything look beautiful, what a feast for the eyes!'

'Isn't it just, the flowers are gorgeous, I would never have thought of putting red and orange together but it looks so right.'

'Yes and those little purple and white touches just stop it being too heavy. Oh I do love flowers!'

'I'll have to introduce you to Julie in my class, she loves them too.'

'Oh yes, Peter's told me all about her. Bless her.'

'If you think all this looks good, wait until you see the buffet,' says Harry, 'it looks sumptuous.'

'Typical,' replies Hannah, 'always thinking of his stomach. Oh I love this one,' she says as the music group begins another worship song,'

'Be still for the presence of the Lord,
The Holy one is here.'

I remember singing it at the conference, warmth floods through me, and something else – a sort of peace, a great contentment. I've never felt that before today.

Soon the service begins and church wardens and clergy process down the central aisle. My eyes search out Peter, resplendent in his white surplice. His hair is like distilled moonlight and he looks so very happy. As he passes he catches my eye and winks, his mum squeezes my hand and I look up to see tears marching down her cheeks. Harry's eyes, also, glimmer with liquid love.

The organ bursts forth and we join our voices in great celebration. Later, Peter makes his vows and I am suddenly aware of the great step he is taking. His life will never be the same again. This is what he feels God has called him to do. He will be at the beck and call of all these people. He will never belong to me, He is promised to God.

I feel like I have sucked on a lemon.

*

Harry was right about the buffet it could have graced any banqueting hall.

'Oh Meg,' I whisper, 'it all looks stunning.'

'How could it not with so many people working together. Would you believe a total of thirty three people have baked cakes and at least a dozen ladies have been making sandwiches for five hours?'

'You must be shattered.'

'Do you know, it's very strange, but I'm not. We've had such a good time chattering, telling jokes and singing. It's been worth booking a day's holiday from work.' She turns, her eyes searching for John. 'Eee, just look at him. I might have known, did you ever see such a plateful. No doubt he'll keep me awake again with indigestion.' She flushed as she realized what she had said. I looked quizzically at her and she grinned. 'Well, he didn't have it *all* night.'

'Meg Warriner, what are you saying and in a church as well?' I teased.

'Oh, Kathy, I'm so mixed up. I'm that 'appy but I feel so guilty as well. My poor Keith, not dead twelve months and me in love again.' I hug her tightly.

'Meg, Keith loved you, you were a wonderful wife to him. He wouldn't want you to live the rest of your life in misery; he would want you to be happy. Just enjoy every moment.'

'Oh I will. I will.' And she looks at John with such brightness that I have to turn away.

*

It's a while before I get a chance to talk to Peter. He always seems to be surrounded by an adoring flock of elderly ladies. Then there is the mayor and other dignitaries and also several rather attractive and not so elderly ladies. But his love lit smiles from across the room keep me going.

As the crowds thin out, Harry and Hannah come to say goodbye. They are going across to the vicarage where they are staying the night.

'We've just come to say goodnight, love. We're both absolutely whacked so it's an early night for us and we have to catch the ten o'clock train from Leeds. Take care of yourself, dear. We hope to see you again soon,' says Hannah.

Harry gives me another bear hug. 'It's been a great pleasure meeting you Kathy; you're a real breath of fresh air.' I feel myself blushing.

'Thank you. I've loved getting to know you both. Have a safe journey.'

After I wave them off I go to the kitchen to see if I can be of use. There are cardboard cartons of clean cups on every surface and a bag of used tea towels stands by the door.

'Too late, lassie, the fun's all over,' says Meg. 'Time for bed, I think.'

'Speak for yourself,' says I, 'some of us are not so far along the journey.'

'You'd better get going then, I can see a young man waiting patiently.'

I turn around and look up at Peter's smiling face. He holds out his arm.

'Can I walk you home, fair maid?'

'You can indeed, sir,' I reply.

We walk companionably through the darkened streets.

'So,' he says when we reach my door, 'wasn't that just amazing, all those wonderful people being there for me. I only hope I can do a good job. I don't want to let anyone down.' I snuggle into his chest and put my arms inside his coat.

'You won't, I'm quite sure of that.'

Oh Christmas Tree

It's wonderful watching the children coming into the hall and catching sight of the tree for the first time. It is huge, almost touching the high ceiling with plump, thickly needled branches. They know what comes next and sit, chests puffed out, legs crossed, arms folded. It is so special to be chosen to help decorate the tree.

Julie looks like a stiff-backed scarecrow, her washed out cardigan too small and her thin wrists poke out of shapeless sleeves. Even though the frost is thick upon the ground outside, she wears only a thin cotton dress.

Miss Heaton stands quite still, only her eyes move as she views the rows of waiting children. She solemnly points at chosen individuals and they walk proudly towards the tree. We begin to sing our carols as a snaking line moves forward and each in turn climbs the steps and hangs a bauble or places a skein of tinsel. Julie lights up when she is chosen, her face as bright as the daytime moon. I watch as she reaches for a branch and slides her fingers tenderly across the springy needles, I see her sniff and can't resist a smile; she seeks out the scent of every growing thing she comes across.

Robbie strides out and chooses the biggest bauble he can find, whacks it into place, gives us all a cheeky grin and bows like a clockwork toy.

Soon the tree is resplendent in scarlet and gold and silver and blue. The children are no longer silent; an excited buzz zooms around the room. Miss Heaton stands quite still again and eyeballs each row in turn. The hubbub subsides, silence reigns.

'And now...' the head announces, 'we will choose the person who will put the fairy on the very top.' We wait with baited breath. Wayne looks like he'll burst a blood vessel; so much effort is put into sitting straight.

'I think I'll choose... Linda Brown.'

'Yes!' choruses my class, proud it is one of their own. Linda rises, steps over several pairs of feet and walks shyly to the front, her face carefully composed but with eyes like stars. Karen and Janet help her up the steps then place the fairy on the hook of the window pole and help Linda to guide her into place. As the large hook slides over the topmost spire a great cheer goes up. Linda walks back, a stream of sunlight.

Don, at the piano begins a jazzy introduction and we burst into song;

> *'Oh Christmas tree, Oh Christmas tree*
> *How lovely are your branches.'*

Back in the classroom there is more excitement, right in the middle of a maths lesson. The children are weighing and measuring a number of 'Christmas parcels'. Julie is busy watering the plants, including the hyacinths which we all planted weeks ago.

'Miss, Miss there's a fwower coming; Oh Miss there's a fwower at last!'

'Whose is it?' shouts Robbie. 'I bet it's mine.'

'Tisn't.'

'Oh don't say it's yours, your fings allus grow best.'

'Tisn't mine, it's Linda's and I fink it's ganna be a pink one, Linda cum and look.'

Linda stands quickly, knocking a box of crayons to the floor. She looks like a scared rabbit caught in the headlights.

'It's okay,' I say. 'Linda, you go look at your hyacinth. Now, everyone else, back to your maths please.' Whilst they all settle back to work I enjoy the scene enacted between Linda and Julie. Julie holds the flowerpot and eagerly points at the fat bud. Linda smiles in delight then they bend their heads and sniff, another moment for me to treasure.

*

At lunch time I pick tiredly at my cottage cheese salad. The door opens and in walks Mike, overly jovial; he greets us in Dixon of Dock Green mode.

'Evening all.'

Don jumps up in welcome, 'Hello lad, to what do we owe this visitation?'

'Stolen goods, I'm afraid. Someone's nicked all the church silver, so I've come to see where you've hidden it.'

'You mean you think it's one of our lot? Surely not!' Don says sarcastically.

'Well, put it this way, it's someone with a size three shoe and judging by the graffiti, felt-tipped around the place, someone who can't spell very well...they missed off the kicking K at the end of a four letter word.'

There are hoots of laughter. Mike pours himself a cup of tea and comes to sit opposite me. Prickles rise upon my neck; I stare intently at my salad.

'What do you want us to do then, Mike?' asks Don. 'A bit of search and rescue?'

'When did the stuff go missing?' asks Steve as he delves into his Pot Noodle.

Mike pulls a face, 'Well, I spoke to that new curate chap this morning. He doesn't seem to have a clue, a bit wet around the ears, if you ask me.' I bite back an angry retort but Sandra gets there before me.

'Oh I don't know, he looks pretty tasty to me, he can listen to my confessions any time.'

I glance up and catch Mike looking at me, with the wrong sort of look, coveting me.

'Well Sandra, I hate to say this, love, but I think you'll have to get in the queue behind Kathy, she's the one who seems to light his fire,' quips Steve. I feel my face redden and look up; Mike's eyes have darkened to a frightening shade of North Sea grey.

I gather my things together, 'Well, this won't get my classroom sorted; we've got a nativity rehearsal this afternoon.' I make for the door.

Once back in the classroom I lean against the wall and breathe a sigh of relief. This is ridiculous, now I can't even bear to be in the same room as him. I busy myself moving child-size chairs and sorting the children's costumes. Suddenly the door flies open and Mike just stands, looking grumpy and full of loathing.

'Is that the way the land lies then? Are you messing around with this curate chap?'

'His name is Peter, Peter Bield and I am not *messing around* as you so elegantly put it. We are friends.'

'I bet you are. And how long has this been going on then?' I decide that honesty is the best policy.

'We met at the conference I went to at half-term. So obviously, when I found out that he was coming to Becklefield, we struck up a friendship.'

'Oh, we struck up a friendship,' he mimics in a stupid falsetto voice. My palm itches to slap him.

'Oh, go away, you stupid man. Get lost!' Suddenly his face

crumples, his pride hurt, his dignity mulched. He slams the door and I am left with a bitter taste in my mouth.

A School Christmas

On Wednesday evening we gather at the church for the school carol service. The moon is mustard in a charcoal sky and the ground is hard frozen. Inside, the church is full of twittering children in a state of imploding excitement. Once attired in tea towels or bejeweled crowns and halos, we lead them to their positions around the building. Parents stand open-mouthed like baby birds, necks stretched, eyes searching, children wave and bounce.

Every sill holds a lit candelabra and flower arrangements abound. A huge tree stands behind the piano, dripping grandeur. Reverend Tom walks to the front, his cassock puffing out gently because of the underfloor heating. He holds out his arms; 'Welcome, welcome everyone. It's good to have you here at St Michael's and a great joy to have so many children with us.' He turns to them, eyes twinkling, 'Now, which one of you is going to sing?'

There is a forest of eager hands.

'Well, aren't we lucky, so many of you, my goodness there's enough of you to raise the roof!'

Then we begin and they sing their little hearts out. I spot Wayne's dad on the front row, bullet head of thick black hair, cream shirt open to the waist, hairy chest and gold medallion. A tough nut, but with tears coursing down his cheeks. And Wayne? Well, he is suddenly every cathedral choir boy, scrubbed face, candle-flame hair and shining eyes.

It's difficult to know which song has the edge, 'Away in a manger' or the Johnny Mathis classic 'When a child is born', but when the children finish singing the tears flow freely on many faces. Janet has done an amazing job with the choir and my class is exceptional as they reenact the Christmas Story. True, Steven is a tad too violent as he refuses Joseph entry to the inn, and Robbie, as Joseph, does rather spoil the image as he wipes his nose on his sleeve. Linda makes a delightful Mary and Sally, the angel who, appropriately 'delivers' the baby to Mary, does whisper rather loudly, 'Me mam's 'avin one of these.'

Soon it's over and never has 'O come all ye faithful' been sung with such gusto. The school choir stride down the aisle carrying lit lanterns hooked on sticks. Peter walks up the chancel steps, raises his arm and blesses us all, and then he catches my eye and smiles. My heart turns over.

*

The next day the staff perform their pantomime. As we wait behind the curtain, Steve, who is acting the part of the dame, does an impromptu can-can revealing his sexy black stockings.

'Very nice,' quips Reg the caretaker, 'are you doing ought tonight?'

Steve walks to the curtains, thrusts one leg through the opening and does a few high kicks. There are roars of laughter from the children and then a high-pitched voice is heard to shout, 'I know who that is, it's Miss Johnson, she allus wears tights like that.' The staff falls about laughing. I look at Steve's knobbly knees and profess to feel insulted. Then the curtains inch back jerkily and we begin our opening number, 'Happy days are here again', the applause is tremendous.

It's good to see the children laughing so much and to hear them joining in all the shouting. Alison has come back to school for the first time since the fire and she is holding her sides with laughing, I see Robbie clutching at her as they rock back and forth with mirth. Sally sparkles, Wayne guffaws and Christopher covers his mouth in horror as custard pies career back and forth.

Suddenly I spy a frozen trio, Julie has her arm around Jamie and Linda is holding his hand. Their faces are paper white and they are so still, what on earth is wrong there?

At home time I help them into their coats and worry, not for the first time, about how cold they must be in such thin anoraks. Jamie is stiff and doll-like as I fasten his zip.

'What's the matter, Jamie, aren't you feeling well?' He shakes his head staring at the ground. Julie puts her arm around him protectively.

'It's awight, Miss. I wook after him.'

'And what about you, Linda, are you feeling poorly too?' She stares back at me miserably, huge brown eyes welling with tears.

'Don't wowwy, Miss, we be okay. Have a mewwy Chwistmas. See you after the holidays,' says Julie.

'Happy Christmas, then, hope you have a lovely time.'

They trudge into the winter's night and I feel at a loss about what to do or say. However, the term is at an end and the staff party beckons. We are having a trust banquet where each person contributes a favourite dish and we all share. I've brought my specialty, a salmon mousse, and feel quite proud as I ease it out of its fish mould and onto

69

an oval plate and garnish with cucumber. The buffet table looks spectacular; Sandra has brought an amazing chocolate cake and Barbara, a raspberry Pavlova. Mrs Biggins has brought sausage and stuffing pasties and Miss Heaton, an assortment of quiches. Everyone has gone to so much trouble, and the wine flows freely. The only fly in the ointment for me is that Mike is here as one of our special guests and of course, Peter is here too, I find it difficult to behave naturally.

Christmas Eve

'Mam! What time is it? Mam, will he be here soon? Will he Mam?'
Nellie Boon tried to focus her thoughts through a whisky haze.
'He? Who...?
She tried to surface through the mists of confusion at the small
pyjama clad figure before her.
'Mam! Wake up will yer!' Ali tried shaking her shoulder.
'She's been drinking again,' said Amber, twiddling her hair, as she
stared blankly at the television. Robbie was quick in his mother's
defence.
*'Well, it's Christmas ent it. People allus drink at Christmas. That's
why we 'ave it.'*
'Me mam drinks any time, you know that,' said Lisa.
'OK,' agreed Robbie reluctantly. *'Help me get 'er on't settee, our
Dwayne'll be 'ere soon and he'll see to her.'*
Lisa jumped up and down impatiently, *'Yes, we'll have to get to bed
soon else Santa'll be 'ere.'* Nellie saw Robbie and the others disappear
through the door like hazy visions, then the tears of self-pity began to
fall.
Allus drunk, *that wasn't true. She only drank sometimes, to dull the
pain. If Bill hadn't left there wouldn't have been any need. She had a
sudden rosy picture of them both, as they might have been, sitting close
in the firelight. They would fill the children's stockings, talking and
laughing like they did on the telly. She shook her head, sadly life
wasn't like that. Real life was about struggling and longing and
loneliness, in spite of having six children. It was boarded up windows
because you were tired of having a running battle with the vandals on
the estate. It was raucous evenings in the pub when you tried to forget
the past. It was occasionally meeting someone new and your heart
filling with hope and reaching out for loving only to find yourself
saying goodbye after yet another one night stand. Nellie sat up and
reached for the whisky bottle. It was nice of her boss to have given it
her for Christmas. She would have liked to have gone out tonight but
she had to be careful, ever since the fire. She shuddered to think of
what might have happened. Thank God she had really been working
late that night, or they would have taken them all into care.*
She thought of Ali's lividly disfigured body, 'Poor little beggars,'

she mused, 'poor little sods, stuck with a useless bit of shit for a mother.' She addressed the whisky bottle solemnly, 'My trouble is that I'm no good. Absholutely no goo. I'm a failure, did you know that? I'm a fucking failure, a slut, a whore, a really, really, really bad mother. And you know what else? I'm a heathen,' she giggled inanely, 'that's it, a heathen celebrating Christmas.'

She had a sudden picture of her childhood home, a comfortable detached house in the salubrious area of Adel. They'd had big bay windows. The curtains had been fixed so that they pulled across the bay, leaving an empty space behind. How she and her sister had loved that space. Every Christmas it would become their stage and they would entertain all the assembled uncles and aunts with their tap dancing and songs.

They had everything children could wish for, dancing classes, piano lessons, skates, brand new bikes, beautifully tailored coats with velvet collars and shiny patent shoes with silvery buckles. She remembered how, on Christmas morning, they would all go to church, clutching the one new toy they were allowed to take and how their parents' friends would fuss over them and how there would be lots of smiles and hugs and warmth. She took several more swigs of the soothing liquid before adding, 'Still, at least I managed to get the twins a doll each, beautiful dolls with blonde hair and startling blue eyes. Just like...just like I used to be.' She surveyed the rolls of fat undulating down her body and squelching out above the waistband of her tracksuit bottoms and her doughy breasts thrusting above and below her bra.

'Shit!' Her reverie was broken by a shout from upstairs.

'Mam! What time is it? Are you sober yet, Mam?' Nell squinted at the clock on the mantle shelf, she could just make out the big hand.

'It's a quarter to Christmas!' she bellowed. 'Now belt up and get to sleep!'

It was always quarter to something. That just about summed up her life. Always waiting, always being nearly there, nearly ready, almost organised but never succeeding. It was always a quarter to something and tomorrow never came.

'Mam!'

'What now?'

Robbie's voice quavered down the stairs, 'He'll be bringing me train set soon, Mam, won't he? I do hope he brings me a train.'

'It'll be a blooming miracle if he does, son,' Nell said quietly to

herself and then sat for a long time staring at the cold grey bars of the gas fire.

Suddenly the door burst open. Icy air rocketed through the house. A flurry of coloured balloons entered triumphantly borne by her grinning eldest son, her lifeline, support and whipping boy. Her spirits soared.

'Hi Mam! Merry Christmas! Ere's your ever loving son bearing gifts of gold, Frankenstein and whatever the other one was.'

Nellie giggled, 'You are a fool, our Dwayne, whatever 'ave you been up to?'

Wayne winked and touched a finger to his nose, 'Never you mind. Now, 'eres a prezzy – not to be opened 'til tomorrow, mind.'

He continued to pull out unwrapped gifts from a large, black plastic bin bag with the air of a magician pulling rabbits from a hat.

'Here are teddy bears for Jade and Ruby and some crayons and an Etch-a-Sketch for our Ali and... he imitated a trumpet fanfare before pressing something into her hand, '...and a gold watch for our Robbie.'

For a moment she was speechless, then she kissed him, tears falling wetly down fat cheeks.

'Oh our Dwayne, you're a wonder, a bloomin' wonder.' She wiped her eyes with a grubby fist before continuing, 'Fancy, miracles do 'appen, after all.'

They spent the next hour happily wrapping the children's gifts and decorating the living room with crepe paper twists and balloons. They ate a Chinese takeaway and drank more whisky and Nell felt happier than she had for a long time.

'Eeh, but I wish our Tracey were 'ere,' she said wistfully as the clock struck one.

'Nay Mam, they don't take kindly to breakouts from Borstal even at this time of year, but I expect they'll let her 'ome once she's 'ad the baby and its been adopted.'

Nell looked at her son, thoughtfully, 'I'm a failure, you know, Son. I've been no bloody good at all as a mother.'

'Belt up, mam,' said Wayne through clenched teeth as he blew up yet another balloon.

At two thirty the police arrived and with indisputable authority arrested Dwayne for robbery and assault. He went quietly, his cheeky grin hardly slipping. His mother was not so calm and spent the last of her energy hurling abuse at the police, the neighbours, the government and anyone else she could think of. The children slept on, used as they were to sleeping through trauma.

Alone once more she slumped in a chair, rocking back and forth as she wept, the whisky bottle clutched tight to her chest. The bulging stockings that Dwayne had hung precariously over the fireplace seemed to mock her. Soon she dozed fitfully, dreaming of Santa Claus and Christmases long past. Oh how she had believed in Santa Claus. She woke suddenly, and realized that in some silly way she had believed even as a teenager, right up until she got pregnant with Tracey and Dwayne at sixteen and had embarked on her disastrous marriage. She had believed in God then too, a kind, Father Christmassy sort of God who looked after you and answered all your prayers, when you remembered to say them. She didn't believe in anything any more.

At around four fifteen she drifted into a lovely dream. The church bells were ringing and there she was in slow motion moving towards the church. She was wearing a smart suit and a white furry hat. The children floated sedately by her side dressed in fur coats and shiny boots. The bells were getting louder. She could hear singing, 'Christians awake, salute the happy morn!' It was going to be all right, the Christian people were sure to help. The music rose to a crescendo as she arrived at the door. She reached out her hand to take the hymn sheet proffered by a respectable looking man in a suit. Suddenly, it was snatched away. His smile froze and he shook his head muttering, 'Too late! Too late! No!' and then the door crashed shut in her face.

She woke up, shaking violently, her mouth felt like a sewer. The radio was blaring loudly.

'Mam! Mam! Wake up will yer. It's Christmas!' shouted Ali.

'Uuuugh. What time is it?'

Nellie had difficulty forming her words and her head was hammering.

'It's quarter to something. Never mind the time Mam, has he been, has Santa been?'

Jade and Ruby stood by the door sucking thumbs, sleepily. 'We can't find us presents, Mam,' they said worriedly.

She nodded towards the fireplace, 'They're 'ung by the chimney, stupid! Where did you think they would be?'

'Oooh,' two grubby little faces lit in wonder, 'they've never been there before, you usually forget.'

'Mam! Oh Mam look!' shrieked Jade as she tore at the wrapping

paper revealing the blue-eyed doll. *'Cor! Int she lovely! I'm gonna look after her real good, aren't I Mam, cos she's my very own baby.'* She gazed down tenderly at the doll in her arms.

Nell choked on her tears and remembered her dream. Would the man really have slammed the door in her face because she was a bad mother? She didn't expect that he would, but she knew that tongues wagged behind her back and she could read condemnation in so many faces.

There was a stupefied silence from Robbie as he opened his present, he had known years of disappointing Christmases, the non existent bike, the invisible football and now, a parcel that was obviously not the longed for train set. Robbie had learned to steel himself against pain when opening presents. Nellie watched with bated breath.

'Mam, oh Mam. It's a watch, a real one. Cor Mam it's fantastic!' He fastened it proudly to his wrist and gazed steadily at her. *'Will...will we even 'ave a turkey as well?'* Nell hesitated before saying apologetically, *'Sorry Love, I er, I forgot to thaw it.'*

Robbie shrugged and his bottom lip trembled. *'No Fuss, we'll 'ave it tomorrow. Will our Dwayne be coming?'*

'Not today, love.'

He patted her arm, suddenly looking old beyond his years.

'Never mind, we'll have a good Christmas, just the five of us, you'll see.'

Then he held out his arm proudly for her approbation, *'And I'll be able to tell you the time whenever you need it.'*

A Real Christmas

I haven't had a family Christmas for years, not since the 'awful time' wiped happiness from my blackboard and left only dark. For the last two years Meg and I have celebrated quietly, two lonely neighbours finding solace together with a few bottles of red and a packed television schedule.

This year everything is different. Meg is spending Christmas with John at his daughter's house and Peter and I are spending Christmas with his parents. I'm so excited. But, before all that, we are helping to host Christmas lunch for all those in the area who otherwise would be alone and don't want to be.

First there is Christmas morning worship, the only one I've ever attended. Then we set out, armed with names and addresses, to pick up those who cannot make the journey under their own steam. When we arrive the hall is warm and welcoming. Savoury smells waft from the kitchen, coloured lights quiver and presents tumble invitingly from a large sack near the Christmas tree. Tables are spread with red and gold cloths and white and gold flower arrangements sit placid on every table.

'Eeh lass,' croons Elsie my passenger, 'it looks a treat and no mistake and I tell thee what, I'm going to right enjoy this, I am that.'

'Do you know, Elsie, I think I am too.'

And I do, much more than I expected. It is worth all the hard work to see the joy on so many faces. I hear lots of stories and laugh so much my muscles ache, but best of all, as I occasionally glance around the room, I catch Peter's eye, he smiles and my heart dances. After Christmas lunch we play silly games. The elderly revel in pass the parcel with forfeits between every sheet of wrapping and have no inhibitions about reciting limericks or singing. One group treats us to a crazy version of 'Knees up Mother Brown' complete with zimmer frames and an old man dressed as a Chelsea pensioner recites the sorry tale of 'Albert and the Lion'.

While we wash up, the participants watch the musical 'The Sound of Music' and we all join in with the songs as we scrub and scour.

At last, with all our charges safely home and everything cleared away Peter and I embark on our journey to North Yorkshire and the village near Helmsley where Peter's family live. It is already dark and frosty and the Christmas moon shows off the jewels of night to perfection.

'It was fantastic today,' says Peter, 'thanks for helping; it meant so much to have you there.'

'I enjoyed it, they're lovely people. I can't remember when I last laughed so much. Elsie Bottomley is such a character and so is Albert White. Sitting between the two of them was like being with Morecambe and Wise, a laugh a minute; I nearly choked on my turkey.'

The miles speed by in cheerful conversation and soon the lights of Limmiton shine before us.

'Here we are, home at last,' says Peter, pulling me close as we walk up the garden path. Suddenly the door opens and light and music flood out. Peter's dad holds wide his arms and enfolds me in an enormous hug.

'Now isn't this nice,' he says. 'Come on in, come in and warm yourselves. Let me take your coat, here sit down by the fire. Oh lass, you must be fair worn out.'

Peter's mum squeezes my arm and bends to kiss my cheek, 'Good to see you again, love, Happy Christmas. Now would you like a sherry? Harry love, get Kathy a glass of sherry.'

'Right ho, coming up, your ladyship. Would that be sweet or dry?'

Peter and I settle down on the sofa next to a roaring log fire. Hannah and Harry sit opposite both rather flushed and smiling benignly but whether from sherry or exertion I cannot tell. I catch the scent of cinnamon and apples and the savoury smell of turkey and feel surrounded by love and comfort.

'Now then, what do we have here?' says a fierce voice from the doorway.

'Oh Mum, I wondered if you were awake yet, it's Peter and his friend Kathy. I told you they were coming. Come on in and sit by the fire.'

'Aye, I will do, it's colder than a monkey's doo-dah out there, by the looks of it.'

She makes her way slowly and steadily across the room, leaning heavily upon her stick. Peter jumps up to greet her and folds her to his chest, or tries to, her head reaches to just above his waist. He strokes her sparse white hair gently.

'Hello you,' he croons, 'how's my favourite old granny?'

'Less of the old, you cheeky rascal. Well, I'm hanging on, you know, just hanging on.'

Peter places his hands upon her shoulders and bends right down to look closely at her face.

'Yes I can see that, it must be the weight of all those wrinkles that's getting you down.'

She raises her stick threateningly and he pretends to duck, holding up his hands and calling, 'Truce!' And then, 'Granny, allow me to present my beautiful girlfriend Kathy. Kathy this is my little Gran, Granny Bield.'

I rise hurriedly to my feet and take her two gnarled hands in mine.

'It...it's lovely to meet you,' I stammer, suddenly overawed by the gimlet eyes and fierce face. Then she smiles, her face lighting up as if she has inner batteries and all my fear evaporates. She has a finely corrugated skin the colour of oatmeal but her eyes are the same singing blue as Peter's and her hair is soft as dandelion fuzz.

'You'll do,' she says solemnly, 'happy Christmas, sunshine, I'm very pleased to meet you too.' I smile back, pleased at the approbation. As I drink my sherry I feel a great weight slip from my shoulders. I'm home; I have a family once more. Oh please God, let this be my family, I have been so alone.

*

We eat until we're stuffed. The turkey is tender and moist with plenty of chestnut stuffing and cranberry sauce. I cut through a roast potato, crisp and gleaming on the outside fluffy within. There's cauliflower cheese with crispy strips of bacon and chunks of sausage, sprouts and baby carrots and beautiful roast parsnips.

We eat slowly and chat and laugh and it feels like I've been here for ever. We finish with a traditional Christmas pudding. Glasses refilled we toast each other, Christmas and Becklefield and I wonder briefly how my pupils are faring. Is Robert playing with a train set, right now? Has Linda shoplifted an adequate Christmas buffet and is the family enjoying it? Is Julie tending the hyacinths she's taken home? And what of Jamie? For a moment a wave of despair sweeps through me and I shudder but Peter takes hold of my hand and squeezes it tightly and I'm back in this lovely place again. His eyes twinkle with mischief as he hands me my cracker.

'Come on, woman. Let the serious business begin!'

He cheats of course, winning both lots of paper hats, gifts and mottos. I retaliate by making him wear both hats at once and he gives me a plastic ring that has fallen onto the table, placing it solemnly on my thumb as it's too large for any other finger.

Later, in my narrow bed in the little room under the eaves, I place it on my ring finger and lay staring out at the stars as I push it round and round with my thumb. It has been a perfect day.

Post Celebration Blues

We have to leave Limmiton after lunch on Boxing Day, as Reverend Tom is having a well deserved rest and Peter is taking over his duties for a couple of weeks. It's a butter yellow day that turns the Yorkshire stone cottages to gold and gleams orange on red pantile roofs and everything glitters with frost. I love this village and am reluctant to leave but as I sigh Peter grins, his face is crammed with light.

'Don't tell me that you're not aching to be back in Becklefield, you know you love it.'

'I do, but it's so beautiful here and I think I've fallen in love with it and it all passed so quickly.'

'You'll be back, sunshine, and we'll spend much longer next time, I promise.'

'I do hope so.'

All too soon we are back. The sunshine has gone and ominous grey clouds scribble charcoal across the sky.

'Looks like we're in for a snowfall,' says Peter. I do hope he's wrong, around Limmiton it would have been idyllic but here in Becklefield it will just be another problem with which to cope.

'Well sunshine, here we are.' He turns off the ignition and leans towards me, he cups my face with his hands and his lips are so warm and soft. The kiss goes on and on and I long for him to take me inside and up to my bed.

'Are you coming in?' I whisper.

'You know I can't, we have to do things properly.'

'But...' He places one finger on my lips.

'Kathy, I know all the buts, I want you so much, just a while longer. It won't be long now, I promise. Take care, my love. I'll see you tomorrow.' I squeeze his hand

'Thank you, thank you for a wonderful Christmas.'

'The thanks are all mine.'

He hurries away as if chased by devils.

*

My Christmas tree bears no resemblance to its former shimmering glory. Denuded of everything but brittle branches it lays pathetically at the end of the garden. I look at it with distaste having just struggled the length of the lawn with its mass in my arms. I am scratched and sore and appear to have a bra filled with pine needles.

'Oh well, there's not much else in there,' I say and go back into the house and survey the mess. The carpet still bears a thin film of needles but the baubles and other paraphernalia are safely packed away. I vacuum the carpet enthusiastically and order is restored once more.

I sit cross-legged on the carpet and sort through my Christmas cards. I'll keep the majority for future classroom work. Among the glossy and the gilded are the cards from my pupils. A fat Santa, sitting astride a motorbike bears the legend 'Luv form Trevor.'

I can't help but smile and can just see his cherubic face and sparkly blue eyes. I pick up another, an ascetic angel heralds 'I love yoe, from Lisa', clingy Lisa, moon-faced, big-eyed with a pudding basin haircut.

There is a bulging stocking card from Robbie and I wonder again if he got the longed for train set. I reflect again on the idea that all advertising of children's toys should be banned. What agonies these orchestrated longings cause both children and parents. I know that many of my class would be happy with less sophisticated toys and their parents would be less likely to push themselves into debt if it were not for this insidious persuasion.

A fat robin bears an illegible message from Julie…has she had a good Christmas, I wonder? And what of Linda, has she spent it with her mother in the Women's Refuge as she did last year? I sigh and make mental notes for the coming term. They all need a massive input on writing and many of them have no motivation for reading coming as they do from homes where books are as rare as dishwashers and are probably seen to be a lot less useful.

I look at the clock and begin to clear my teaching files from the kitchen table. I hate January; everything seems so flat after Christmas. Now what shall I have for my tea? There is a peremptory knock and the door opens bringing in flurry of snow and a blast of cold air. Suede boots stamp ineffectually on the mat.

'Hello friend,' says Meg sweeping me into a hug, 'and how was your Christmas?'

'Come on in, I'm all-agog.' I kiss her cold cheek and smell the fresh scent of 'Blue Grass', the perfume I bought her.

She plonks a bottle of Beaujolais upon the table; 'Are you busy, can I invite myself to tea?' She peers into the pan that I have just set on the cooker, 'Aaah, spaghetti. Fantastic. Is there anything I can do? Shall I grate the cheese? You don't mind, do you? I'm at my wits end, been talking to the microwave again.'

'Of course I don't mind, I was beginning to think that you were never coming back, that John had swept you onto a white horse and that you'd both ridden off into the sunset.'

'I wish! Oh Kathy, it was awful. His family didn't want me there, they think it's too soon after their mum's death and I can understand that. I know he loved her very much, as I loved Keith, but why can't they understand that the greater you've loved the bigger the hole when they have gone.' She bangs her fist upon the table and bursts into tears. I sit down beside her and reach for her hand.

'Oh Meg, I'm so sorry, poor you, it must have been awful.'

'It was, we ended up having a huge row on Boxing Day, then John told them all to "go to hell" and we marched out. We've been at John's ever since. But he is so low, they've never rowed before and he loves them all so much and he dotes on his grandchildren. Oh Kathy, they're so sweet, Matthew and Rebecca. Matthew's nearly one and Rebecca is four. I thought that I could have a share in children at last, if not my own, then step grandchildren. Now it's all spoiled and, Kathy, I love John. I didn't think it possible to love like that again. What am I going to do?'

'Well for a start you're going to stuff yourself with spag bol and pour some of the red stuff down your throat and then you can tell me everything.'

Meg is usually like a whirlwind, a very welcome one, as practical as a pan scourer and as down to earth as a loaf of bread. She is my staunchest ally and loves nothing better than to hear me witter on about the kids in my class. She tackles the cheese with great ferocity whilst I peel spring onions, shred lettuce and do chopped apples and walnuts for a Waldorf salad. She quickly steers the conversation into safer territory.

'So, are you all ready for the fray, all lessons planned and ready for execution?'

'Nope.'

'No? That's not like you, you're usually all organised by now, work cards made, pictures filed, duplicated sheets at the ready. What's the problem?'

'The kids are the problem. I'm not getting through. How can I expect them to write their news each day when it's probably more suitable for the front page of the News of the World. Their lives are so barren, there's nothing they *want* to write about...except what they saw on the telly last night.'

Meg laughs throatily, 'From what you've told me, their lives are a lot more colourful than mine; rape, robbery, incest. What more do you want?'

My face feels frozen with concern.

'You know what I mean, Meg, there's no magic in so many of their lives, no joy, no bloody childhood even.'

'Then put it there, you ninny,' said Meg. 'If anybody can do it, you can, Kathy. You're like a big kid yourself. Give them some dreams.'

'It's easier said than done. I mean, what topic can I do? We did *ourselves* last term. It was a disaster, how can you make family trees when your mum is not sure who your dad was and you've had half a dozen *uncles* in as many months. How can you write about your home when it's so damned derelict and uninviting and your electricity's been off for weeks?'

'Is it really as bad as that?' asked Meg, stirring the bolognaise and inhaling its rich herby scent.

'I'm afraid it is. Oh Meg, it was so beautiful at Peter's mum and dad's, so peaceful and picturesque but all I could see were the contrasts. How some people live and what others have to put up with. Meg, it's pulling me down. I kept thinking, I wonder what Wayne is doing, did Santa come to Robbie and is Julie's mum on the streets this Christmas or did she have a couple of days off sex?'

Meg licked the spoon and grinned wickedly, 'Talking of which, did you...?'

'No, we didn't...unfortunately.'

'Never mind, I feel very confident that you will. As for all those poor kids...their lives won't come to an end just because *you* can't do everything, they're not your dependents, you know. Now sit down, you ninny, and eat, I'm starving.' With deft movements she drains the spaghetti and serves up the meal on warmed blue and white plates. I sit down heavily. The Beaujolais is opened, cheese sprinkled and we eat with gusto glorying in taste and texture, herbs and spices, hot crunchy garlic bread and the tangy freshness of salad. Cliff Richard caresses us with song and Meg regales me with tales from Bowitt and Hamble, the lavish world of stockbrokers where she used to work, which seems a million miles from Becklefield Primary School.

'...and so I said to Gerald Pembroke-Lewis, "Excuse me Sir, I don't know if you are aware but your shoes appear not only to be completely different colours but also completely disparate in style." You should have seen his face, there he was, all pinstriped yuppiness, filofax in hand, with one grey shoe with a silver buckle and one black lace-up...' Meg laughs heartily as she tells this tale and I dissolve into giggles '...and after that,' she splutters, 'I didn't have the heart to tell him that his flies were undone!'

Later, over thinly sliced brie, black grapes and coffee my mind goes plodding back to school. 'I wish I could take the kids somewhere like that, Meg, show them what the world *can* be like, leather swivel chairs, smart suits, polished mahogany and I could show them what computers really look like.'

'Why not? It would probably do those yuppies good as well, though maybe a stockbrokers office is not quite the right place, how about the bank or the post office or behind the scenes at Marks and Spencer's. I know, why don't you do people's jobs as a topic?'

'Of course, that's a good one. I could invite parents in to talk about their jobs, well, those that have them. We could visit the local shops and talk to the shop keepers and we could...'

'OK, OK, now, tell me about your love life.'

'Mine is good, thanks, except for the frustration issue, but what about you Meg? You'll be all right, surely. John loves you to bits. It'll all work out, I know it will.'

'Oh I know he loves me, we make one another laugh, we like the same things, we even share the same faith and that's something I've never had before. But what if they make him...you know, choose. What if he has to choose between his children and me? What will I do?'

I'm thoughtful for a moment, wondering how to phrase my feelings.

'Perhaps, if we have this new found faith, and I feel it too and it's not just because of Peter. I feel something deep inside me a great sort of special love. Maybe if we do believe, we just have to trust and, and...pray.'

Meg looks up at me, her eyes large and soft, 'Perhaps you're right.'

The World of Work

I arrive early in school and set to work on some minor furniture reorganisation. The room is small and cluttered with little or no storage space. Several feet are taken up with a raised platform which fifty years previously had housed a large, upright teacher's desk. Today it serves no purpose except that the blackboard is fixed to the wall above it and when I stand there I have a perfect view of everyone.

There is no sink or piped water in the classroom or even in the immediate vicinity and so paint, clay and water play require a major organisational effort. The walls have peeling paint and flaking plaster and one wall in particular has a large, smelly fungal growth. The floor is wooden and untreated and when the weather is wet becomes extremely damp, apparently due to an underwater stream. The school was built above old mine workings and a variety of cracks in the brickwork are evidence of subsidence.

When I first came here, it wasn't the building but the smell that most assaulted my senses. It was the smell of human urine seeping through cracked urinals, crumbling plaster and dirty underwear. It was wet rot and dry rot, decay and neglect, the smell of unwashed bodies and dirty clothes, stiff with last week's baked beans, gravy and fish and chip grease. It was stronger and more pungent than anything I had previously experienced. It made me physically sick and yet, once I was part of it, I ceased to be bothered by it. I smile as I think of visitors who have opened the door of my classroom and baulked as the stench assailed them. Don't get me wrong, there are clean, sweet-smelling children with scrubbed faces and carefully groomed hair, I think of Christopher, Sally and Linda. There are caring parents who try desperately to give their offspring everything, which they, themselves, have not experienced. But somehow the air of squalor and deprivation seems to encompass them all.

I busy myself moving tables across one corner of the room to serve as a post office. I affix the large shop sign I have made in the holidays and lay out the forms and leaflets I have filched from several real post offices. The completion of all these will make wonderful writing practice and at least they'll know then how to write their names and addresses. There are sheets of sticky paper to serve as stamps, these I've perforated using my sewing machine. Five pounds of my own money, made up of various denominations, lies in the cash register, risky I know, but I found out long ago that such streetwise children despise plastic money. Only the real thing is good enough for them. I stand back to survey my work. There are sheets of brown paper for wrapping, Sellotape and string and lots of boxes which will become parcels. Pens and felt-tips are at the ready. Pencils sharpened and laid ready in every place and weighing scales for every group. I consult my watch, eight forty, just time for a quick coffee in the staff room and then...*into the frey.*

*

I open the staffroom door to a chorus of 'happy new years'.

'Hello Don, did you have a good Christmas?'

He pats his spreading girth and twinkles from behind his spectacles. 'Aye, it were grand! Did you?'

'Oh yes. Hi Sandra, oh I like your hair, what a lovely colour. Did you have a good Christmas?' She is busy trying to strain the last of the lukewarm tea from the large pot into her cup.

'Look at this,' she thrusts the cup under my nose, 'it looks like witches pee, still, no time to make any more. It's time we got a boiler in this place we spend half our precious breaks waiting for the bloody kettle to boil. Oh sorry, happy new year and all that, though I don't hold out much hope for you with class five, what a bloody shower!'

Is this what teaching does to you, I think, this cynicism? I look at Sandra's down turned mouth and permanent frown and my spirits sink. Suddenly there are hoots of laughter from the corner of the room, accompanied by a few shrieks.

'What on earth!' shouts Sandra and then she collapses laughing against the wall her finger pointing. In the corner by the sink there is a plastic washing line on which we hang tea towels to dry. Running along this tightrope as nimbly as any circus performer is a fat grey mouse...the New Year at Becklefield Primary has begun.

*

'Miss, do you know what I got from Santa? I got an Action Man then our Paul pinched it and our Colin bashed him and then our mam got mad and she 'it him and then...' says Wayne as he bursts into the room.

Sally can't wait to share her news either, 'Miss I got this flippin doll and it's dead rude and it's got a willie and everyfing. Me mam says its called Rea Listic but I don't like that name so I call it Sam, but

86

I wish he were a girl.' This was greeted with raucous laughter by Robbie until Lisa interrupted with, 'You shouldn't call it a willie, its proper name is a pea nis; Uncle Bill has got one and it...'

'OK! OK! Everyone, sit on the mat please, then we can have a proper chat, Wayne, I'll have the gun, thank you, now sit here by my feet. Lisa, turn round I'd like to look at your pretty face not the back of your neck. Right, now we'll do the register...Robbie Boon.'

'Yes, Miss Johnson.'

'Well done.'

I continue to call the register in a businesslike manner praising those who answer politely. I try to smile, nod, or give some kind of facial response to all my charges so that they are each personally acknowledged.

At 'sharing time' more details of Christmas emerge. Darren and Christopher have both received bicycles, Lana, who is Darren's twin, has not been so fortunate.

'I only got a doll, it's not fair, I wanted a bike. I only got a flippin doll, not even a pram to tek out in't street.'

Linda is sitting close to my feet, head bowed throughout this discussion. She looks up and our eyes meet, she holds out her hand, 'Do you like my golliwog, Miss? She says, her eyes imploring as she cradles the little brooch, protectively.

'It's lovely,' I lie. 'Was it a present?'

'Yes, my auntie got it for me; she had to send away loads of marmalade labels to get it. It's great isn't it Miss?'

Before I can agree Wayne bursts in; 'Eh, what did my dad buy you, Linda? Did he get you ought?'

'Course he did, he got me an 'andbag, my dad did.' She pulls the cheap plastic object from beneath her matted sweater and thrusts it proudly beneath his nose. 'See, he bought me this,' she says triumphantly. Wayne looked scathingly at the shiny pink handbag.

'He bought *me* a bike,' he replies and turns away, no longer interested. His dad's other family, of which Linda was a part, no longer poses a threat to him. His father's love he measures quite simply in terms of what he buys. Linda knows this and crumples like a burst balloon.

Damn! I think, feeling the familiar tug at my heart, damn and blast the man, *why the hell can't he see what he's doing to these children?*

I bring the discussion to an abrupt end and explain about our class post office and then organise who are going to be the first three people to play in it. All the children sit up very straight and I pretend to look for the best behaved.

'Oh Linda, you're sitting up beautifully. You can be in charge of the post office and...let me see, Jamie, I think you will be very good at selling stamps and Julie you can be in charge of weighing the parcels.'

There are forms to complete in every place and a parcel wrapping station is organised by my desk. Soon all the children are working with some excitement, order restored and we all look forward to visiting the real post office later in the week.

During the morning I glance worriedly at Linda and Jamie from time to time.

Jamie particularly looks unwell. His skin white and waxy and his eyes look as if his childhood has leaked away. Julie is quiet and withdrawn and stares obliquely at nothing in particular whilst pulling continually at her hair. My stomach lurches, something is terribly wrong and I haven't got a clue what it can be.

Fear

Jamie lay fully clothed, huddled against his brother Dean on the narrow bed with the thin plastic mattress. He pulled at the blanket, stiff with dried urine and the Superman quilt slid to the floor. Jamie prayed that Dean would not wet the bed tonight. It was awful when he did, at first it was all warm and trickily and ran down his legs and onto the sheet. Later it went cold and made him shiver. It made the sore places on his legs hurt. Oh, he hoped that Dean did not wet the bed tonight!

The light from the street lamp flooded through the uncurtained windows and the shape of the frame was reflected on the wall. When cars passed there were shadows, huge, monstrous shadows that danced and swooped. He pulled the covers over his head and trembled. Now he could hear the drums again, thumping slowly, menacingly, perdum, perdum, perdum. *They were coming to get him, he was sure they were coming and if they did they'd hurt him again. He lay there in terror, for he had no way of knowing that the noise was merely the beating of his heart.*

Christmas had made it worse. When his mam had been here, Christmas was nice. He searched in the depths of his memory. Yes, Christmas had been good then. There had been warm sausage rolls and sausages on sticks and salmon sandwiches. They'd had fruit cake all juicy and thick with cherries and marzipan. He feasted his memory on cake; it had a shiny red ribbon round it and a Santa on the top. She'd baked it, had his mum, he remembered this with pride. She'd made it in a big bowl and he had helped to stir it. The mixture had been heavy, stiff with currants and other things and the smell, well that had been really lovely. The cake was in the oven for a long time and Mam had said not to make a noise or bang the doors or it would go 'sad' so they'd all walked on tip-toe and had been really, really quiet because they did not want a 'sad cake' they wanted a happy one. Jamie sighed, remembering...remembering the smell and the warmth and the taste, remembering licking out the bowl and his mam's smile. He thought of the hugs and the laughter and clean sheets that smelled nice. Yes, those Christmases had been good with angels and singing and presents, Father Christmas and turkey. Not like this Christmas, this had been all monsters and shouting and men with breath that smelled of beer. This Christmas had hurt him and he didn't like it. He felt the tears running down his cheeks, their saltiness dribbling into his mouth. His nose was running too but he didn't care. He wanted his mam; he wanted the hurt to go away.

Suddenly the bed was filled with hot wetness and a pungent smell.

'Aaagh, our Dean, I told you not to wet the bed tonight,' he moaned.

Hypothermia

Fog lies like organza through which glows an amber sun. I join Meg for our early morning walk, her old dog, Bessie, waddling and sniffing alongside. The cold claws at my cheeks and nose, frost crunches underfoot. Meg stamps her feet to summon up some warmth.

'Bloomin 'eck, it'd freeze a monkeys balls off. Oh, just look at that, Kathy, what a picture.' She leans forward to examine a spider's web swollen and suspended in the hedge. 'It's like a piece of antique lace,' she observes. 'Aren't we lucky to have all this?'

I nod my head to indicate the strip of countryside by the edge of the motorway. 'Aye, but I'd prefer it without the whoosh of wheels on tarmac, what a racket.'

Bessie leaps suddenly jumping at the hedge, paws flailing, the web shudders and falls on frozen leaves. We shiver and quicken our steps. I feel invigorated and ready for anything as I make my way to school.

An hour later it seems as if all hell has broken loose!

*

'I'm not working without any heating on a day like this. It was bad enough yesterday with the boiler going in fits and starts, but today without any heat, it's bloody ridiculous.' Barbara is our union rep and her anger zips like electricity, her face bare of make-up and angry red blotches rising on her long neck. Her hair, carefully gelled and spiked, gives the appearance of someone who has suffered an electric shock.

'How about doubling up?' asks Mary, her face troubled, her question tentative. 'It'll soon warm up with two classes in a room together.'

'What sixty eight kids in a room barely big enough for thirty,' storms Sandra. 'We're here to teach not bloody babysit. I say we send them home as soon as they arrive.'

At that moment Agnes Heaton, our esteemed head, makes a grand entrance, a plump, imposing figure, carefully corseted and Jaeger clad she commands our attention.

'Today it is very cold,' she announces unnecessarily. 'I have rung the education office and they are to send someone out to review the situation apropos the broken boiler. I suggest that in the mean time we inform the parents of the situation and let them decide whether or not the children should stay. We are of course obliged to keep those who are unaccompanied in school. I suggest that you…er…keep your coats on and…you could exercise, that's very warming,' she finished brightly.

'So is bonking,' whispers Sandra, 'and I know which I'd be rather doing.' I giggle and receive a frosty glare from the head. Oh dear!

Don, as deputy, leads the way into the playground to inform parents. Agnes Heaton returns to her inner sanctum, complete with kettle and two bar electric fire. We shiver on the periphery of the playground as Don addresses the parents. They are unimpressed.

'Forty-five degrees Fahrenheit, what's all the hassle? It's a damn sight colder than that in my house. We haven't had any leccy for a fortnight, not since they cut us off.' Mrs Cappum hurls her words as she hitches up her ample bosom and rests it on her fat folded arms.

'We don't 'ave no fancy central 'eating…the kids are bloody better off 'ere, at least they'll get a hot meal,' shouts Trevor's mum.

'Yes, if we take 'em 'ome what about their dinners? Mine are all on frees,' asks another mum pointing her finger threateningly.

Sadie Turner adds her four pennyworth, 'Aye they're best here anyway. I've got someone coming at ten.' Sandra and Barbara exchange glances and grin. Sadie is the mother of four of their pupils and a renowned prostitute. I find myself mesmerised by her heavy lashes, which stand in stiff black spikes about three centimetres long. They give her a weird tarantula like appearance, which, added to the miniscule red leather skirt and white fishnet tights makes me shiver anew.

'Perhaps she doesn't feel the cold,' whispers Mary.

Huddled in my fur lined duffle coat I feel suddenly soft and inadequate surrounded by all these resilient people. I look around and see Linda's mum standing apart from the others. She is painfully thin with waxy unwashed hair and gives me a sad, absurd smile. I walk towards her.

'Hello, Mrs Long. Have you heard the news, we've no heating and the building is very cold. You can take the children home if you want.'

She grips the pushchair with gloveless hands. Her coat is summer thin and her legs are bare. My heart clenches with pity.

'Aye, I heard,' weariness envelops her like the fog, 'but I can't face 'aving them all at 'ome, I've enough on. I'm pregnant again, you see and so sick with it I can't keep a thing down.'

I glance at the toddler and baby in the pushchair and tears grapple with my eyes. I bend to tickle the baby and am rewarded with a smile.

'She's going to be a heart breaker and that's for sure, she's got the same eyes as Linda hasn't she?' I fix a smile and Linda's mum smiles wearily back.

'Aye, they both tek after me, well around the eyes anyway. Lads both tek after their dads.' The plural is not lost on me and I search the face of the toddler for a clue as to his parenting. Oh yes, he bears a striking resemblance to Wayne, same pale blue eyes and thick black hair, same cheeky grin. Wayne's dad is certainly leaving his mark on this estate.

Mrs Long is speaking, 'I just can't 'ave them all at 'ome, not with babies an' all. I've wet washing 'anging everywhere,' she bites her lip, 'can they stay?'

I pat her shoulder in sympathy then notice something odd. My blood runs cold. A small figure is loping strangely across the playground, it seems like there is an ache in every step, a slow, malnourished walk. I mumble an excuse and run. Jamie is wearing a thin shirt minus several buttons revealing cold, blue flesh. His thin summer jacket is several sizes too small and he walks stiffly as if his legs are in splints. I reach out and draw him towards me. The material of his trousers is a solid, frozen mass.

'Jamie!' I gasp. He turns a frozen face towards me, his eyes glazed and sleepy. He moves his blue-tinged lips but no sound comes. I tear off my coat and engulf him in its furry warmth. His stiff arms are fisted in fragile pockets and he appears too heavy for his legs. He sinks to the ground.

'Don! Help me,' I shout, 'quickly!' Jamie is now a dead weight and appears to have slipped into unconsciousness. Don takes him from me, his face dark with fury. With long strides he marches into the building. I run to keep up. He reaches Miss Heaton's door before me and kicks it with his foot. It opens wide and Don lays his burden gently in the armchair before the glowing bars of the electric fire.

'What the-' begins Miss Heaton with affronted dignity and then lapses into confusion.

'An ambulance,' barks Don, 'now!' He kneels on the floor and begins to massage the child's frozen limbs.

'Blankets!' I shout and run towards the medical room. I return and swaddle him at the same time retrieving my coat. My teeth are chattering and I'm shaking with cold and fear. I would have liked to stay with him, cuddle him and whisper words of comfort but I have a class to teach. I'm in shock and long for a cup of hot, sweet tea, or brandy or anything to take away the trembling inside. I want to weep and shout and scream out my anger against a society that allows children to suffer like this. Instead I walk back to my classroom, once more hunched inside my duffel coat and with warm woollen gloves encasing icy fingers.

*

Lesson plans are abandoned, the situation calls for something different. We need movement to generate heat, music to lift our spirits, laughter. Feeling more like a Butlin's redcoat than a teacher I strive to fulfil our needs. We jump and hop and jog and jiggle, our feet drumming on bare icy boards. The echoes travel from class to class as the process is repeated, neither staff nor children are novices at this game, keeping warm has become part of the curriculum. Some parents have taken children home and no doubt they are now safely ensconced in easy chairs pulled close to glowing gas fires and watching cartoons on television. Their mothers will hoover around them, wash kitchen floors and prepare lunches. Other mothers will huddle together for warmth in shambolic rooms, smoking cigarettes and gossiping until it is time for the pubs to open. Some, like Linda's mum, will face the daily combat with dirty nappies, little hot water and no money for detergent with which to wash them. They will be thankful for just a few hours respite from the rest of their brood, souls as well as bodies crying out for any kind of warmth.

I hear the whining of the ambulance and long for news of Jamie, my brain on a perpetual turntable silently singing out his name. *Oh Jamie, please God help him, put your arms around him, show me how I can help!* But there is no news and I am helpless, trapped in my classroom with a rapacious audience clamouring to be entertained.

By break time the fog has lifted, but the insides of the classroom windows still bear their elaborate frost tracery testifying to the temperature within. Even the cramped staffroom is chilly. I clasp my steaming mug of coffee with both hands in a vain attempt to keep warm. Mary's face has a blue tinge; her usually flawless complexion looks pock-marked and pinched. Alison's short spiky haircut reveals two ears which are reddened and raw and she confesses that she wishes her hair reached down her back like mine. 'In fact, I wish I were a bloody gorilla, covered all over in fur.'

'Well at least you are well cushioned whereas I, poor creature that I am,' says Don, 'have hardly an inch of spare flesh to cover my poor freezing bones.'

'Except for the paunch of course,' quips Mary.

We all laugh as if everything is normal then I ask; 'Don, what's happened to Jamie? Is he OK?'

'I doubt it, the doctor from the clinic came over while we were waiting for the ambulance, hypothermia he said, he's never seen a case so bad. It would seem that he had slept in his clothes. Apparently he also shares a bed with Dean. During the night they evidently peed themselves, lay in it all night and then walked to school. Jamie was the wettest and his clothes froze on the journey. His little legs were raw and bleeding when we got his trousers off' He shakes his head and his voice breaks. 'The poor little blighter is in a terrible state.'

I gaze around at my colleagues. A thick silence pervades the room. Tears leak.

'What about his dad?' I ask after a while. I know that his mother left home over a year ago. Dad has full custody of all four children. 'What does he have to say?'

Don shrugs, 'Well I went round there of course, but there was no reply to my knock, I suspect he was still in bed.'

'It never ceases to amaze me,' declares Alison, 'that some of these kids can get themselves up, dressed, fed and off to school without any adult intervention.'

'Aye,' replies Don, 'and a lot don't, that's why we have so many absences, but I know what you mean. How old is Jamie, six? Seven?'

'He's seven in March,' I reply wearily, 'if he gets that far.'

Don squeezes my arm sympathetically,

'He'll be ok, love, social services are on to it. They'll sort it out I'm sure.'

Maybe they will. But something else is nagging at my brain, some important fact just out of my reach which I cannot grasp. Something is very badly wrong with Jamie, if only I can figure out what it is.

Desperation

Jamie has been in hospital for a week and all the time I'm worrying about him.

In addition, Julie is quiet and withdrawn and not even the discovery that a pot of hyacinths are in bud can raise her from her reverie.

'Are you all right, Julie?'

'Yes Miss.'

'Have you seen the new hyacinths, they're going to be pink ones this time.'

'Yes, I know.'

'Oh Julie, I've just had an idea, shall we give them to Jamie's dad so he can take them to hospital.'

A look of fear passes over her pale, pinched face.

'No, he can't.' She rubs her hands together in a frenzied washing movement and then rubs her face,

'Julie, can you tell me what's wrong?'

She gazes up at me and in her eyes is pure terror.

'Where's Linda, why's Linda not here today? Where's Linda gone?'

'Her mother rang to say she has a doctor's appointment, why Julie, what is the matter?' My stomach curdles with a sick fear.

Suddenly the door opens and Miss Heaton is there, looking suddenly old and worn out.

'Miss Johnson, I wonder if I could have Julie Thorne please, there's someone here who needs to see her.' Julie walks slowly across the room, white faced and shaking.

'It's all right Julie,' says Miss Heaton kindly, 'there's a very nice lady here who needs to talk to you for a little while. Miss Johnson will come and get you at playtime.' Then, to me she says, 'Get your coffee first and then come to my room.' I look at the clock, there's a good hour yet, how will I get through another sixty minutes?

At break I hurry to the head's office and I'm surprised to see she's the only occupant.

'Sit down Kathy. It's bad news I'm afraid. Julie has been taken into care, together with Linda and Jamie. It appears that they have all been,' her voice breaks, 'sexually assaulted on a number of occasions.

Apparently a lot of this abuse happened during the Christmas period. The police and social services are investigating and it seems very likely that none of the children will be returning to school. I would appreciate it if you keep this matter to yourself at the moment, I will of course be informing the staff as other children may also be involved but I'll do that at the staff meeting on Monday, when, hopefully I will have more information.'

I feel numb. My tongue seems to have grown in size. I cannot form words. I begin to shake uncontrollably. It's happening again. I can't bear it. I stand abruptly and the next thing I remember is lying on the carpet, with Don leaning over me and then pushing my head between my knees.

Don takes me home and I go straight to bed, I pull the duvet over my head and resolve to stay in the dark forever.

Lost

The days pass in a fog of pain. There are two empty places in my classroom, Jamie and Julie are gone, spirited away by social services and my heart shudders and groans at their loss. I will probably never see them again, these children that I have loved. My thoughts are mashed together and I'm unable to separate them, one from the other. I know again that creeping fear, like a frost blackening all the plants around me.

'Eh, Miss, where's Julie? 'Er plants are looking proper poorly,' commented Wayne. 'Is she coming back or what?'

'I don't know, Wayne, we'll just have to wait and see.'

'Well, the plants can't wait; they'll soon be dead as door nails.'

Linda tugs at my skirt, vast brown eyes pleading, 'Shall I do 'em Miss, 'til she gets back. Shall I see't flowers?'

'Please Linda, that will be very helpful, just 'til she gets back.'

Of the three children concerned, only Linda has been allowed to return. The others are in care. I recall my conversation with her mother. Anguish seeps through like an awful damp.

'I couldn't believe it when they told me,' she said, tears soaking her crumpled face. 'How can they do that to a little one, filthy, 'eartless bastards. I 'ad no idea. It were a Christmas party they said. I took her there – Oh God! I actually *took* her there, only a few houses away, but I didn't want owt to 'appen to 'er in the dark. God, when they opened that door it looked like fairyland, she were that excited. Oh my poor little love...' She let out a thin roar of grief before bursting into violent tears.

I held her. I was up to my neck in horror. We both wept. What else is there to say?

Life goes on, but for me all the joy has been sucked out. Every day in school is like walking in treacle. We all feel it; every one of us is wounded. We're told not to discuss the subject outside school; it's all a vast, dirty, inexplicable secret.

In the meantime tables have to be learned, reading schemes read, creative writing created and children praised and chastised. We are well into our topic on people's jobs and have visited the post office; posted our parcels to some elderly residents and the letters we've written to the Queen, Starsky and Hutch, President Nixon and Kojak to mention but a few. The visit to the bus station was a great hit as was the butchers, where we saw how sausages and beef burgers were made. Today we visit the Police Station.

Sergeant Bingham shows us around, he is a large, square-faced man with ample white hair which he keeps smoothing, laughing brown eyes and dimpled cheeks.

'Now you lot, I expect you'll want to be seeing the cells.'

'Is that where you keep the murderers?'

'On occasions, yes, we've also had quite a few naughty boys in here.'

Wayne looks thoughtful, 'Er...what exactly had they done?'

'Oh, the odd burglary, joyriding, drunk and disorderly, that sort of thing.'

Robbie nodded and I wondered if he was thinking of his brother, Dwayne.

Christopher says, 'Joyriding, that's very bad; I mean stealing people's cars and then wrecking 'em. Some fellas took our car once, me dad wasn't arf mad. Do you know what they did? They crashed it into a tree and everything burned, the tree an all.'

'Oh that's disgusting,' says Robbie, 'crashing into a tree. We're supposed to look after the environment aren't we Miss? When I'm bigger and pinch a car I won't crash it into a tree, that's awful.'

Sergeant Bingham catches my eye and rolls his own. 'Right, let's go see how people are fingerprinted.'

'Coo-el!' says Robbie, 'I've allus wanted to be finger-printed.'

After that excitement we return to a large office upstairs.

'Right,' says the policeman leaning on a desk, 'any more questions?'

Christopher's hand is up immediately waving like a flag, his chest puffed out, eyes sparkling. 'Yes, where do you keep the speedboats?'

'Er...what speedboats are those?'

'You know, Sir. The ones you chase the drug dealers with on the Thames.'

'But we're nowhere near the Thames, that's in London, we're in Leeds.'

'Yeah, but it's a long river, I saw it on the telly and the police had these speedboats with blue lights and sirens and everything and they went really fast, it were cool.'

'Well I'm sorry to have to tell you that we haven't got any, we're a couple of miles off the river anyway. Any more questions?'

Wayne was next. 'Is it 'ard getting your trousers on in a morning?'

Again Bob looks puzzled, 'What do yer mean, lad?'

'Well you told us there was this pocket thing in yer trousers to carry yer truncheon, right. Well it's a long thing, right? Well dun't it get in the way when yer putting yer trousers on?'

I notice that the sergeant is beginning to sweat profusely. He wipes his forehead with the back of his hand. 'Well I think that just about concludes this visit. I'll have to be going I'm afraid got lots of criminals to catch. It's been very interesting. Yes, very interesting indeed.'

After Linda has given a very appropriate vote of thanks we return to the coach and our journey back to school. As I turn to leave I see Mike in earnest conversation with Sergeant Bingham, now what's that about I wonder?

The Telling

The enforced silence is gluing up my tongue. If I can't talk to the people I love about what's driving me mad, I feel I have nothing else *to* talk about. Peter is worried but what can I say, other than what I do say.

'There are serious problems concerning some of the children in my class, it's really upsetting me but I'm not allowed to talk about it.'

He puts his hands on my shoulders and looks into my eyes and there is so much to read in his, concern, gentleness, even fear. I go willingly into his strong arms, rest my head on his chest and the tears fall, yet again, but this time there's a measure of comfort. I cling to my rock.

Later, as we walk in the winter air, he broaches another subject - Mike.

'That community constable chap, Mike, came to see me the other day; ostensibly it was about the stolen church silver.'

'Oh really.' I can think of nothing else to say.

'He *said* a lot of things.'

'Oh.'

'Yes, about the estate and all its problems, the uselessness of the church, that sort of thing.'

I grimace, 'That sounds like Mike.'

'And, he talked about you.'

'Me?' Fear clutches at my heart.

'Mm, he says that you and he were an item until I came along and that you were close, very close.'

Words build a wall around me that I cannot climb, all the past pain rises up and gags me.

'I...I...'

A frown penetrates the smooth skin above his solemn eyes.

'He *said* you were lovers, that you were "at it like rabbits" as he so delicately put it.'

'No! Definitely not, I didn't, I can't, I couldn't. I never have because I just...can't.'

My voice splinters, I'm unable to string words together any longer. I begin to sob, a dark, desolate crying that I feel will never stop. He holds me, crooning, stroking my wet cheeks and tangled hair and I'm filled with despair. He takes my arm and leads me to a bench overlooking the park lake. Ducks skitter on the thin ice, crows swoop and call, but apart from a few dog walkers the park is deserted. Peter looks earnestly into my eyes

'Look sunshine, why not tell me what you can. Never mind the children in your class for the moment, just tell me what's eating away at *you*.'

'I can't, I never have, no-one knows, no-one alive that is.' He looks at me with a steady unwavering gaze. 'OK, I'll try. It was my dad, he...he abused me, sexually.'

I glance up quickly, he looks as if he has had an electric shock, he even jerks, suddenly he has dull black windows for eyes.

'I don't understand. You always speak of your dad with such affection. You've even said he was a wonderful father.'

He grips my hands and his knuckles are white, my breast beats as if a trembling sparrow is trapped there.

'He *was* wonderful, he loved me very much and when I was a child he couldn't do enough for me. He read me stories, took me cycling, we went for picnics and long walks. We often played silly games and I adored him, I...' Suddenly it's too much and I am crying again my face a wet mask of grief.

'Then, Kathy I don't understand what happened, what changed?'

'I don't know. I don't understand either. One day my mum was out, dad came in and he'd had a bit to drink. I was thirteen, I'd been in the garden sunbathing, we were fooling about and suddenly everything changed and... he...raped me.'

'Oh God! Oh Kathy I'm so sorry.' His waterlogged eyes hold mine. 'What did you do?'

'I was so shocked I just ran. I ran away to my grandma's. I ran four miles without stopping. She was my mum's mother, I doted on her. I was distraught, hysterical. Thank God she believed me, I don't know what I would have done if she hadn't. I never went home. I never saw my dad again.'

Peter is still holding my hands, gently stroking them with his thumbs. He shakes his head as if to rid it of bewilderment.

'So what happened, what happened to your dad?'

I start to cry again, my ribs ache with the sobs that rip through me.

'Well after she'd settled me Gran went over there. She talked to my dad and she told my mum. By all accounts there was a terrible row, my

Mum came back to stay with Gran. Later that night Dad went into the garage, sat in his car and switched on the ignition.'

'Oh no, suicide! And your mum?'

'Had a complete nervous breakdown, she was admitted to a psychiatric hospital but never recovered.'

Shock renders him speechless for a while. Then he stands, pulls me to him and hands clasped tightly we walk.

'Where are we going?'

'To the Vicarage, you need looking after.'

'No, really, I'll be fine!'

'Kathy, how many years have you held this in. How long have you tried to cope with it all by yourself? You need help, expert help. But right now you need to be looked after. May I tell Father Tom and Alice?'

I feel anesthetized with pain and humiliation. I nod and then remember little else, just Alice's gentle hands, a warm bed, hot chocolate, tablets and sleep. I am exhausted, sick of feeling, trapped in bereavement and pain like an insect in amber. I sleep and sleep.

Carrying On

I am back in school by the first week in February and feeling emotionally much more able to cope. I have a meeting with social workers dealing with the case and it would seem that Jamie, Julie and Linda have been targeted by a gang of pedophiles led by Jamie's dad. I tell those at the case conference how devastated I am not to have picked up the clues earlier. Gwen, the social worker in charge of the case is quick to reassure me.

'Don't worry, love. We are only just beginning to pick up on these cases ourselves. It was thought, in the past, that such things were rare. Unfortunately, it now seems that they are more common than anyone thought. It's a lousy world sometimes.' She pushes back her frizzy fair hair, revealing large hoop earrings, sits back in her chair and stretches, raising her arms high. She has a pleasant, open face devoid of make-up and sprinkled with laughter lines.

I clear my throat and continue, 'But I *saw how* amazing that house looked, it was really over the top and so out of character for Mr Coggs. I should have realized something was wrong.'

'Don't beat yourself up about it, Kathy; there will come a time, I'm sure, when all teachers will have training in detecting abuse. In the meantime we must all be alert to the signs and try to protect children as much as possible.'

I think of my dad and of what happened and reflect that some things can never be detected or prevented.

*

On Tuesday morning there is some good news at last.

'Miss! Miss! Me mam's had it, she's 'ad the baby at last *and* it's a sister and she's lovely. Six pounds twelve ounces she is, Miss, and I went to the 'ospital and I've seen 'er. Actually, she is a *little* bit ugly at the moment, 'er face is a bit squashy and red and she 'as these little black 'airs on her ears, a bit like a werewolf, but me mam says they'll come off. Oh and she doesn't smile and gurgle like Brenda's sister but me mam says she will adventurally.' I smile secretly and wonder if malapropisms will always be part of Sally's speech patterns.

'Oh that's lovely,' I get in quickly as she pauses for breath, 'and what are you going to call her?'

'Well that were funny that was because when me dad got 'ome

from the 'ospital he says, "It's a girl and she's called Margaret" and I
were *dead* angry cos I'd decided to call her Susan, it's a right nice
name is Susan, anyway me dad were right prized and he said he'd talk
to me mam and he did and she said, "Well we'll call 'er Susan
Margaret". Anyway, me mam 'as to stay in't eternity ward for ten days
then she can come 'ome and I'm making this banner thing to 'ang on't
door and it says *Welcome 'ome Mam and Susan Mar,* I didn't have
room for *garet* cos it's a long name for a baby so I'm reet glad we
settled on *Susan* and Miss do you know what?'

I take a deep breath, 'Sally can you sit down now, please we're just
going to have registration. You can tell me all the details when you do
your writing.' Phew! I thought I'd never be able to stop her. After an
initial sharing time on the mat the children settle down to write their
news. This can be very interesting and I look forward to reading their
journalistic endeavours later.

During the next lesson, which is maths, I ask Wayne to do a job for
me.

'Wayne could you just pop next door, please, and ask Mrs Sutcliffe
if we can borrow the Unifix blocks as we haven't got enough.'

He looks at me, a little blankly and says, 'Unifix?'

'Yes, you know, those coloured plastic blocks that we fit together to
help us add up and take away.'

He is not at all his usual lively self and leaves the room. Five
minutes pass and he still hasn't returned. I go to the door and peer out.
He is standing in the middle of the corridor looking disorientated.

'What's wrong, Wayne?'

'I can't find no unisex blocks cos I'm not sure which is next door.'

This is not like Wayne at all and I am very worried.

'Are you OK, Wayne? Is something wrong?'

He pushes grubby fists into his eye sockets and rubs ineffectually.
His face is smeared and muddy, he begins to shake. I am reluctant to
pull him back into the classroom but dare not leave the others
unsupervised. Fortunately Don appears at the end of the corridor. I
beckon him over and whisper the problem. He goes into my classroom
to ask mathematical questions. Oh joy!

'Now, Wayne love, whatever's the matter?'

'It's me dad Miss,' he sobs, 'the one that used to be Linda's. He's
gone Miss, he never came back after't pub last night and me mam said
he's gone to be Robbie's dad, she said Robbie's mam's the estate bike,

and....and he's tekken *my* bike wiv 'im.'

Oh wonderful, I think. How many more children in my class are going to be harmed by this man called, would you believe, Elvis Preston? He needs locking up.

'Oh Wayne, I'm so very sorry,' I say, when what I want to say is *good riddance*! I can't help but wonder what this 'super stud' looks like. He's never bothered to come to any parents' night, but he must really be quite something to have such an effect on so many women.

*

In the afternoon I take the children to the public library. I have arranged for the librarian to tell us about her job. She gives us a lively talk and tells us about the importance of alphabetical order for fiction books and a little about the Dewey decimal system for arranging non-fiction. Then a variety of children are given the opportunity to find things using both those systems. They love it and we build up a race atmosphere with children vying with one another to see who can find it the quickest. Then of course comes the exciting bit.

'Are there any questions about working in a library?' As usual there is a forest of thrusting arms. The librarian is a tall, silver-haired woman with a hook nose and horn-rimmed spectacles. She has great presence.

'Do librarians have to be tall like you to reach the shelves cos I want to be one and I'm only little?'

'Oh no,' she answers kindly. 'The two things that you need to be a good librarian are a love of books and you have to like people.'

Steven is next with his question.

'I heard on the telly about a book called Lady Chatterboxes Lover, they said that libraries could have it now but it used to be banned.' The librarian looks rather pink.

'Er....yes, I heard that too. Well, I think that it's time for you to be going, now,'

I choose Sally to give the vote of thanks;

'Thank you very much for telling us about libraries. They are very good places, me mam comes a lot for a bit of peace and quiet. So thanks.'

Suddenly Robbie leaps up, 'There's me new dad. Eh, Wayne, there's yer old dad.'

Linda presses her lips together and goes very pale. Wayne examines the Velcro fastening on his shoes.

Robbie runs up to the new arrival. He's a thick-set fellow with a square, red face, a fleshy nose and an abundance of very black hair in the style of Elvis Presley. His cream, embroidered shirt is open to the waist and a gold medallion completes the look, nestling against a thick covering of black chest hair. A brass studded belt is slung around his protruding belly and yes, he *is* wearing blue suede shoes.

'Now then young un,' he says to Robbie, ruffling his hair affectionately.

At this Wayne jumps to his feet and runs towards him. 'Dad,' he yells, 'we've been doing all about people's jobs. Will you come and tell us what it's like in't pit?' Wayne waits with baited breath, blue eyes sparkling, bottom lip trembling.

'Talk about t'pit?' shouts Elvis. 'There's nowt to talk about lad, it's just a great big bloody hole.'

Wayne shrinks back to his seat. Robbie *high fives* his new dad and swaggers back, smiling. Two little boys who have suddenly switched roles and one of them is visibly shattered.

'And a very good bye to you all,' Elvis shouts cheerfully, he has no antennae for grief.

Steven

Steven put the cassette back in the tape player he'd got for Christmas, he couldn't stop playing it. Beethoven's Fifth, he loved it. *Ever since the man had taken the back off the piano and played part of it, the rhythms had vibrated in his heart.* He'd never heard classical music before, his mum listened to Elvis and Cliff Richard and stuff like that, he liked that too, but it didn't leap about in his brain like Beethoven did. He hadn't told Miss Johnson at sharing time, he knew the others would laugh. He could hear the radio right now, but he'd never heard it play Beethoven. But now he had a problem, he wondered if Beethoven had made any other records. He wanted to find out more but didn't know where to look.

'Steven, come on love. Don't forget we're going shopping and we'll have to go straight away if you want to be back for Dr Who. We need to get to the bus stop, NOW!'

'OK I'm coming. Will you buy me a comic? Plee...ease.'

'We'll see, now come on, let me look at you.' She spit on a tissue and wiped at a smear of jam on his face and ran a comb through his hair tut-tutting as she did so.

Steven grinned cheekily at his mam and gave her a great smacking kiss on the cheek as she bent down to do up the zip on his anorak.

'Pack it in, Mozart,' she laughed, giving him a mock smack on his bottom.

'Mam, why do you call me Mozart?'

'Well didn't he write that music you're allus playing?'

'No, that's Beethoven.'

'Oh, I must have got it wrong, it were all a long time ago. You see I once went on this holiday with the Girl Guides It were really expensive and I had to save up for a long time and do all sorts of jobs for me mam and dad and my aunts and uncles and everything. Eeeh I was that excited to be going to Austria!' His mam's eyes were all fairy tale looking, staring into the distance like she saw something nobody else could.

Steven had never seen her look like that before. She was a great big comfy settee of a woman with lots of bulgy bits you could cuddle up to and her face was bulgy too with lovely soft skin and pink cheeks and when she laughed she wobbled. He called her Marshmallow Mum and *then she would laugh and laugh and give him a push and say, 'Cheeky little bugger!' and then she'd laugh some more.*

When they were on the bus he cuddled up and said, 'Was it nice in ostrichland?

She looked puzzled for a minute and then she laughed like a cackling witch. 'Ostrichland! Ooh you are a card, Ostriches...' and she wiped her eyes with a hankie and laughed and laughed. 'You are a duck egg, *our Steven. The place is called Austria and that's where I first heard about Mozart. It's a lovely place, really nice, with mountains and rivers and beautiful palaces. I loved it and the people were so nice and that's where I met your dad.' She pushed her conker coloured hair back from her face and he could see that her eyes had that fairytale look again.*

'My dad! That's where you met him? Oh wow, does that mean he was foreign?'

'Yes, he was Austrian. Oh he was beautiful.'

'Yuk! Men aren't beautiful.'

'Well he was. He was very tall and he had thick blonde hair and the darkest blue eyes you ever saw and he danced like a Prince.'

'A Prince!' Steven could see him in his mind although he had never seen him in real life. He thought of his own golden hair and deep blue eyes and he felt suddenly very proud to look like his dad.

The bus rumbled on but neither of them saw anything beyond the windows.

'So how did you meet him, Mum, how did you meet the Prince?'

'He wasn't really a Prince, silly. The Guide Captain took us to a concert in Scheonberg Palace. Eeeh it were so beautiful, it had red velvet seats and big glass chandeliers and there were pictures right up on the ceiling, how anybody ever got up there to paint them I will never know. And do you know, there were flowers everywhere and a great big orchestra with violins and flutes and all sorts of stuff and they were playing all these Mozart bits and Strauss waltzes and there might even have been a bit of your mate, Beethoven. Eeeh it were lovely. Afterwards we were all giddy and we were singing and laughing and there was this big ice-cream place, still open at ten o'clock at night and we all had some and Captain said, 'We'll take a short cut back to our hotel through the park. So we did.'

'Wow, in the dark, was it scary?'

'No because there were lots of twinkling lights and we saw a golden

statue of Mozart. Do you know he was a great composer and musician when he was just a little lad like you?'

'Then what happened?'

'Well, we were walking through this park passed the trees and suddenly there was this clearing and lots of coloured lights and an orchestra playing Strauss waltzes. People were sitting at tables drinking beer and champagne and lots of people were dancing. Captain said we could stay for a while and I was dancing with Christine Rogers and we were laughing and suddenly, he was there, your dad.'

'What did he say?' mam's eyes went all dreamy again.

'He said, "You will dance with me, yes?" and I said "Yes" and that was it, we waltzed and waltzed and waltzed. After that I saw him every day until we came home. My Prince,' she sighed.

'And what happened then?'

'Then I came home and after that you were born.'

Steven sat very quietly, bouncing a little with the rhythm of the bus. He wasn't quite sure how the Prince got to be his dad, but some instinct told him not to ask any more. He cuddled up to his mam and he gave her a big hug.

'Do you know, my little man, when we get to town I'm going to buy you another tape, I'm going to buy you a Mozart one and we'll listen to it together.'

'Coo-el and can I have a Strauss one an all?'

'Don't push your luck, my little prince, don't push your luck.'

But on the bus going back Steven held two precious parcels. He couldn't wait to play them both.

Unfinished Symphony

Another Monday morning and the children are sitting on the mat for sharing time. Robbie is raring to go, arm waving in the air, chest puffed out, and eyes like stars. *What a difference a dad makes.* I ponder, even if it is only temporary as in the case of Elvis.

'Go on then, Robbie. What would you like to share?'

'Well, me and me dad, right, we went cycling in the park. We went down every roadway and we had races on the downhill bits and it was cool, really cool and then...do you know what we 'ad then?'

'Fish and chips,' called Linda softly without meeting his eyes. Wayne was playing absent mindedly with his grey woollen socks, pulling them, in turn, up and down his leg.

'No, not fish and chips, it's better than that.'

Steven laughed mischievously, 'There in't owt better than fish and chips.'

'There is! Me and me dad 'ad a picnic in the woods and we 'ad.....' he paused for effect, 'hard-boiled eggs. When me dad got 'em out of the bag I said "we can't eat them we've got nowt to cook them in" and he said they were cooked already. Then he showed me 'ow to peel 'em. I didn't know you could do that, it were brill. And we saw loads of birds, even a robin like on a Christmas card.'

Steven is playing with Sally's hair, her plaits are gorgeous and he obviously loves the feel of them. Suddenly he realises Robbie's story has come to an end and eagerly puts up his hand.

'Come on then Steven. I wonder what you have got to tell us?'

He scratches his blonde head and grins widely. 'Well, do you remember that man that came and took the back off our piano in the hall?'

'Yes,' they chorus.'

'Well can you remember that music that we all loved, you know that da da da daah thing?'

'Do you mean Beethoven?' asks Christopher.

'Yes.'

'Well why didn't you say so then?' Like Robbie, *I'm* beginning to lose the thread.

'Well on Saturday me and my mam went in town and...' he produces two cassettes from his pocket as if performing a magic trick,

'I've got some more composers. I've got Mozart and Strauss and they are both dead good. Miss, can we listen to 'em this afternoon and draw them listening pictures again. Please Miss, can we?'

I glance quickly at my planning, 'Mm, maybe we can do that instead of story time, but we'll only be able to do one of them. We'll have to save one for another day.'

*

At lunchtime I get the classroom ready for painting. Not an easy task without a sink and a tap but we do the best we can. I spread the tables with news paper trying to ensure that all page three type material is face downwards, then I set out the bun tins, ensuring that each space is filled with a different colour of powder paint and that there are several non-spill water pots on each table and an array of different sized brushes.

When the children come in from the playground, I explain the task before us.

'Now, over the past few weeks we have been thinking about the very important jobs that people do to help us. Who can remind us of some of the things we've found out?'

'Well there's bus conductors like my dad,' says Sally.

'And bus drivers and train drivers and lorry drivers and van drivers and...'

'OK Paul, I think we've got that,' I say

'There are nurses, Miss, and doctors,' says Lisa. 'I'm going to be one of them cos I like bandaging, I bandaged our dog up and it took ages to get undone.'

'Right, thank you for that Lisa.'

'There are composers, Miss, and piano players, 'specially those that take the backs off the pianos, I'm going to be one of them. Or I might be a vile inits.'

I puzzle over that for a moment then say, 'I think you mean a violinist.'

'Yeah, I do.'

'Now on the blackboard I've put a list of lots of jobs, I'd like you to choose just one of them and draw a big, bold picture of that person, like this one.' I show them the figure that I have drawn. 'Now, if this person were a butcher, what might he have in his hands?'

'Well it depends,' said Wayne, he could have a chopper in one hand and a string of them sausages in the other.'

'That's brilliant' I say. 'Now I'll be walking around to help you if you get stuck, so don't be afraid to ask for help. Right, off you go.'

Oh wow, some of these are like caricatures. Steven has drawn a fantastic violinist with long flowing hair and a beard which cascades like a river beneath his violin. Robbie has done an amazing butcher, an enormous pie in one hand and a string of sausages in the other. He is round and fat with a huge, smiling face, complete with teeth.

'Oh that's lovely Robbie, but what are all these red bits?'

'That's the blood, Miss, it gets everywhere. Me dad keeps getting it on his pants, he's got piles.' Mm, too much information, I think Elvis would not appreciate everyone knowing that!

By afternoon break we've got lots of fabulous pictures, lollipop ladies, people up ladders, firemen, policemen, nurses brandishing huge needles and cleaners with mops and feather dusters. A good afternoon's work but I haven't managed to hear one person read. I'll have to make up for it tomorrow.

After break we listen to Mozart's *Eine Kleine Nachtmusik* and we make our felt-tip pen patterns and Steven is in his element, eyes bright, head bent towards the cassette player, listening and moving his body in time to the music. I smile; today has been what teaching is all about.

The children go into the cloakroom, gather up their things and set off home.

Janet comes into my room to view the paintings that I'm busy mounting to display on the classroom wall.

'Oh fantastic! I love this one of Steven's with the man playing the violin, just look at those teeth.'

'I know, it's brilliant, just have a look at Robbie's and tell me who that is.'

She shuffles through the papers and laughs heartily, 'It's Elvis Preston to a T, I love the embroidered shirt and the gold medallion and all that hair topped off with a miner's helmet. Eeh there's nothing like childrens' drawings, is there?'

There's a sudden shrieking sound, the screech of brakes, then a tremendously loud bang.

My stomach curdles and turns to dread. We drop everything and thunder through the playground. Already a crowd has gathered and a woman is keening like a wounded animal. I elbow my way through the crowd and see the inert, bleeding figure on the road. My thoughts plummet through a canyon of grief, 'Oh dear God, Oh no! Please no, not Steven!' His mum kneels beside him, her big doughy face the colour of putty, her eyes swimming in sorrow.

'My baby,' she sobs, 'oh Stevey, my baby.'

The ambulance arrives in a fluster of noise and the paramedics take over, calm, organised, efficient. I look down at Steven's mum and squeeze her shoulder, shock renders her speechless. I put my arms around her and feel her deep trembling. She looks so frightened, so lonely, lost and haunted. All I can do is hold her, whilst weeping silently, myself.

When the ambulance is ready to depart she whispers, 'Will you come with me, please? I've no-one else.' The paramedic nods and I climb into the vehicle. With blue lights flashing and sirens blaring we head for the hospital.

It's not long before Steven is rushed down to theatre. Then the waiting begins. On the way to fetch coffee I see a telephone booth and ring Peter. 'I'll come straight down,' he says. Immediately I feel stronger.

Later, as I hand Steven's mum the coffee, I say, 'My name's Kathy by the way, what's yours?'

'Sorry, I'm Lisa, thanks so much for coming; I didn't want to be on my own.'

'Don't worry, I want to be here, Steven's a lovely little boy with an amazing mind. I'm sure he'll be a great musician one day, I've never known a child of his age have such a passion for classical music.'

'Mm it's very strange, it must be in his genes, his father was Austrian. We met at a Strauss waltz night, in a park, in Vienna.'

'Sounds very romantic.'

'Oh it was, but I was only fifteen. It was a fleeting holiday romance and now it seems like something I dreamed, a fairy tale.'

I glance at this sweet, lonely woman, who looks at least twice her age and I'm filled with compassion. How strange, that each decision we make, has the power to affect us for the rest of our lives. How easy to make mistakes. But then, how can someone as special as Steven *be* a mistake?

'What was his name? This handsome Austrian boy?'

'Oh, he was called Ludwig.' She manages a smile. 'Weird isn't it, when you think about Steven's passion for Beethoven.'

Suddenly Peter is here and relief floods through me. I introduce them and then we are chatting easily. But, every time a door opens or someone walks towards us, our eyes follow every move. We wait, hungry for information. At last it comes.

'Miss Hirst?' Lisa stands up hurriedly. The doctor takes her hand. 'Steven's as well as can be expected. Both legs are badly broken, I'm afraid, and he has lost a lot of blood through a wound in his shoulder. But, fortunately there was no concussion. He is conscious but in a lot of pain. He's asking for his cassettes, do you know what he means?'

'Oh yes,' says Lisa, tears flooding once again down her white, tormented face. 'They're all crushed too.'

'Don't worry,' says Peter, 'we'll make sure he has some replacements before the night's out.' And with that we leave Lisa to spend precious time with her son. We stumble out into the dark.

It's at the door of my house that we usually say goodnight, Peter wanting to conduct our courtship properly because of his position in the church. But tonight our emotions are raw and we both need comfort. He opens his overcoat and I slip my arms around his waist. I shudder and he wraps his arms around me. Suddenly we're kissing softly and deeply, his tongue slips between my lips. I can't meet his eyes and when I do it is like putting a match to a firelighter and seeing it flare up. As we gaze at each other a ripple of heat rises up through me and I feel his manhood leap against my belly. I melt like wax and suddenly we're through the door, lying on my bed. Our kisses are urgent, sensual and I am warm, wanton and waiting. We meld together like two parts of a jigsaw, one picture. Now we are stroking one another, skin warm and silky, he smells of apples and spice and sweat. His lips seek out my nipples and I feel them harden and tingle, I am wet, he enters, we are one body.

Swansong

Miss Johnson was using the rubber again as she made invisible
*some rubbish from Darren's book. Wayne cursed under his breath. He
could see Christopher smile across the classroom and he wanted to
wipe that silly smile from his face. Trust Christopher to think of buying
her a rubber and a pen and a notebook for Christmas.*

*Trust him with his soppy, pretty, blond mother and his smart
briefcase dad, they even 'ad a car. It wasn't fair! Wayne loved Miss
Johnson more than anybody even if he was only seven. When he grew
up and she grew down he would marry her, yes he would and then
Christopher wouldn't be laughing, Oh no! Then he would be dead put
out and it would be his own fault.*

*'Oh Wayne,' said Miss Johnson quietly, 'what on earth are you
doing. You've even put the margin in the wrong place. Come on now,
you're one of my best story writers. I know you can do better than
this.'*

*Out came the blasted rubber again, it wasn't even an ordinary
rubber. It had a pink plastic holder and a neat transparent cover.
Wayne thought back to the day Christopher had brought it. The parcel
was all wrapped in gold stripy paper and there was a shiny blue
ribbon with a huge bow on it. If Wayne had been rich he would have
brought her a present wrapped up just like that...but bigger.*

*'My, this looks exciting, it's looks almost too good to open,' she had
said, her face all pink and smiley and Christopher had grinned
happily.*

'Open it! Open it!' they chanted and of course she did.

*'Oh Christopher, that is so beautiful,' she had said lifting out the
pink-flowered notepaper, the rubber and the matching pen and pencil.
'This is just what I needed and it will all be so useful, why, I'll be able
to use them every day in the classroom.'*

Wayne groaned inwardly, 'Oh no, not every day.'

*Everything had gone wrong lately, since his dad had left, his mum
was crying and shouting all the time and there was no money for treats
and now this, bloody Christopher Harmon.*

*That night, at home in the bed he shared with his brother, Wayne
thought about it. He could steal one of the pink-flowered present things
from the classroom. The trouble was, if he did, she would be upset and*

he couldn't bear for her to be unhappy. Late that night he arose stealthily when everyone else was peacefully snoring. Carefully he prised up the broken floorboard by the window. The tin box was still there, it was here that he kept all his plunder. He lifted it onto the cold linoleum and began to count the contents.

Six five pence's and twelve two pence's that was...Wayne counted slowly and then shook his head and began again. Decimalisation had only just come in and it was very confusing.

'Fifty four pence,' he whispered, 'not a lot, but by Easter I should have enough for a grand egg. She'd like an egg, he was sure, because she really loved chocolate. He slipped the box back into its hiding place and climbed smilingly back to bed. He did not get any pocket money of his own. When you'd six kids in the house it wasn't easy, especially without a dad. He'd got the money from the trays of the other kids. If you hung about in the classroom at the beginning of break it was easy, the others were in the cloakroom then and miss 'ad to be with 'em else there'd be a riot. He was very careful and he tried to be fair. He never pinched from anyone twice in a row. No, he let them 'ave their spends sometimes. He was not a bad lad, he thought comfortably as he drifted towards sleep.

By Easter he had enough for a really nice egg. It was not very big but it was full of Smarties, he'd seen it in the post office window. The trouble was that everyone seemed to get Smartie ones, what if someone else bought the same? What if that blasted Christopher did? No, that wasn't good enough. He wanted his egg to be special, extra special.

The next day he saw it, in the window of the Majestic Bingo hall, the most special egg you could ever imagine. It was a beautiful swan, sculptured in chocolate. It was enormous and covered in shiny silver paper. It seemed to float in a gorgeous box as blue as a summer sky and the whole, glamorous confection was topped with a beautiful blue bow covered in silver stars. Wayne stared in openmouthed adoration.

'Oh she'll like that, she really, really will.'

His longing eyes sought out the price and his heart sank, seven pounds twenty and he only had, one pound, seventy five. He pocketed the sweaty coins once more and dragged himself wearily home. All that evening he searched for an answer but could think of no way of realising the extra cash. His hopes of showing her how much he loved her were dashed.

The day before the end of term dawned and the precious coins still lay in the sticky depths of his trouser pockets. A quick sojourn into the trays of his classmates at break had brought forth three pesetas, a ten pence piece and two, rather nice, bluey marbles, nothing that would buy his heart's desire. On the way home that afternoon Wayne wrestled again with his problem. Should he buy the Smarties egg or should he wait in case anything else turned up? As he reached the corner by the library he was surprised to see Murray Jenkins blocking his path. Murray was a mate of his brother, Craig, eleven years old and something of a hardcase. He was well known in the area for his skill as a burglar and for his ability to knock down anyone in his way. Wayne felt the goosebumps rise on his skin and his heart began to thump wildly.

'Want to buy summat?' Murray asked casually.

'Might do, what is it?'

'Easter egg, quality stuff, none of yer Smartie rubbish. Fell off a lorry.'

Wayne's hopes began to rise,"Ow much?'

'Watcha got?'

Wayne's business brain began to grow, this was his first major contract.

'One fifty'

'Yer on. Meet me at the *back of Sandy's Garage in five minutes.'*

Wayne waited there until Murray arrived carrying a large black plastic sack.

'Where's yer money?'

Wayne handed over several coins. Murray rummaged in the bin liner and handed over his purchase. Wayne let out a low whistle when he saw it. There was the large chocolate swan shimmering in silver and blue in a magnificent box. Over seven quid and he'd got it for one *fifty; he even had thirty five pence left.*

'Ere wrap it up,' said Murray quickly, 'we don't want anyone to see.' He handed Wayne a copy of The News of the World and he wrapped it swiftly. His heart sang.

He couldn't wait to get to school the next day. He knew that Miss Johnson was always there about eight o' clock, he had seen her many a time when he'd been hanging round the streets after his mam had set off for work. He decided to go early so that he could give his precious gift in private. The extra thirty five pence had bought pink wrapping paper liberally scattered with blue flowers and hearts. It also had twenty one written all over it but he wasn't sure what that meant. He watched her through the classroom window. She seemed very busy; sharpening pencils and writing the date on the blackboard. She set out the maths table and put out new work cards, mixed paint and put clean paper in the art area. Suddenly he was aware that if he gave the gift now, no-one would know. But he wanted them to know. Above all he wanted Christopher Harmon to know, exactly how caring and generous he was. It was important that they knew that Wayne Brummet could buy beautiful gifts, even if he was on free meals. Miss Heaton had said in assembly that it was more important to give than to receive. He had always wanted to give. Well, for the first time in his life he was going to do it!

*

As soon as Wayne arrives in the classroom he thrusts a parcel unceremoniously into my hands and then looks hastily away.

'Wayne,' I gasp, surprised, 'is this for me?'

'Yea, a happy Easter,' he mumbles without looking up.

I touch the top of his head, his eyes appear glued to his feet. I gently lift his chin, ensuring that he will look at me. His eyes are full of …excitement?

'Thank you, Wayne. Thank you very much. Can I open it now or do I have to wait for Easter Sunday?'

'You can oppen it now, Miss.'

I pull the chair from behind my desk and sit at the edge of the red patterned carpet I've bought from a market stall. I sit down, and very quietly the children leave their tables and come to sit on the mat. I place the gifts on a chair beside me and then call the register.

'You know, there is really no need for any of you to buy me presents. I like every one of you; you're all very special people. You know it's what you ARE that matters, not what you can give. However, thank you all very much for all your kind gifts and good wishes, you are very kind.'

So the *opening* begins. There's a Smartie egg from Tracy. 'Mm my favourites,' I enthuse, then see Wayne's stricken face, 'but you all know that I love everything chocolatey,' I amend quickly.

There's a chocolate orange from Simon, I thank him profusely and a rather lovely Cadbury's Milk Tray egg which is gratefully received from Christopher. When I open that one I notice that Wayne has a very strange expression on his face. I pick up Wayne's huge offering and smile at him.

'Cor, it's a big one Miss,' says Robbie.

'Yes it's massive,' agrees Sally.

'It's nice paper, Wayne,' says Tracy kindly, 'you've wrapped it really good.'

He certainly has, I have great difficulty trying to unknot the garden twine. I suspect that there was no such thing as Sellotape in the Brummett household; maybe even the string came from the allotments. As the paper falls away there is an orchestrated gasp. Everyone stares in astonishment. Wayne grins like a Cheshire cat, for a moment I am lost for words.

'Why Wayne...it is absolutely beautiful, a lovely, graceful swan all made of chocolate. It looks almost too good to eat. Thank you *very* much.'

I am puzzled by Wayne's gift. How on earth has he have afforded something so obviously expensive? At break time I take it to the staffroom, perhaps someone else will be able to shed light on it.

I open the staffroom door; lift my gift above my head and shout, 'Look what I've got,' then stop in my tracks.

'Snap!' yell a chorus of voices as they each hold up what amounts to a flock of identical chocolate swans. There are sniggers of raucous laughter.

'Oh hell, here we go again,' laughs Don.

'Indeed,' interrupts a laughing voice from the doorway, 'caught in the act! Receiving stolen goods is a very serious offence as well you all know.'

Oh dear, here is Mike again, my stomach twists.

Easter

My first Easter in church and not at all how I imagined it would be. Every windowsill is crammed with spring flowers and as we enter we're each given a daffodil. A large, freestanding wooden cross, about seven feet high, dominates the sanctuary. But, unlike Friday, when it stood stark and unadorned, today it is swathed in greenery. Beautifully embroidered banners hang from the stonework each depicting an aspect of the Easter story. The church is packed and as we sing, 'Christ the Lord is risen today' we are invited to place our daffodils amongst the greenery of the cross, a living symbol of resurrection.

Peter preaches an impassioned sermon about the need for Christians to be there for the poor, lonely, sick and despairing, to go beyond all the trash and frippery and to live out the love of Christ. During the next hymn we place our Easter gift money in a basket, for the suffering people of Bangladesh. Marnie, a young, single mum, stands at the lectern to lead the prayers, speaking with quiet sincerity. Then we sing our final hymn, 'The Servant King', we are blessed and go into the church hall for coffee and buttered hot cross buns.

*

We are to spend the rest of Easter in Limmiton, where Peter's family live. As we drive we sing along happily to our tape cassettes, all our favourite Abba songs, the Beatles and of course Elvis. Peter chuckles happily as I describe the 'other Elvis' and we take bets on whose dad he'll be when school resumes for the summer term. Then we are there and I'm in my little flower-sprigged room with the sloping roof. The mullion windows overlook the garden with its carpet of forget-me-nots, early red tulips and blossoming trees. A blackbird sings, its sweet, silvery notes dipping and soaring in the soft evening air. I feel like I'm bursting out of my skin with happiness.

During tea Hannah brings us up to date with village news. The post office has extended into the cottage next door and become the village shop, a much needed resource in the village. Harry tells us about the walking group they've joined and the places they've visited.

'Well, you're both certainly looking fitter,' remarks Peter and Harry points out that's probably due to the regular dog walks rather than the Wednesday walking group.

'Oh, talking of energy,' remarks Hannah, 'you know Bradley and

Jennie Carr, Peter? Well, they're fostering again, *at they're age*, they must both be in their late forties. They've got two lovely kiddies at the moment, such frightened little mites they were at first, but now they're fair blossoming.'

An enormous lightness takes hold of me.

'That's good to hear, what are they called?'

'Oh I forget, do you know, Harry?'

'Do I know what?'

'The names of those kiddies that Brad and Jennie are fostering?'

'Oh, let me see, oh I know, Charlotte and Grace, lovely kids they are.'

Peter catches my eye and shakes his head gently. Later he says.

'You know, my love, you're going to have to accept that we'll never see them again. We just have to trust that God will look after them in their new homes *wherever* they might be.'

'You say *homes;* don't you think they're together, then?'

'I think it's extremely unlikely, it's not as if they're brother and sister, is it?'

'I suppose so, it's just that I miss Julie and Jamie so much and it would be lovely to know they are happy and safe and together.'

As previously, Peter's family envelop me with love and his mum particularly dispenses the tincture of comfort in every way she can. I don't know if Peter has told them the details of my past, I just know that I am embraced, totally, without any cloying sentiment or judgement. When Peter goes off walking with his dad and the *hairy hounds*, as he calls them, I spend some time with Hannah. In the kitchen we bake scones together and she shares her family recipe, using buttermilk in place of ordinary milk. I love the feel of the elastic dough and the skill required to handle it as little as possible whilst rolling and cutting out. I love the smell of home baking escaping from the Aga and wrapping us around with contentment. Ada, Peter's Gran, sits in the rocking chair by the stove, occasionally dozing but often treating us to her acerbic wit. When we are discussing the new village shop and its owners she remarks, 'She's a nice enough lass, I suppose, but yer know, she's all fur coat and no knickers.' I giggle helplessly.

'A bit different from Becklefield then, there it's no coat and no knickers in some cases.'

'Aye well, poverty can be a great equaliser whereas with some folk around 'ere it's *what* you wear that defines you. That Dora Dawkins, you should 'ave seen her last Sunday when I wore me demob suit, she were right lemon-lipped.'

'I thought it were only soldiers and the like that had demob suits...after the war.'

'Aye, well it were, but I had the chance to buy this suit backend o' nineteen forty seven, a lovely heather coloured tweed it were with a fuchsia-satin lining. That there Sarah Finnegan had it made by Jessica Martin's cousin's wife and she was right well thought of in dressmaking circles. Some folks say she once worked for Hardy Amies but then she married and came north, sensible woman. Anyway I bought it off Sarah after't war so I calls it my demob suit. And there's still a lot o' wear in it.'

Hannah looks across at me and winks, her face the colour of scones, her cheeks flushed in the kitchen warmth.

Later we kneel by the flower beds, loosening the soil around the daffodils and primroses and transplanting forget-me-nots so they make neat drifts instead of unmanageable clumps. I inhale the scent of new grass, the turned soil and the haunting perfume of hyacinths.

'You have a beautiful garden, I love it here.'

'Me too, after so many years of rushing around it was a joy to settle and I love nothing better than kneeling here trying to pin down all the colours of heaven in my own little patch.'

'I'd love a garden of my own and a greenhouse, I love planting seeds and watching them push through the earth, it always seems like magic to me to see them grow; especially things like busy lizzies, the seeds are like specks of dust, but in no time at all you've got these big, strong plants with such vibrant flowers.'

'Yes, they're a favourite of mine, especially in pots and hanging baskets. Oh look, the wanderers have returned.'

'Yes,' says Harry, 'and would you believe it, it's lunchtime. I wonder what we're having?'

'You know very well what we're having and you know who's making it, so get on with you, you rascal.'

Soon, we're all sitting down at the old pine table to a lunch cooked by Peter and his dad. Goose egg omelettes, (which are huge), with cooked ham and cheese, crusty bread and salad. I don't know why but I always have a huge appetite when I'm here.

'What topic are you doing next term?' asks Peter

'I thought about doing holidays. I know that some of the children won't be able to have them, but I've planned an educational visit to the seaside, so we can get a lot of work from that, and, we can make use of the park and talk about games and sports and maybe that'll give them some ideas for the school holidays.'

'Sounds good to me. Will I be allowed to come to the seaside?'

'That would be great, the more helpers, the better it will be. It's your favourite place anyway, Scarborough.'

'Oh great,' says Harry, I hope you'll take them to see the Battleships on the lake at Peasholm Park. Then seeing my questioning look he explains. 'Well they've got all these wooden replicas of battleships from the war and they stage this battle on the lake with fire and explosions and everything, kids love it.'

'I bet they do,' I reply, thinking of the bright lit faces of Robbie, Wayne and Steven.

The next day Peter suggests that we spend the day in Scarborough. The sun is warm on my back. We drive over the moors towards Whitby, a long way round but a stunning drive. We get out of the car to appreciate the view over the Hole of Hocum, a strange crater like bowl with moors beyond, dazzling and spectacular.

'Oh gosh, I'd forgotten how beautiful it all is. It makes me feel so small.'

'That's what creation does for us; it puts everything else into proportion, puts humankind into its proper place.'

'Which is?'

'Just being *part* of something far greater than itself. So often we run away with the idea that it's *we* that are the reason for everything, that somehow *we* are in charge whereas actually we are just one small part of creation.'

'Well, it certainly makes you think when you see a sight like this,' I sigh, 'it's just all so beautiful.'

We arrive in Scarborough in time for elevenses and head for the Harbour Bar, milky coffee and beautiful, Italian ice-cream. Then decide to walk up to the castle, a steep climb but worth it for the view from the top. We can see both bays, curved and comely, golden sands edged with foam. The water shimmers into infinity, calm and silver-grey, the salt-wind rubs at our cheeks and the seagulls scream for fish. We find a rocky outcrop beneath the old stone walls; spread our coats and cuddle, drinking in the view, the scents of springtime and the distant sound of waves, crashing. You can idle away many hours, just kissing.

Later, we walk through the churchyard, in search of Anne Bronte's grave and stand there for a while, thinking of that family who left such a treasure trove of literature, yet whose own stories were even stranger than fiction.

We amble through the town and choose posters, pictures and postcards suitable for my holiday topic. Then visit a Travel Agent and collect brochures, buy cheap knick-knacks that will look good on a classroom display and play silly games in the penny arcade.

We drive back over the moors as the sun casts its last rays and dusk falls. I'm sleepy and take little notice of where we're going when Peter stops the car on the lonely road. He grins at me, cheekily.

'Won't be a moment, just need to see to something,' and disappears through a gate beside an old stone barn. We seem to be on the edge of a village, I can see the lights of several houses surging over the cobbles, like waves. I look at my watch, where on earth has Peter gone? From somewhere close I hear the dulcet tones of Frank Sinatra singing 'You Will be My Music', one of my favourite songs and as I listen I think of Steven with his poor crushed legs stretched out and the violin cradled under his chin, his clear, soft skin suffused with pink and his utter joy in music of all kinds.

Suddenly the car door opens and Peter's standing there wearing a dinner suit, what on earth is going on?

'What are you doing, I don't understand.'

'That's what I was hoping,' he grins wickedly and reaches for my hand, 'come on, my lady, I don't have all night.'

I love the warmth and strength of his hand, the way his hair flops across his forehead, and the little dimples that fold around his smile. There is no other man in the universe I want and I squeeze his hand. We reach an old oak door, he pushes it and it creaks alarmingly, we both laugh.

'Where are we going?'

He places his hands over my eyes and edges me forward with his body,

'Right, now you can look.' We are in an old cruck barn, warmth is funnelling from a convector heater and flowers are massed on the table, but what takes my breath away are the candles; lots of them, tea-lights in glasses, candles in bottles, candlesticks on every window-sill and all the way along a huge table spread with a white cloth. Little flickering beams of light everywhere. It is so beautiful.

There are dishes of salmon and chicken, crusty bread, a variety of salads, raspberry pavlova and champagne on ice. I am dumbstruck, this is totally unexpected. Frank Sinatra croons on, Peter sweeps me into his arms and we dance.

'Then you will be my music,
You will be my song,
You will be my music.
I can't wait any longer if I'm wrong.'

He holds me tightly and the candlelight sends dancing shadows on the walls and ceiling. Then Elvis serenades,

Love me tender, love me long.

Eventually the music stops, we stand slightly apart holding hands, and all that he is, is in his eyes, honesty, care, compassion. Slowly, without taking his eyes from mine he kneels,

'Kathy, I love you so much. I have done since the first moment I set eyes on you. Will you marry me?'

'Yes! Yes! Oh Peter, you're my best friend in the world, I trust you with my life.'

'And I, you.' And from his pocket he takes a faded velvet box, opens it and slips an exquisite diamond ring upon my finger.

'I hope you like it, it was my gran's, I love it, and she's always said that one day I could give it to the girl of my dreams. She's beside herself with excitement, we'd better not be late back or she'll never forgive us. In fact, there's something I must do immediately.' And with that Peter opens the door, picks up an old school bell and rings it joyfully. Suddenly we're surrounded with family and friends.

Gran is the first to hug me, 'Eee lass, I'm reet made up. You're a grand lassie; our laddo couldn't 'ave found anyone better.'

Tears spring to my eyes and there's a lump in my throat. This is what I've craved for so long, to be part of a family again.

Malice

I prefer to do my supermarket shop on a Tuesday evening, it's usually quite quiet and our nearest one is several miles away, so after the journey I need a bit of peace. I push my trolley on automatic pilot, my head full of Easter and Peter and of the lovely times we've enjoyed. I reach up for a pack of Persil, someone else does at the same time, and I turn towards them with a smile that freezes on my lips. I think for a moment that my heart stops, my blood suspended on the journey to my brain. Then a fierce dark rage moves through me. How dare he be here? How can he? Surely he should be locked away somewhere? How can he be here, buying Persil?

Mr Coggs, Jamie's dad.

Small, wiry with greasy hair, round black spectacles and eyes like glittering coins. He stinks of rancid fat and historic sweat. My blood chills. How can he be here? How can he be doing normal everyday things whilst his child and goodness knows how many others are severely damaged, snatched from all that they know and from all who love them? I'm engulfed by a terrible darkness, a sea of hate such as I've never felt before. I gaze at his nauseating, pock-marked face and vomit spurts into my throat. His icy eyes gaze back at me but there's not even a flicker of recognition. He doesn't even *know* that I'm his child's teacher, even though we've met on countless occasions. Or is it just a trick to avoid confrontation? I don't recognise you, so you can't recognise me.

A great flame flares in my brain and I feel its power to the end of my fingertips. I grab at his flapping anorak and pull him towards me. Hate gives me strength.

'Hello, it's Mr Coggs, isn't it?' I growl through gritted teeth, 'How is Jamie?'

He stares into my eyes with a look of undiluted poison, his hatred equal to mine. Yet I feel no fear. He defiles everything he touches.

'You bastard!' I whisper. 'You will never, ever hurt a child again. I will make sure of that. Very, very soon someone is going to tear you limb from limb, very soon you will suffer unbelievable pain. You will never know when it's going to happen, you will never be free or ever enjoy one moments peace, you will never sleep soundly again, ever.'

He stares, empty-eyed and it seems as if he is already beyond vengeance and retribution, as if all life and goodness has been sucked from him and only a zombie remains. I shiver in the face of such evil and long with all my heart for justice to be done, quickly and efficiently, preferably before he goes to court.

The Summer Term

A new term and Steven returns to school, one leg is still in plaster and he's on crutches and will need to stay in at break times, but his sunny smile and exuberant personality are still very much in evidence, thank God. Our sharing time has widened to include world events because many of the children love watching John Craven's Newsround and I find it fascinating to hear what interests the children.

'I went to the pictures last night,' says Sally, 'we got a babysitter for our Susan cos she's too young for the pictures and we went to see Herbie Rides Again, it were about this little white car what was like a person, it had eyes and everything and it were dead funny. I had a choc-ice as well. It were smashing, I like going to the pictures, Miss.'

'That sounds fantastic, Sally. I think we'll be making our school hall into a cinema again soon. I wonder what we'll see this time?'

'I think it'll be a cowboy film, I hope it is, I love them kind and we can all shout "Boo" when the baddies come on and "Hurray" when the goodies chase them on their 'osses. It'll be dead good will that.' The others nod their heads and say 'yea' and it's obvious they're looking forward to our annual film show.

Christopher is sitting up very straight; one finger of his left hand on his lips and his right hand in the air, his back is ramrod straight.

'Oh Christopher, you are sitting nicely, you can have your turn now.'

He flushes with pride and everyone else suddenly sits straighter. It's amazing what a bit of praise will do!

'I was watching Newsround and I found out some very interesting things.'

'Oh good, so what's going on in the world Christopher?'

'Well it's a bit disgusting really, you see President Nixon, that's him in America where the cowboys come from, he's been a lot naughty. My dad says he's been telling lies, anyway he's got to resign, that means he has to *stop* being the President.'

'Oh dear, that's not good is it?' says I.

'No,' says Linda virtuously, 'I never tell lies.'

'That's a lie,' says Wayne, 'I remember when you told a lie.'

'Didn't.'

'You did, you said my dad...'

'That's enough,' I growl, in my scariest voice. 'Is there anything else, Christopher?'

'Yes, and this is in America, too. They have built a building even taller than the Empire State Building, it's called the Sears Tower and it's in Chicago.'

'Them Americans are always doing things bigger than everyone else, my dad says,' shouts Wayne.

'Oh that reminds me,' says Robbie thoughtfully, 'Is me dad sleeping with your mam tonight or wiv mine?'

'Er... Steven, you've got something very exciting to show us haven't you,' I interrupt quickly, though I have to confess I would have liked to hear the answer myself. Fortunately everyone turns towards Steven as he unloads his treasure from a large kit bag.

'It's a funny shaped box,' remarks Lisa.

'It is indeed, shall I help you open it, Steven, it's a bit difficult when you've got plaster on your leg, isn't it?'

All the children wait with bated breath. Steven unzips the case to reveal a violin, its wood polished and golden, and its strings taut.

Steven beams at the assembled children. 'So, who knows what it is?'

'It's a musical instrument,' says Wayne. 'I saw some on the telly once.'

Steven can't wait to display his knowledge, 'It's called a...violin. And, guess what...I'm going to learn it. I've had some lessons already; I can play "Twinkle, Twinkle Little Star."'

'Go on then,' says Wayne, 'go on and play for us.'

'Shall I, Miss?'

'Please Steven we'd like that very much, wouldn't we, children?' They beam their replies.

Steven lifts the violin almost tenderly and gently puts it under his chin. He places his fingers on the bow, expertly spread to balance the weight, and begins to play. The tune is recognizable and the tone pleasant. The children are obviously delighted and clap enthusiastically.

'Right folks, now we've all got lots to write about. Let's see if we can do beautiful handwriting and don't forget to use your dictionaries if you're not sure about spellings and if you need help what do you do?'

'Put up our hands,' they chorus.

'Right, all the pencils are sharpened so there's no need to waste time with that. So let's see who can write the most before I say stop at ten o'clock. Ready, go!'

They are all busily engaged and I walk around the classroom with my rubber and pen, ready to erase mistakes or supply spellings as needed. I find if I break lessons up into small portions like this, the children are much more likely to remain on task. As I walk I try to keep up a constant litany of praise.

'Well done, Lisa, you *are* writing a lot today.'

'Oh Wayne, that writing is *so* beautiful.'

'Kirsty you're keeping right up to the margins, well done, it looks so neat.'

On the dot of ten o'clock we pause to share some of what we've done. Various children volunteer to read out their work, others prefer me to do it for them.

Wayne always volunteers. 'Last yesterday me and my dad and my bruvvers watched Dr Who, it was dead scary. It's a different Dr now because every so often they metamorphose like when we did the metamorphosis of a frog. The new one is called Tom Baker cos I read it in the Radio Times. Our Dean won't sit with us and watch it, he goes behind the sofa and he always has his gun, he hates the Daleks.'

'Goodness me, you had some interesting words in there, Wayne, well done. I'm so proud that you remembered metamorphosis. You can put a well done sticker on the chart.' I hand him a sticker, he puffs out his chest and grins widely. Things do seem to have settled down a bit now that Elvis is bestowing his attentions on a fairer basis.

Linda puts up her hand and asks me to read her work.

'My dad came back on Saturday. He was really happy cos he's got an extra job. He's going to be an impersonator and work in all the clubs when he is not in the pit. We went to the club with him. He did, 'Are you Lonesome tonight' but that made my mam cry so after that he did, 'The girl of my best friend' and that made her smile. When I asked why, she said it were because of our other dad, the one who is Trevor's dad, he used to be Elvis's best friend. Anyway we stayed there 'til eleven o'clock and had loads of crisps and orange squash and then dad came 'ome with us so that was nice.'

'Well, that's amazing Linda, you have written a lot.'

'And she used a big word, that *impersonator* one. Can we put it on our list?'

'That's a good idea, Trevor. I'll just get my fat felt-tip pen and write it.'

I had pinned a long sheet of card to the wall by the blackboard and it was there that we wrote down all the interesting words we discovered.

'Now, who can tell me what *impersonator* means?'

'Does it mean a man with a lot of wives?' asks Christopher.

'No, it means someone who pretends to be someone else, like, *my* dad is like Elvis,' says Robbie scornfully.

'Yes, like *our* dad,' Wayne corrects firmly.

Grrr I think, *does that man realise how complicated he makes my life?*

A Load of Old Rubbish

Stuart and Trevor loved playing on the pit hills and also on the tip now that it was all joined together. Sometimes they found really interesting things like the day Stuart had found all those little balloons. His brother said they were condoms and told him what they were for but he thought that was gross, beside which, they made smashing water bombs. They had been digging a den all morning and now they were busy furnishing it. They had found two plastic boxes which they could use as seats and an old cupboard door thing that they balanced on a cardboard carton to make a table. They'd brought two plastic cups and a bottle of dandelion and burdock pop and some jam and bread sandwiches and ginger biscuits.

'This is brill,' said Trevor, 'it's like 'aving our own house.'

'Den,' corrected Stuart, 'houses are just for ordinary folk, dens are for gangs.'

'But there's only two of us, can two people be a gang?'

'Yea, cos it's not big enough for more of us, that's why we've got to keep it secret, so cross your heart and hope to die.'

'Do we 'ave to?'

'Yea that's what gangs do; it's called "swearing an oath."'

'OK,' Trevor stood to attention, 'cross my heart and hope to die.'

'Right, then I get my pen-knife and I slit our wrists and mix our blood together, and then we're blood brothers.'

'Hang on a minute, I saw on the telly someone slitted their wrists to commit suicide, I don't want to do that, *it can be lethal.'*

'Are you sure?'

'Yes, I'm very sure, I think.'

'All right, I tell you what, then, we'll slit us hands and then high five and we'll have done it.'

'Done what?'

'Mixed us blood together.'

'Will it hurt?'

'Nah!'

Hesitantly, Trevor placed his hand, palm upwards on the table. Stuart drew out the pen-knife blade and cut a cross on both their hands. Both drew in their breaths at the stinging pain but neither wanted to appear cowardly to the other. They slapped their bleeding palms together and Stuart said, 'One for all and all for one.'

'What does that mean?'

'Don't know but that's what you're supposed to say.'

They repeated it together and then Trevor shouted, 'Oh 'ell it's raining. Quick, we need a piece of a roof, find a piece of wood or summat.'

They scrabbled around until they found a piece that looked about right and carried it together to cover the hole. Quickly they crept underneath. In the sudden darkness they bumped heads. Trevor searched around for his torch and switched it on.

'That's better now, we can 'ave us picnic.'

'No,' said Stuart, 'we'll use up too much battery. Better light the candles, did you bring the matches?'

'Yes they're in my anorak pocket. Here you are. Eh, it don't half stink in here.'

'It's all reet.'

The candle was placed in an empty bottle. The match rasped against the box. There was a flame and then...a loud explosion.

*

I was just returning home from the shops when I heard a huge bang. A group of men went running towards the tip and shortly afterwards I heard the sounds of an ambulance and fire engine. I stood at my kitchen window, long after I returned home, pensive and afraid. I chewed the inside of my cheek and drummed my fingers impatiently on the worktop.

What if it is...anyone of several hundred children? What if they've been messing about on the tip? What if one of them is hurt? My thoughts were like a fairground ride but without the thrills.

There is a sharp knock on the door and Meg lets herself in.

'Doesn't sound so good, does it?'

'What have you heard?'

'Just that a few kids were playing over there and that there was some sort of explosion.'

'We're always telling them "don't play on the tip it's very dangerous," "don't go near the pond in the park," "look both ways when you cross the road." Sometimes I think we're just wasting our breath.'

'They're just kids, Kathy, looking for adventure. Their heads are full of crocodiles, they inhabit a different world.' I know, but no-one told me when I started teaching that I'd care so much.

Peter comes to pick me up at eight. We're going out for a Chinese meal with John and Meg.

'Did you hear the explosion earlier?' I ask. 'Any idea what happened?'

'I think you'd better sit down, love.' He guides me towards the settee. 'I've just got back from the hospital. It's not good I'm afraid, Stuart Hanson is badly burned, he took the brunt of it. Fortunately Trevor was thrown clear, though obviously he's very shocked and concussed. He hit his head on a door they'd been using to build a den. It was the methane; it ignited when they lit candles.'

'Oh dear God, am I going to have any children left by the end of this year?'

He puts his arms around me and I rest my head on his chest. Who would have thought that teaching on this estate would be so hard? I love these children, but I wonder if I can go on coping with all the pain and suffering that they go through.

Recycling

Naturally, Stuart and Trevor are the main topic of conversation when we return to school on Monday and it takes a while for me to settle the children.

'Eh Miss, have you 'eard about Trevor, he got blowed up and he's got comprehension.'

'No he aint, stupid, that's what we get when we're reading, reading comprehension. Trevor's got that other thing, er...'

'Concussion,' I finish. 'Trevor has got concussion so he needs to stay in hospital until he gets better.'

'I feel reet sorry for Stuart though,' says Robbie, sadly. 'I know it really 'urt our Ali when she got burned and it makes a real mess of your skin.'

We talk more about the accident and I warn the children, yet again, about the dangers of playing on the pit hills and the tip. Then I quickly move on to our new topic.

'Right everyone, our topic this term is about the sea, so let's make a list on the blackboard of everything that we know already about it.' There is silence for a while and I am made even more aware of the tremendous gaps in their experience.

'It's wet, Miss,' says Sally thoughtfully, 'cos when I went in it I didn't have a costume and then my knickers got wet and we had to hang them on a rope between two deckchairs to dry and we'd no pegs so my mam had to pin them on with the safety pins from our Susan's nappy cos she didn't have one on cos me mam says baby's can go naked on the beach and it were a nice day, well a bit windy and-'

'Thank you Sally,' I interrupt, 'that's very helpful, so the sea is wet.' I write *wet* on the board. 'Now, what else do we know about the sea?'

'I saw a picture once,' says Linda, playing with the Velcro fastening on her shoes. 'It's kind of frayed at the edges.'

'No it's not frayed, you're daft, you,' says Wayne. 'I went once with me dad, we didn't actually go on the beach, only in the arcades, but the sea were a bit like beer, you know, it's like that foam on the top of beer.'

I try to stop myself from sighing, oh gosh, they know so little. But Christopher, bless him, comes to my rescue.

'In some countries the sea looks dead blue, I've seen it in holiday brochures, but our sea is mainly grey. When the waves break on the sand they are foamy and sometimes the sea is coming in and sometimes it's going out.'

So then I'm able to talk about tides and the moon and then, with the help of a beautiful picture story book I introduce some of the creatures of the sea. Soon there's a busy murmur as children write about what they've learned. Then do their own versions of the fish and sea creatures I have produced for them with the help of a spirit duplicator.

Maths becomes more exciting as we calculate the volume of sand needed for a variety of sandcastles. Then, using magnets, we play the fishing game and add up the numbers of the 'caught' fish. Another group of children are drawing fishes of an exact size using tape measures and rulers, while yet another group, are seeing which boats float and which boats sink in the water play I have borrowed from the reception class. There is a general air of excitement and enjoyment and the day passes quickly.

After afternoon break we all sit down ready for a story. Today we have 'Topsy and Tim go to the seaside' and I use it to prepare them for my exciting news.

'Do you think Topsy and Tim had an enjoyable day at the seaside?'

'Yes, I think they liked the sand best,' said Robbie. 'I'd really like to build a ginormous sandcastle with a moat all the way round and it would have soldiers on the top and-'

'Well, Robbie, you will be able to do that very soon *because* all of the people in our class are going to go to the seaside.'

'Are we off on a trip?' asks Wayne, getting down to the nitty gritty. ''Ow much will it cost? Cos me mam allus says "we 'aven't got enough money and that's final."'

'I'm going to give each of you a letter that contains all the important information. It will tell you *where* we are going, *when* we are going, *how* we're going to get there and *how much* it will cost. But the good news is that it will not cost very much because the school is paying for most of it.'

'Do you mean it's like a bargain, Miss?' asks Christopher, a great frown furrowing his brow.

'That's exactly right Christopher. Our school trip will be a real bargain, BUT if you want to go you have to bring this form back all filled in and signed by one of your parents. If you don't bring the form back you won't be able to go.'

When the bell rings, signaling the end of school, the children are buzzing with excitement. I feel enormous enthusiasm too, what a privilege to take so many children for their first ever view of the seaside.

I've backed all the display boards with poster paper in various shades of blue to represent the sea. Needless to say, I got into trouble for this. Poster paper is an expensive resource. It was only when I pointed out that I'd bought some of it from the art shop in Leeds, with my own money, that Don appeared mollified. Resources are a constant bone of contention between teachers and management, there is so little money and far too many children to make it go round.

'We'll be fetching our own bloody toilet rolls soon, if it goes on at this rate,' moans Sandra. 'How are we supposed to create an exciting, stimulating environment if we haven't got the stock? I asked for a dozen more pencils last week and I was told I haven't been making them last long enough.'

'Good grief, don't they get it,' grumbled Janet, 'when children bloody well write, the bloody pencils wear down.'

The teachers here are incredibly generous and think nothing of buying resources from their own pockets and supplying books, home corner equipment and even paint for the walls.

Don listens to all this with his usual gentle smile and twinkling eyes and says, 'Well there's only one thing for it, folks. I feel a jumble sale coming on.'

There are hoots of laughter and more groans, this annual fundraising event is not a pleasant affair but one of the only ways open to us for raising money.

'Well, I'm definitely not doing the shoe stall, that was gross,' says Sandra. 'I reckon Kathy's due for that, it'll be good practice for being a Curate's wife.'

'What's that got to do with it,' I protest laughingly.

'All that foot washing,' grins Sandra.

At the staff meeting after school we plan the jumble sale together. It's a massive event using both assembly halls and there are stalls of every kind. Sandra is delegated underwear.

'You might well laugh, Kathy Johnson, but there are some very choice pieces, remember, we have several ladies of the night on our books.'

The evening of the jumble sale is hectic. Several mums are very organised and have lists and move around school in a very purposeful manner. Meg has offered to help on shoes and one of our first customers is Linda's mum.

'Hello Miss Johnson, can I have four pairs of wellies please, one size eleven, one size eight, one size six and one size three.' I gaze at the mountain of wellington boots and wish I'd thought to sort them into sizes. Just at that moment Don passes by and hands me some piece of card and giant felt-tips. 'Quick see if you can order them in sizes before all hell breaks loose.'

I wend my way into the thick of the Welly Mountain leaving Meg to make sales and collect the money. Then I seem to spend hours pairing white stilettos, children's sandals, fur-lined boots and moth eaten carpet slippers and securing them with clothes pegs. The stench is awful, my back is tender, my feet aching and yet many of these women fill me with awe. They are struggling against so much, poverty, illness, too many children, violent partners or none. Government may be toying with equal rights for women but it'll be a long time before these women get a sniff of it. And yet, women like Linda's mum, have, in spite of everything, a quiet dignity, pride and an attention to detail in the behaviour and manners of their children that are sadly lacking in many.

Mrs Duckworth, a loud, rotund woman with chin upon chin and a laugh that causes her whole body to vibrate, shouts over the paired shoe masses.

'Eh love, I'm after one o' them bacinny things. Where am I likely to find one?'

'I'm sorry, didn't catch what you said.'

'You know, the bacinny things, what you take on your holidays. I'm off to Benidorm with our Betty's cousin's friend's daughter.' I stare in bewilderment.

Meg steps into the breach, 'You'll be wanting beachwear, love. Bikini's and such are down on that bottom table.'

'Ah thanks, sweetheart.' She glances down at her list, 'Will they have beach towels as well, oh 'ell and I'll need a sun hat.'

As we pack up at the end of the evening, Robbie passes by and gives me a cheeky grin.

'It were well good tonight Miss, I've got a load of stuff for the seaside.' He pops a pair of giant sunglasses onto his snub nose, and holds up a beautiful bucket and spade. 'Aye, I'm all set, bring on the sea.'

At the Seaside

I can't sleep on the night before the Scarborough visit. There's so much that can go wrong and my brain seems to think that I have to imagine each awful scenario before I'm allowed to rest. I *think* I've planned for everything, sick bags and buckets, toilet rolls and tissues, lots of towels, spare knickers and underpants in various sizes, clipboards, paper and pencils, blankets and beach balls and a first aid kit. I think that's all. Meg, John and Peter are all coming to help and I have extra staff in Mrs Lambing and Don and I've asked Sally's dad the bus conductor and Linda's mum, Jenny. Jenny didn't think she'd be able to come but her mother agreed to look after the baby and the twins and she came to me yesterday, as excited as a child saying; 'Miss Johnson, I've managed to make arrangements so, yes please, I can go to the ball,' and then she'd laughed at her own joke. I wanted to hug her.

*

So, here we are, all packed up and ready, each of the adults responsible for four children and we set off with two on each side all holding hands. The coach is on time and with much laughter and squeals of excitement we settle into our seats. One final check to make sure everyone is here and off we go. As we travel we sing all our favourite songs and then keep our own groups occupied by playing 'I spy', 'alphabet shopping' and other tried and tested travel games.

'Are we nearly there yet,' shouts Robbie, 'me stomach thinks me throat's cut.'

'Can we eat us lunch, yet?'

'I need a wee.'

'Will there be ice-cream when we get there?'

'Miss what if the tide's in and we can't go on't sand.'

Well, obviously they've learned something; three weeks ago they didn't even know there was a tide.

'Oh wow! I can see the sea! I can really, I can see it.'

No that wasn't a child it was Jenny, Linda's mum.

Meg and I exchange a smile. Then I have to stop all the children running to one side of the coach so they can all see.

The coach drops us on the North Shore. The tide has just gone out and the sand is deliciously rippled and damp. Don leads us to a

141

secluded area and we spread our blankets and sit down in our groups. Leaders distribute cartons of orange squash and biscuits and we are all quiet...for a while.

'I knew it'd be big Miss but I never thought it were big as this. I mean you can't see the end of it can you?'

'Isn't it shiny, Miss, it looks just like a silver cloth that hasn't been ironed.'

'Miss, you see that line where the sea meets the sky, well a boat just dropped over the other side.'

Note to self, teach about horizons later, and remember the 'silver cloth' comment for poetry writing.

Soon all the children are barefoot, sand-grizzled, happily digging and sculpting, enjoying the glory and majesty of the British seaside on a beautiful sunny day. I slip off my own shoes and socks, rub my feet in the sand and stretch out my legs. Bliss!

'Ee lass, you'll have to stop wearing stilettos just look at the corns on your feet,' laughs Meg

'I know, I hadn't realized they were so bad.'

Sally pauses on her way back from collecting seawater in her bucket and peers at my feet,

'Ah, Miss, haven't you got lovely feet, oh look Linda, Miss has got little bubbles on her toes, they're ever so nice.'

I can't resist a triumphant glance at Meg.

We are booked into the fish market later, so after about an hour of sandy creativity and collecting treasures, we bundle all our paraphernalia into our beach hut, (borrowed for the day) and head for the harbour. We bounce along in our groups of five, like a fairground caterpillar ride.

As we reach the first stall where the fishmongers are hard at work excited chatter becomes awed silence.

'Wow look at that enormous fish and he slit it in just one whoosh of his knife, cool.'

'Yea, you can even see its giblets.'

The fishmonger takes a second fish and with one chop, the fish head is severed. There are cries of disgust, awe and amazement, 'Eh, mister, what do you do with all the heads?'

'We throw them away, son.'

'Can I have one?' The man catches my eye and I shake my head.

'Nah, sorry lad, they all have to go to make pet food.'

'Look at them eyes they're like black marbles,' says Darren, the fishmonger squeezes one out to demonstrate, Meg and I shudder, Peter laughs, but the children are awe struck.

'Sir, what kind of fish is that?' asks Linda,

'This one, love, is a cod, the most popular fish we get.' He holds up another. 'This ones a silver hake, this a lemon sole and here,' he shouts triumphantly, 'are fresh Flamborough crabs.'

'Er, they look dangerous, look at their big claws; I don't fancy eating one of them,' says Lisa.

'Oh they're grand,' says the fishmonger, 'pure heaven on a plate.'

'How did they get here?' asks Robbie.

'See those boats out in the harbour, they are the trawlers. They go right out to sea, further than you can see, then they let down their nets and catch the fish.'

'Is it a hard job?' asks Christopher.

'Very hard, sometimes the waves out there are like mountains and the ships are tossed about as if they were matchboxes and the fishermen are battered by the wind and the waves. It's a very dangerous job. They have to listen to the shipping forecast very carefully, before they decide where they can go.'

'What's a shipping forecast?'

'Oh... yer teacher will tell you about that,' he says with a grin and a wink 'she'll tell you *everything* about that.'

'I will indeed. Right children, it's time to go, what do we say to the fishmonger?'

'Thank you sir!' they chorus.

'Aye it's been reet interesting,' adds Robbie. 'I think you're a wizard with that knife, ave you ever killed a person?'

As we make our way to Peasholm Park where we are to eat our sandwiches we pass several fish and chip shops. The scent wafts on the warm air and we all sniff appreciatively, before tucking into our potted meat or salmon paste sandwiches.

As I watch my class, so happy and excited I think, yet again, of those that are missing. How Jamie and Julie would have loved all this. I imagine Julie's delight at the neat flower borders in the park and the awe with which she would have greeted the azaleas and rhododendrons, *Oh Julie, where are you?* I think and just pray that she is surrounded by kindness and affection. And what of Jamie, does he laugh now? Does he run around freely like a normal boy getting noisy and sweaty and overexcited? I hope so. Then there's Stuart? How many more weeks and months will he spend in hospital?

My eyes seek out Trevor. He is rolling over and over in the grass, like an excited puppy whilst Robbie and Wayne pelt him with grass cuttings.

'All right, that's enough!' I call. Don is busy setting up a rounders pitch and his group of helpers organise the class into two teams whilst Peter has been to a nearby kiosk to organise welcome cups of tea for my half of supporters.

'Come on sunshine, time to stop brooding and enjoy a cuppa. Pity about the fish heads, we could have had a great battle. He pulls five mangled heads from a plastic bag.

'What on earth?'

'It's ok, it wasn't me, Miss,' he chirrups, 'just confiscated them from Raymond Pickles, apparently he was taking them home as a present for his mum who really, *really* likes fish heads.'

'I bet she does,' laughs John, 'I don't expect she'll enjoy washing his trousers, though. Ooh what a pong.'

'He's a funny little lad,' says Meg, 'he was crying when we were on the beach and he wouldn't take his coat off, or play in the sand.'

'I saw you talking to him,' I say. 'He is a very quiet boy; he's not been with us very long. I try to draw him into discussions but it's like trying to plait treacle.'

'Well, he said he didn't want to get dirty and that sand was messy. Then, later on he just sat there crying and when I asked him what was wrong he said his granddad has died.'

'Oh, poor kid,' says Peter, 'when did that happen?'

'Well that's just it,' chuckled Meg, 'that's what I said and-' she breaks off and can't stop laughing.

'What?'

'He said he... got shot in the war.'

Peter laughs heartily, then looks thoughtful, 'Oh, of course, there's a Raymond Arthur Pickles on the war memorial, I bet that was his granddad.'

'Oh dear,' I say, 'that's Raymond's full name too, Raymond Arthur Pickles, I wonder if he's seen his own name up there written in stone, and if that's upset him, poor lad.'

After a while it's our turn to organise the entertainment, something vaguely resembling a cricket match, whilst the other adults have a tea break. Raymond is crying again, he doesn't want to bat. Meg stays with him whilst John bowls gently. She guides his arm and the ball is whacked some distance away. Raymond's face blooms with delight and he performs a comical dance, his round wire spectacles fall crookedly across his nose, he pushes at them impatiently. As John bowls again the sun glistens Raymond's mousy hair and illuminates his T-shirt, a smiles curves across Meg's lips and yet again she assists him to sporting prowess. This time the ball spins across the grass and there is a great cry of, 'Run Raymond, run!' He doesn't need telling twice, he raises the bat like a javelin and careers across the grass, his little legs pounding like pistons. When he reaches the other end the whole class is cheering wildly, 'Go Ray! Go! Ray! Ray! Ray! Ray!' His face when he gets back to the wicket is a personification of joy and Meg sweeps him into her arms and swings him round like a whirligig. Peter and I are caught up in the moment too; he hugs me in sheer delight and my whole being jitters and booms.

A loudspeaker announcement informs us that the *Battle of the River Plate* will soon be starting and we quickly gather up all our belongings and make for the seats we've booked by the lake. The boys, particularly, are excited.

'Will there be real torpedos and bombs, Miss?' shouts Robbie. I notice that Trevor's face is the colour of porridge and that his eyes exhibit fear.

'Trevor, come and sit here between Reverend Peter and me. I don't like loud bangs very much'

He grins weakly, 'Neither do I. I used to like 'em on Bonfire Night, but not any more.'

'I'm not surprised,' says Peter. 'You've been very brave.' The colour returns slowly to Wayne's face.

Soon we're all caught up in the mock battle though I'm sure that many of the children are relieved that the battleships are in miniature.

'I'm glad it was only pretend, Miss,' says Lisa, her little moon-face earnest and worried, her yellow hair like burnished silk, 'I don't like it when they keep having wars. It's a waste of time when you could be playing.'

'I agree,' says Peter, 'you've got it right there, Lisa. We all need more time for playing.' He turns to me with a heart-stopping smile, 'What's next on the agenda, Miss?'

'We're going from the ridiculous to the sublime; it's the fairy glen, just around the corner.'

'Oh good,' says Peter and gives me a cheeky wink.

'Oh Miss, do we have to, I don't like bl...flipping fairies,' says Darren kicking at a stone.

'It's only fair in't it, Miss. We've 'ad to sit through a bloomin battle, now the boys 'ave to go look at the fairies,' replies Lisa.

'Now children, we are going to go into a very special place. All the houses and buildings and people that you see are just like real ones but they are all in miniature, which means they are very tiny. I want you to look at how beautifully and carefully they have been made. Then when we get back to school you *might* be able to make something similar for yourselves.'

'What, tonight Miss? I think I'll be too knacke...too tired, Miss.'

'No, not tonight,' says Don impatiently then under his breath he mimics *Captain Mannering*, 'Stupid boy!'

So we begin our walk, in single file, along the narrow paths of the model world of Fairy Glen.

'Miss, you won't forget to give me my travel sickness pill will you?' shouts Christopher from somewhere near the back of our crocodile.

'No I won't forget.'

'You won't forget my valium, will you?' calls Trevor worriedly.

'No I won't forget.'

'Eh, it's a good job we're not staying the night,' quips Robbie, 'else I'd be saying, don't forget I wet the bed, wouldn't I?' He grins cheekily and I try to smother my laughter.

Needless to say, the children are enchanted by the Fairy Glen and are busy making plans for their model making when we return to school.

'I'm going to make a lighthouse,' says Christopher seriously, 'I noticed that the first one was built in 1804, that is a very long time ago.'

Wayne shakes his head and frowns. 'I'm going to make a lighthouse also,' he sticks his nose in the air, 'but *mine* will actually light up.'

'Mine will too!' shouts Christopher angrily. 'Who ever heard of a lighthouse that didn't?'

'I'm going to make a church that lights up so that you can see all its stained glass windows,' said Linda.

'You won't be able to use glass, it's too dangerous and you could prick your finger and die, I bet Miss makes you use plastic,' pronounces Wayne.

'Now children, there's one more exciting thing before we get on the coach to go home. We're going to travel on a very small train on the North Bay Railway, so we need to cross this road very carefully.'

'I've changed my mind,' enunciated Christopher, '*I'm* going to build a model railway.'

'I've already got one,' said Wayne.

At the end of the day we drop the children outside school, being very careful to reunite children with their appropriate adult. Not easy when you try to work out which one Elvis has actually come to collect. It must be Jenny's lucky night as he greets Linda with a kiss and 'Hello Babe' in a false American accent and surprisingly, he is pushing a double buggy. 'Priscilla's still with your mum,' he informs her.

She turns round and with a big smile says shyly, 'Thank you for having me, Miss Johnson, I've had a lovely time.' Linda, with thumb in mouth and face flushed with sleep flutters her fingers and snuggles up to Elvis. In one swift movement he hoists her from the ground and sits her on his shoulders, holding tightly onto her hands. She beams like a lighthouse and nods her head from side to side as if listening to invisible music.

'I didn't realise the new baby was called Priscilla,' remarks Meg. I grin,

'Neither did I but, come to think of it; she's always just referred to as, "the baby."'

'Well, glad to see them all looking so happy.'

Me too, perhaps Elvis is so incensed by what's happened to Linda, he's determined to protect her in the future. I hope so.

Meg and I walk back to my house; the men go to pick up the fish and chips we've been craving all day. The sky is like a china blue bowl, streaked with peach and apricot and crisscrossed with vapour trails. We gaze upwards as yet another plane wends its way through the warm air.

'I wonder in what exotic place that one will land?' considers Meg.

'Don't know, but do you know what?' I reply.

'What?'

'I'm glad I'm not on it, I'm glad I'm here in Yorkshire, I couldn't have had a nicer day.'

'Or a more exhausting one, I'm absolutely knackered,' quips Meg.

Ships, Sharks and Sea Shanties

Scarborough seems to have reinvigorated all my class for they arrive in school buzzing with ideas of what they're going to do. I've never seen them like this before.

As they gather on the carpet for sharing time I'm amazed by the strength of their motivation for work.

'Miss, can I write a story about sharks and pirates because I was thinking about it in bed last night and I'm going to call my chief pirate, Greenbeard and he's going to have a ship just like the pirate ship we saw in the outer harbour where all the treasure boats go.'

'Good, but it's *leisure* boats, Wayne, not treasure boats. The harbour master said the outer harbour was used for leisure boats.'

'Oh, I thought he said treasure, anyway that's what they'll be in my story and the pirate won't have a parrot cos that's common, all pirate's 'ave them, no, *my* pirate is going to have his own monkey. And then they're going to go to Africa and-'

'That sounds brilliant, Wayne, but don't tell us anymore just yet, then, when you read it to us we'll have a lovely surprise!'

Although I'm surprised all ready, I've never known Wayne want to write a story before!

Linda's hand is held high and straight.

'Linda, what have you got to tell us?'

'Have you heard of mermaids, Miss? Well me dad told me about them. They're girls but they don't have legs, they have fish's tails like the silver hake we saw yesterday, or even the cod I expect. Anyway can I write a story about them?'

'Do they have mermen?' asks Robbie thoughtfully.

'In stories they do.'

'Right well I'm going to do an underwater war between mermen and another army; I think I'll call them...sub-men.'

I stand and walk to the blackboard. 'I'm going to write down some of your ideas, so that we can see how to spell the words and then I think we had better get on with it, because we want to know how the stories end before we have playtime. Well done everyone, you've got some very good ideas.'

*

In the staffroom I remark to Janet about how keen to write, my class are today.

'Well that's what politicians don't understand isn't it. They think you just lift up the top of the kid's heads like inkwells and pour the facts in from some great jug called 'Curriculum' and that's it. They don't seem to have any understanding about kids who never get to go anywhere or do anything.'

Mrs Lambing joins in.

'I know, I kept thinking yesterday, if only Edward Heath could see them now, kids who've never seen the sea before, whilst him and his ilk have been messing about in their own boats practically since birth.'

'Yes, if you'd seen Raymond Pickles yesterday afternoon, minus the famous anorak with fur-lined hood, standing in the sunshine in a white shirt, playing cricket, you'd have been amazed, he was like a different child,' said Don.

'And Wayne came in this morning *begging* to write a story. I couldn't believe it.' I smile, remembering.

'Well, it's like we've always said, if they don't get the experiences at home, we have to make sure that we give them as many good adventures as we can. Though how we can be expected to cram it all into the school day, I don't know?' says Sandra.

Don stands up and grins broadly, his eyes fizzing like sparklers on bonfire night.

'Ladies, you forget, we don't *have* to cram it *all* in the school day, that's why we do so much at other times. That's we have the film shows, pantomimes and trips to the theatre. That's why we go to the ballet and concerts, zoos and supermarkets. We bring the world to them or we take them into the world. That's why *you're all* such fantastic teachers and don't you bloody well forget it. Don't let *anyone* destroy your enthusiasm, because an apathetic teacher is as much use as a chocolate teapot.'

There is the sound of applause from the doorway. Oh blast, it's Mike.

'Hear, hear. I'm all for a bit of enthusiasm, in every area. He wiggles his eyebrows and grins suggestively. Some people laugh. I turn away and start to wash up the coffee cups; I can't bear to look at him.

'Would you like a cuppa?' asks Don, 'I'll get you one.'

'Thanks milk and two sugars, I'm sure Kathy will have told you I'm not sweet enough.'

'Not by a long chalk,' I whisper, but even so I find myself shaking inside.

'So, how's the crime rate?' asks Don companionably. 'Anything we can help you with?'

'Well, I've just come from Robinson's, the greengrocers. They had a break in during the early hours of this morning; there was nowt in the till, so they didn't get any money. There are a couple of these new electronic calculators missing, a television that they had in the back, a portable radio, and here's the funny thing, a poster about fish that they had on the wall by the wet fish counter. Weird isn't it?'

My heart thuds and clanks. The bell goes signifying the end of break and I beat a hasty retreat. *Oh no! Who is it this time?* Well, if they run true to form I won't have long to wait for an answer.

During maths we weigh fish made from a variety of materials and decide which are heaviest and which are lighter. We have a wet fish shop in the home corner and Wayne and Darren serve in there whilst the other children take turns at buying. Other groups of children add up shopping lists for fish products and I walk around, marking books, chivvying and sorting out the occasional disagreements. Mrs Lambing is hearing readers and when the children settle down to draw careful pictures of fish I hear readers too.

Just before lunch we settle down on the carpet again to discuss what we have learned and to plan for the afternoon.

'Miss, can I make a college?' says Linda.

'A college?' I ask puzzled.

'Yes, you know one of the college things about fish, I was looking in the library and I found some more different kinds and they are all lovely shapes and colours and patterns.'

'Oh you mean a collage; yes that's a very good idea. Will you show me the book before you go for lunch? I wonder what kind of materials we'll need to make fish.'

'That silver foil stuff will be good, we could draw on the scales with felt-tip pens and what's that shiny material called?' asks Sally

'Satin,' says Lisa, to my surprise, 'that's what my bridesmaid dress was made from. Yes it will be like that one Jamie made for the harvest only bigger and when he comes back he'll be dead pleased.'

'Yes and can we start on our model seaside town, like the Fairy Glen, because actually I'm going to make the lighthouse,' says Christopher, 'and it will actually light up if I can get hold of any batteries.'

'Oh Miss, that's not fair, I was going to make the lighthouse,' argues Wayne

'I think we'll have to make a list of all the things we'll need and who is to do what.' I pin some large sheets of sugar paper to an easel and we begin to plan. Wayne is easily persuaded to build a castle with Robbie because that's one of the most important buildings.

I spend most of my lunch hour searching for materials and setting them out on tables. I am really pleased by the excitement that this topic has generated and looking forward to some quality work. As I stand with my back to the door, surveying my handiwork, I suddenly feel hot breath on my neck and turn quickly. He is far too close for comfort.

'I had an idea that if something fishy was going on; it would be in this room.' Mike's voice is heavy with sarcasm. A cold silence seeps in. 'Come on then, where is it?'

'Where is what, may I ask?'

He echoes my words in a silly voice then replies, 'The poster, what do you think I mean, or have you got all the electrical goods as well? The bloody fish poster. I know you are aware of the thief's identity, but you're so goody-goody these days you're probably protecting *all* the thieves on this patch.'

'Don't be ridiculous, I've got no idea who the thieves are. How dare you walk in here and start throwing accusations around!'

'Because I know what a soft, sentimental fool you are, always trying to help the poor little kiddi-winks. You're just too daft to see what's in front of your eyes. This estate is just a den of iniquity, full of thieves, prostitutes and ponces and it's people like you that help them get away with their crimes.'

'And there speaks the *community* constable!'

He leans against the wall, his hands in his pockets, a sardonic grin on his face, a large, peevish somnolent man. We chafe at each other like mismatched cogs. Did I ever feel any attraction for this man? Fortunately the bell for afternoon school rings loudly.

'I think you had better go. If you need to interrogate me again you should let me know in advance and I will make sure my solicitor is present.'

He grins again and slides his hand slowly down my arm as he passes, I shiver.

*

By the end of the week the classroom is looking fantastic. The wet fish shop is full of realistic looking model fish and one wall displays an amazing underwater scene with a vast array of fish, crabs, seahorses, whales and sharks. There are some wonderful paintings of pirates and pirate ships and the children have produced their own sea fantasy books about mermaids, sharks, pirates, underwater witches and sea monsters.

Most rewarding of all, for me, was the reaction of the children to poetry. I tell them the story of 'The Forsaken Merman' and then read Matthew Arnold's poem of the same name, just two verses at a time. They love the language and we began to learn some bits by heart and then they asked to paint some pictures to illustrate the lines they liked best.

'Right everyone,' says Robbie, 'this is my picture of sea beasts cos I like the bit where it says, "Where the sea beasts ranged all round, feed in the ooze of their pasture ground." That means that the bit where they ate were dead boggy.' The children laugh and then Wayne tells about his picture.

'I like the bit where it says, "Where the sea snakes coil and twine, dry their mail, and bask in the brine." So this is my snake, right, all coiled up and these patterns on it's back are it's mail, you know like what soldiers have, and of course we know what *brine* is don't we?'

'IT MEANS SALT WATER,' chorus the children happily.

There are many more of these pictures and no room to display them so I decide to make a big book and on Friday we'll read it all the way through it. I 'm amazed by how much of the poem the children have learned to recite.

It is also on Friday that I discover a little more about the greengrocery robbery. At sharing time I am handed a long, cardboard cylinder. My hands shake as I unroll it and hold it up for the children to see. A large, beautifully coloured poster, plasticised to prolong its life.

'Oh Miss, that's gorgeous and each fish is labelled.'

'Yes, it's going to be really useful in our shop.'

'That was clever, Linda, getting that.'

'My dad got it for me,' she pronounces proudly.

'Oh aye, he's good like that is Elvis,' says Robbie,

'Yes he is,' says Wayne, 'I don't know where he gets some of the stuff!'

Holidays

There's a whole fortnight's holiday in the spring and Peter and I are both weary. It's been a long and painful half-term, Stuart is still in hospital, Steven still limps badly and tires quickly and of course there is no news of Julie or Jamie.

We've decided to holiday with John and Meg and have arranged to stay in a hotel at Bamburgh in Northumberland. I haven't been to this area before, but Meg has visited many times and we look forward to exploring new territory under her guidance. When we arrive the sky is gunmetal grey and the wind is howling across the dunes spattering sand into our faces and gritting our eyes. We walk for several hundred yards and then decide to ensconce ourselves back in the hotel. We are soon cuddled up on huge sofas in front of a roaring fire, enjoying strong, hot tea and toast liberally spread with butter and strawberry jam. Peter and I have inadvertently both bought copies of Tolkien's 'The Hobbit' and are deeply immersed in this fantasy world, but pause now and then to compare notes. Meg and John are curled up together talking softly, except for the times when Meg's great belly laugh rings out, usually closely followed by John's deep, rich chortles.

I've been reading for some time, completely lost in the world of Bilbo Baggins, when I am aware that Peter is looking at me, our eyes meet and lock and if tenderness were liquid we'd both drown. I'm mesmerised. Then he grins and he hooks his arm around me, my head rests on his chest and I know nothing else, until I wake an hour later.

'Oh no, have I been asleep, what time is it?'

'Nearly time for dinner, shall we go up and get changed?' I'm suddenly shy and can only nod. Meg gives me surreptitious thumbs up and we climb the stairs. If anything our lovemaking is better than ever and the pain of the past is buried yet deeper.

Dinner is a lively affair with succulent steaks, fat chips and a lovely assortment of fresh vegetables, followed by bread and butter pudding with double cream. We linger over coffee and inevitably the conversation returns to Becklefield.

'The Robinson's are still upset about the break-in,' says John, deep concern in his voice. 'It's the third since Easter and Myra's really getting depressed about it. They've had new locks fitted and new security bars but all to no avail.'

I clear my throat, but the words just won't come out. Three pairs of eyes are fixed on me.

'Well come on, woman, spit it out,' says Meg. Peter looks surprised.

I tell them everything I know, including my conversation with Mike.

'The cheeky bastard,' croaks John uncharacteristically, 'who the hell does he think he is.'

'A policeman,' I squeak.

'Rubbish,' says Peter, 'he's hardly Starsky or Hutch is he?'

'Yes, but should I tell him? He might do it again, Elvis I mean.'

'But you don't know if it *was* Elvis, the thieves may have dropped the poster or they might have sold it in a pub or a club or simply given it away.'

'That's true, he does work the clubs and I don't really think robbery is his style. But you must admit, a poster about fish is a strange thing to steal.'

Meg laughs, 'He would be a bit obvious wouldn't he, in all that Presley gear as he climbs out the window a deep voice says, "Elvis has left the building!"'

John guffaws.

Later though, I observe that Peter's face is bleak and a frown crinkles the skin above his earnest blue eyes. I squeeze his hand and he meets my gaze.

'Be careful with Mike, my love, he's a devious, deceitful man.'

This is the first time I've ever heard Peter speak badly of another and it worries me.

After dinner we decide to brave the elements once again, wrap up warm and find to our surprise that the skies have cleared. The night is a stunning navy blue, liberally spattered with luminous lights. A gold fingernail moon punctuates the dark and the air has the scent of salt. We walk on the sand and watch the sea billow gently in inky folds with bleached, unblemished edges. All is peace and I realise that I have craved this for *so* long. Becklefield is challenging, lively and yes, exciting, but I feel I've had rather too much of it lately. Peter also meets obstacles and is accosted daily by problems for which there's often no solution. He sits at the bedsides of the sick, tries to offer warmth and comfort to the bereaved, and strives not to be judgemental in the face of often, self-induced predicaments. We walk hand in hand

and breathe the silence and purity of the night air and relish the beauty of the castle, high, floodlit and incredibly romantic.

That night we sleep soundly, spooned together in an enormous four poster bed, lulled by wine and winnowing waves. We wake to the wafting scent of bacon, the sound of seagulls and the smiles of each other; the first time we have been able to do that and all is warmth, feathers and lavender scented sheets. We linger longer.

*

Later we set off to visit the castle, standing strongly majestic, high on a hill. We stare at the ghastly, grey, grizzled sky and feel the wind that scourges flesh and snatches words, that tousles hair and whips the waves. When the drizzle begins we haven't travelled far and suddenly we are doused by driving rain and run laughing, back to the hotel again.

John finds a Scrabble board and we spend a happy hour tussling with words, calculating scores and more laughing, lots of laughing. After lunch the storm abates and a watery sun sits timorously in a pearly sky. We walk for miles along the beach with the gulls wheeling over our heads and the waves thrashing the shore, and then take a boat out to the Farne Islands to look at the seals.

'Now ladies and gentleman, if you just look on your left hand side there are some seals bobbing.' We do and there are, the people shout in excitement and the seals disappear. 'It happens every time,' says the boatman shaking his head. 'No matter how many times you tell 'em to be quiet, when the seals are there they make a racket and the seals disappear.'

Fish and chips next, in Seahouses, and we poddle around the shops where we buy touristy things like puffin tea towels, postcards and keyrings. Of course I have to be different and buy lots of things for my topic, which now, of course has ended. Never mind, they'll go in the topic box marked 'Sea' and will be useful next time.

'So you two, when is the wedding?' asks Meg as we eat our fish and chips from the paper. 'You'll have to give me time to buy a hat.'

Peter and I grin at one another, 'Some-time next year,' I say, 'possibly in the summer holidays, after all we haven't known one another for a year yet.'

'Yes, but what a year,' says John, 'You've both had a real baptism of fire. Let's hope the next school year will be a quieter one.'

'I doubt it; I don't think Becklefield does quiet.'

'Well, John and I have had an idea. Actually it came from Father Tom but we feel it's a good one.' She laughs cheekily, her wrinkles a map of a million smiles and I think how much I've grown to love this friend.

'It was while we were in Scarborough that we thought about it. So many of those children never having been to the seaside before,' John breaks in, enthusiasm radiating from every pore. 'Never been to the sea, never travelled up to the Lake District, climbed trees, cooked on an open fire. These were the things that were meat and drink to my childhood, real adventures and these poor kids are denied all that.'

'So what are you going to do? Start a Scout troop or something?' Three pairs of eyes turn on me.

'That's exactly it,' says Peter the skin crinkling around his glowing eyes.

'Father Tom and the church council have agreed to it and we start after half term, so we can make the most of the summer.' I feel put out for a moment, that all this has been going on and I haven't been part of it. I try to hide it with a laugh but my voice breaks as I say, 'Well, thank you, for telling me.'

John encircles me in a great bear hug. 'You've had enough to think about, flower. We hope that it will all be a help to you.' I smile at the endearment, I love the way that so many of these people have such a wealth of pet names; love, flower, blossom, my love, sunshine and chicken, embroider all their conversations. I sometimes call the children, sausage and it always makes them laugh, I've no idea where it comes from but it's so much better than some of the words that they're called.

'We're going to duplicate some leaflets explaining *where* we'll meet and *when* and we'll see what happens. But if we can encourage lads like Robbie and Wayne, Darren and Christopher and all the rest and we're clever with the fundraising, hopefully we'll be able to take them on pack holiday in the summer.'

'Well, that would be lovely. Where are you thinking of taking them?'

'Not too far away, for the first time. I've heard of a place near Scarborough that's supposed to be very good, purpose built, with dormitories and everything,' says John.

'The only problem with that,' says Peter, 'is that we'd need transport in and out of Scarborough and that would be more expense.' I picked up on the words 'we would' and found myself smiling yet again.

'Do I take it, then, from the *we* that you used just now that *we* are *all* involved?'

'Erm, *darling,* would you like to spend part of your summer holidays with about twenty little boys?'

'I wouldn't miss it for the world. Actually that dovetails nicely with a suggestion that Miss Heaton put to us at the staff meeting. She thinks that it will be good if we each continue with the same children next year. They have so little stability in their lives; an extra year with the same teacher might be a bonus.'

'Seems like a good idea,' says Peter and the others nod in agreement.

'Right,' pronounces John, 'this calls for a celebration, to the pub!' He stands and leads the way, like a ship in full sail. Meg follows in his wake, carrying bags and coats and all sorts of paraphernalia, until he realises, turns back and apologises profusely.

In the pub we are full of plans and Peter takes out his ever present notebook and starts jotting them down. All sorts of exciting possibilities take shape, evenings when the boys will be pirates, cowboys, red □ndians, spacemen and knights. Times for building castles and spaceships, playing rumbustious games and learning, incidentally, about trees and plants, animals, weather and a million other things. We fire one another up and for a moment we forget about the hard work involved, about tiredness, violence and disappointments. There's lots of information from the Scout Association which, *just by chance*, Meg has brought with her. We pore through it whilst working our way through an assortment of lagers and beers.

'I thought it was all about knots and camping and stuff but there's a whole curriculum in here,' I remark.

'Yes and there's all sorts of useful things, like learning to cook simple dishes, the correct way to wash and iron and how to start a fire with only two matches,' John chuckles.

'Excellent training for all our young arsonists.'

'Now who's the cynical one?' quips Peter

'It will be so good, though, to spend some quality time with them. In school we're always worrying about the next thing on the curriculum and making assessments and check lists.'

'Right, enough of all this, how about we get back to the hotel and have a rest before dinner?' He squeezes my hand as he mentions 'rest' and I have no trouble at all in squeezing back.

*

We decide to drive to Alnwick the next day. I have in mind a topic on castles, we need one with a historical bias and I'm sure I'll get lots of information there. I'm sure that the boys will all love dressing up as knights and the girls as princesses and there is a wealth of resources out there. After we've *oohed* and *aahed* about the beautiful castle, examined the cannons on the castle walls and imagined ourselves feasting in the Great Hall we make our way to the castle shop.

'Oh dear,' says Peter in a woebegone voice, 'I've just seen Kathy's eyes, literally, light up. Do you think we should give her a budget and make her stick to it?'

'Impossible!' chirps Meg. 'Anyway there's a lot of stuff here we'll need for the cubs.'

'Foiled again,' says John pushing back his thick white hair and wiggling his bushy eyebrows.

When we leave we have metallic looking helmets complete with visors, rubber swords, plastic shields, innumerable books and some beautiful shimmering flags complete with poles.

'Just enough to set the scene,' I remark, as Peter and John bend and bow under the weight of all our purchases. I'm already excited and can hardly wait to get back to school.

'You know, I've been thinking, I've got quite a few old evening dresses that would easily cut down to make princess dresses for the girls. It won't take long to run them up on my sewing machine,' says Meg.

'Aye, and I've got all that wood in the garage, I bet I could make a turreted wall very easily!'

'Oh Hell's teeth,' says Peter in mock anger, 'they've even got my mate at it now. Some friend you've turned out to be,' and he gives John a push.

It's so good to *share* my excitement.

History and Mystery

All four of us go into school on the Saturday before the new term begins and do a bit of furniture reorganisation.

'This floor is damp,' remarks Peter, 'I'm surprised the caretaker's been mopping today.'

'Oh it's always damp when there's been a lot of wet weather, something to do with the old mine workings and an underground stream.'

'That can't be very healthy,' says Meg.

'No, quite a few of us suffer from painful legs but that could just be all the walking around and crouching down to child level that we do.'

'This fungi growing out of the plaster doesn't do much for the décor, either.'

John remarks, 'Oh stop moaning the pair of you, we're not preparing for Ideal Home magazine, we're just building a castle.'

So we work on. John and Peter transform the house corner into a beautiful castle complete with Gothic arched windows, arrow slits, a portcullis and a bridge that pulls up with chains.

'Amazing what you can do with a few pieces of wood, paint and some very artistic people,' says Peter.

'Looks pretty good, even if I say it myself,' says John.

Meg and I cover all the display boards with grey paper and the 'boys' paint them to look like stone. We hang the flags on the wall above the castle and I put up the titles for the wall displays. So far we have, 'We designed our own shields', 'Look at our castle paintings' and 'Read our exciting stories about Castles.'

The men survey them and John remarks, 'Very dictatorial isn't she, telling everyone what to do. Anyway, what else is on the agenda, shall we forget castles for a while and go out for a Chinese meal tonight?' He pauses, 'What's wrong with you?' He's obviously seen my reluctant expression.

'Well I'd thought about making maths work cards on the theme of-'

'Castles!' they all shout.

Meg Laughs. 'No chance, you're coming for a Chinese, whether you like it or not.'

*

On Monday I'm like a child, anticipating the faces of my class as they come into the classroom and see all that we've prepared for them.

Robbie arrives first, 'Eh up! What's this? Who's changed it into a castle?'

'Do you like it?'

'Aye, it's summat like. I seen 'em afore on't telly, castles.' He starts to sing.

'Robin Hood, Robin Hood riding through the Glen,
Robin hood, Robin Hood with his banda men.'

He bends down to peer through the arched window and nods appreciatively. 'Can I be Robin Hood, Miss, or Banda Men, I'm not bothered which?'

Whoops, he's only been in two minutes and I'm smiling.

'It's not Banda Men, Robbie. It's Band of Men; there were a lot of them.'

'Oh right, suit yourself. Got any bows and arrows?'

'Oh wow, look at this, it's a castle,' shouts Wayne as he bursts through the door. 'Is it supposed to be Scarborough Castle, Miss? Cos, if yer don't mind me saying so, it were a lot more brocken down than this.'

'Broken, Wayne, it's not brocken, it's broken.'

'Aye, that's what I said. It were a right ruin.'

I shake my head; my mouth is curving upwards again.

'Oh Miss, ain't that nice, Sleeping Beauty's castle, oh Linda look! There are ballgowns all 'ung up on a rack. Can our group play in it first?' asks Sally. 'Eh Lisa, come and look at this, Miss has got us a real life castle full of ball gowns and everything.'

Soon we're sitting on the carpet for sharing time.

'Now then everyone, I hope you all had a lovely holiday. Who's got anything to tell us?'

Sally's bouncing like a puppy about to be fed. 'Well you'll never guess where we went, we went to Scarborough and I showed me mam and dad all about the fishing boats and the nets and everything and we saw the lighthouse and talked to the lifeboat men and our Susan paddled in the sea, oh you should have seen her, Miss, in her little costume, she looked right sweet and she loved jumping over the waves and I told her all about mermaids and the merman and everything and I did a bit of the poem but me mam says she thinks she's a bit young for poetry-'

'Belt up, Sally I can 'ardly breathe you're going that fast,' says

Robbie.

'Which bit of the poem did you tell her?' asks Linda, winding her brown hair around her finger.

Sally suddenly stands to attention and in a very different voice begins to quote;

> *'Sand-strew caverns cool and deep,*
> *Where the winds are all asleep*
> *Where the spent lights quiver and gleam;*
> *Where the salt-weed sways in the stream.'*

She finishes with a shy smile and a bob that's almost a curtsey.

'Oh didn't she do that nice,' said Steven. 'You were reet good, Sally. *I* like that bit and all.'

I can feel the tears pricking; these children really are something else!

'Before the holiday we learned a lot about the sea and I was so proud about all that you did learn. I loved reading all your stories and poems and of course you made some wonderful models and lovely paintings. In fact Miss Heaton asked me to put them in the hall so that *all* the children could see them. This term we are going to find out about castles. So, what do we know already about them?'

'Some of them are very old,' said Christopher

'Absolutely, some are hundreds of years old.'

'I think they're mostly built of stone. Actually I've never seen a brick one,' says Wayne.

Raymond is, as usual, huddled at the back, with his jumper over his head like a cowl.

'Raymond, can you tell me anything about castles?' He mumbles something in a voice aimed at his feet.

'Sorry, I didn't catch that.' More mumbling, then Steven interprets.

'He said they have arrow slits for the archers to shoot through and moats around them full of water.' Wow, that's a surprise.

'*Well done, Raymond* and thank you Steven, for helping him. Right, well one of the things that we are going to do this afternoon is to make some model castles and to do that we'll need to be able to measure very carefully. So, this morning we are going to practise all our measuring skills. We'll be using rulers, metre sticks and trundle wheels...' and so the maths lesson begins.

At break time there's news, at last, about Stuart. Apparently he's had several skin grafts on his face and they have taken very well. He is having private tuition on the ward, but only for a short time each day, and is doing as well as can be expected. What a strange term that is. Surely we all expect different things.

'Of course he won't be back in school this year,' Don informs us, 'we'll just have to take it as it comes. Ah...ha look what the cat's brought in.'

'I can have you arrested for insolence, young man,' says Mike, playfully.

'Oh I like the "young man" bit; you can have a cuppa *and* two ginger biscuits. So is this a social call or an *interrogation?*' Mike looks uncomfortable for a minute and I wonder if he's realized that I've talked to Don about him. He clears his throat.

'Ladies and gentlemen, I just thought that you would be interested to know that a certain, William Arthur Spiver has been arrested for the greengrocery robbery and will be appearing in court next week. He will also be charged with several other offences involving robberies around Becklefield.'

'Well that's a relief,' says Janet. 'I've never even heard of him. Do you know I don't think I've ever been able to say that before about local robberies?'

'No it makes a change,' says Sandra. 'I hate reading the newspapers and finding that a former pupil is in prison or on the run, or whatever.'

Mrs Lambing says, 'Yes, it must be really nice to read that one of your pupils has won an Oscar, or played at the Albert Hall or scored a goal for Manchester United.'

'It might happen one day,' I say hopefully.

'Don't write them off; don't ever write them off, some of these kids have got more between the ears than the parson preached about. You wait. Don't *ever* write them off,' says Don passionately.

I feel like cheering, maybe it's because I live in Becklefield myself, or because I have so many friends that do. I think these kids are wonderful.

'By mid afternoon we have several part built papier-mâché castles and some beautiful detailed posters about the parts of the castle. We also have some careful observational drawings of helmets, swords and pots that are supposed to have been used in castles, (probably in Hong Kong judging by the labels underneath). Some children have begun very imaginative stories and I feel really pleased with their achievements.

When we sit on the carpet for story time I have ready the story of two fierce, warrior Vikings.

'Once upon a time there were two strong, powerful brothers called Thorgills and Kormak Ogmundarson . They were fierce and scary and came from a faraway country over the North Sea. They had bushy hair and rough beards and Thorgills looked especially ferocious because he had a hare-lip. One stormy night they landed at a small village beside the sea. It was a good, sheltered place and very soon they decided that it should belong to them and that they should be in charge. That meant that everyone else who lived there should be their slaves. They called this place Skarthaborg because Skarthi was the nickname of Thorgills. They built themselves a strong house on the hill so they could see all around them. Soon the fishing fleet belonged to them too for the fish were plentiful. They often went off to raid other villages to see what riches they could find. Skarthaborg, eventually, became known as Scarborough and many years later a castle was built on the site of the brothers' house but we'll find out about that tomorrow.

'Now we're going to play a game where we make up some stories of our own that include these two characters. They had strange names because they came from a faraway place. Our people in Skathaborg can have easier names, what shall we call them?'

'I'd like to call my person, Darren, like me, he can be the superhero.'

I am sitting with my back to the window and the children are facing me, suddenly I am aware of a distraction by something or someone on the grass outside. Before I have a chance to look behind me, Robbie says, 'Miss, there's a man outside pointing a gun.'

'Don't be silly Robbie,' I say.

Several voices join in, 'There is Miss.'

I peer around the curtain, 'Right children! I want you to lie on your tummies and pretend to be racing caterpillars that crawl very fast right out of the door.' I press myself against the wall and like some American detective follow the children out into the corridor. I can't leave them to run for help. What should I do?

'Children, follow me quickly.' We scuttle silently down the corridor. I open the door of Don's room. He's at his desk. I run to him and gasp; 'Man outside my room on grass. Gun. Police.' He instructs his secretary to dial 999 and then takes off like a bat out of hell. We squeeze into the medical room and sing silly songs. Ten minutes later I see Don through the window. He and Reg, the caretaker, are dragging a man between them.

As he passes, Don winks and shouts, 'You can ring the bell now, it's home time.'

I see the children safely off the premises. After they've gone I race back to the office in time to see the 'man' securely handcuffed between two police officers. As they march towards the waiting police car, waves of merriment come from the staffroom. Steve is red faced, chortling and wiping his eyes. Sandra is bent double, holding her stomach and chirruping and there is laughter alight on every face. I gaze from one to the other and hold up my hands questioningly, 'What?'

Janet splutters and gives a great belly-laugh; I notice her face is smeared with mascara. Mary is beetroot red and looking slightly embarrassed.

'Will someone please tell me what's going on?'

Don moves forward, chuckles, and puts his arm around me. 'It wasn't a gun,' he says. Barbara sniggers and splutters.

'But,' I say, 'it was a long, black thing.' More guffaws and cackling.

Don tries again. 'It wasn't a gun, though it must have looked that way at a quick glance.'

'I don't understand.'

'It was a...' Janet collapses into helpless giggles.

'It was an... it was an erect penis in a black rubber tube.' Gales of laughter.

'What?'

'Kathy, my love, the man was masturbating, right outside your classroom window. But don't worry, the police have arrested him. He won't be doing it again.'

I sit down abruptly and someone puts a mug of tea into my hands. Miss Heaton comes in and places her hand gently on my shoulder. She speaks soothingly, 'Well done Kathy, you followed exactly the right procedure. Poor you, what a dreadful thing to witness,' she shudders 'thank goodness it was in a tube.' And with that she leaves the room.

It takes the rest of us quite a while to recover.

Castles, Cubs and Cucumber

Meg and John did their initial Cub Scout Leader Training at the end of May. They were anxious to start the Pack in the hope that they would be able to do lots of activities during the summer holidays. Many of my boys were of the right age group and we were eager to encourage them to keep them off the streets and out of trouble.

After the first meeting Meg pops in for a coffee.

'Well, how was it?' I ask

'It seemed to go very well, twenty two boys turned up aged between eight and eleven and before you ask, there were several from your class. Robbie Boon, Wayne Brummett, Christopher whatsisname, Darren Peat and Jonathan Andrews. They responded really well to John as Akela, he was wonderful with them.

'They would do, they've so few male role models. Oh that's really good.'

'Oh and I forgot, Raymond came.'

'Raymond, that's a surprise.'

'And he took off his anorak. He got very excited when we talked about working for badges, said he is going to get "loads"'

'Wow!'

'Anyway, enough of all that, I can't wait to tell you. Guess what?'

'What?'

'I'm getting married.' Her face is flushed and her eyes are the green of un-ripened corn shining in sunlight.

'What brought this on?'

'Apparently, Alison, John's daughter, came over on Sunday and she was so pleased to see him happy and content that she apologised profusely for all these months of antipathy and said that they would be very happy for me to be part of the family. So that's where I've been these past few days, over at his house and down at hers and we've made a few plans.'

'Oh Meg, I'm so happy for you.' I give her a big hug; I catch the clean scent of lime and a hint of vanilla. 'So, when is the wedding to be?'

'Well, we saw Reverend Tom last night and he's booked us in for the last Saturday in September. It's to be a *homemade* wedding, not a lot of fuss. The ceremony will be in church and the reception in the church hall. Alison, is making the cake, Melanie, his niece, is doing the flowers and little Rebecca is to be a bridesmaid. I just can't wait! Oh and please will you be my other bridesmaid?'

'I would love to; I thought you'd never ask.'

We stand in the middle of my lounge, arms around each others waists, jumping up and down like a pair of schoolgirls.

'Will you help me choose my wedding dress?'

'You try to stop me!'

*

On Saturday we're in Leeds, on the third floor of Schofield's department store surrounded by dresses in silk, satin, velvet and brocade There's every kind of bridal gown one could imagine, long and flowing, splendid or slinky, bows and bustles, jewel toned silks and pearl encrusted sheers. Just looking and touching is a treat, there are radiant whites, rich creams and fresh and vivid colours and amongst them all my friend, Meg Warriner, scattering joy.

'Oh look at this,' she breathes as she gently parts the hangers on the rack to reveal a pale turquoise dress in a soft, silky material and organza.

'Oh, that's gorgeous, you must try it.' The shop assistant leads the way to the dressing room whilst I amble about touching, smoothing and dreaming. I'm miles away, thinking of my own wedding and I don't immediately recognise the beautiful apparition standing by the changing room door.

'Well?' asks Meg.

'Oh you look stunning, absolutely stunning.' The dress has a clinched in waist and fits snugly over the hips, a sweetheart neckline reveals just a glimpse of Meg's ample cleavage. Then the dress billows out in a soft cloud of organza and ends just below the knee.

'Are you sure I don't look like a blue meringue?'

'No, you don't look like any cake I know. You look like a princess.'

'What, at fifty?'

'Well, a queen then. John is going to be bowled over, in fact everyone will be.'

'Oh, what should I wear on my head? What do you think, a picture hat, flowers, some sort of coronet?'

'I haven't got a clue, let's try some and see.'

*

That evening the four of us celebrate in style with a beautiful meal at a local country club. There are yellow roses arranged in a silver bowl, and gleaming candlesticks hold slim lemon candles. We toast the happy couple with Cava and, as usual, laugh plentifully and often. Talk turns, as usual, to the children on the estate and the planned outing next Saturday to Knaresborough Castle. As it will be the first cub outing, Peter and I are going along as helpers, together with Sally's dad, who is now also training to be a leader.

'I've been in touch with the curator at the castle,' says John and we've got permission to play some battle games on the grass outside. Wait 'til you see what I've managed to borrow. I've got twenty plastic shields, swords *and* helmets. Oh and Kathy, we need to borrow ten hoola-hoops from school. Will that be possible do you think?'

'I'm sure it will, I'll ask tomorrow. And just how do you intend to get all that equipment to the castle?'

'Oh didn't I tell you, I've booked a coach.'

I shake my head and Peter smiles into my eyes, a wave of desire sweeps through me and he reaches for my hand. I notice that, as usual, the sleeves of his jumper don't reach to his wrists. Soft golden hairs are visible against his tanned skin. He has beautiful hands.

'See what you've started, getting people all enthusiastic about castles and things. Who knows where it will all end?'

I know where I'd like tonight to end!

*

Twenty little boys and a huddle of parents wait outside the church on a warm June morning. The path is littered with pink blossom which has all but gone from the trees and Robbie keeps placing clumps of it on Wayne's head and visa versa. A parade of red tulips and orange-gold wall-flowers line the path and forget-me-nots and yellow tulips are in abundance in the flower beds. Christopher and Jonathan are carrying small rucksacks, but the rest have plastic carrier bags for their sandwiches, and raincoats and other paraphernalia.

'Akela, when can we eat us sandwiches?' calls Wayne.

John shakes his head and smiles. 'What did I tell you on Thursday? We eat our picnic when we get to the castle.'

'Ah know that's what thee said, but Elvis says we eat when we're 'ungry and I'm 'ungry now.'

'Rubbish,' says John, 'it's all about control and you're in control of everything that happens in your body, so just say to yourself, "I'm not really hungry" and you won't be. OK? Just practice.'

'Is that right, Sir, I mean Akela, are we in control of our bodies?'

'Yes.'

'What, even when we want to sneeze?'

'Er...yes and no.'

'Oh, right then.'

John mimes wiping sweat from his brow and we laugh. 'All this incisive questioning,' he says, 'I'm not sure I'm up to it.'

'They certainly keep us on our toes.'

Soon, everyone's on the coach, counted, and chattering excitedly. They bounce and bob, staring out of the windows and commenting on roads, rivers, hills, houses, clouds and sky. Peter squeezes my hand and we snuggle comfortably into our seats.

Raymond sits opposite, his head hidden inside his fur-lined hood, his body slouched and cocooned like a caterpillar in a chrysalis. What is he thinking I wonder? Will the butterfly ever emerge?

*

Billy was shouting again, like an angry bull, Raymond drew his coat closer around himself, hunched his shoulders, chin on chest and tried to hide. If he didn't move maybe Billy wouldn't see him. He sat very still. His little sister, Sharon, was playing on the rug in front of the empty fireplace. She was brushing the hair of her Cindy doll. Her hair was golden too and full of floppy curls. Raymond thought she was the prettiest girl he'd ever seen, she was like his mum. His mum was pretty, but sometimes she had big bruises on her face. Once it was so bad her eyes were like little slits and she could hardly see. Then Raymond had dipped cotton wool in warm water and wiped them carefully.

His mum had whispered to him, 'You're a good boy, Raymond' and then he'd been very brave and pulled his hood off his head and he'd kissed each eye in turn.

'I'm kissing you better, Mum,' he said, 'I'll allus kiss you better.' Then he pulled his hood up again in case anyone saw him. Billy stayed away for a few days after that but he came back. Raymond could smell him before he saw him, beer and sick and more beer. He shivered and sat very still. His nose was running but he didn't wipe it. He never did, He just pretended to be a statue.

'Where's me tea, woman?' hollered Billy, 'where's me bloody tea?' His mum got up quickly and started to cook. Billy switched the telly on

and watched the motor racing. Very carefully, Raymond slid off the armchair and rolled behind it, and then he leaned against the back and rested his head on his knees. He was tired. Very tired.

*

Raymond sits very still on the coach. He doesn't react to his friends; he just stares out of the window. There is an empty seat beside him and after a while Peter gets up and sits beside him.

For a long time he says nothing, just matches Raymond's pose and adopts his stillness.

After half an hour he says, gently, 'I like this bus, do you?' From somewhere in the depths of the hood, Raymond shakes his head. Peter hands him a tissue. After what seems an age a hand reaches out and takes it, it disappears into the dark depths. I hope that it did its job. Peter turns and grins at me, then shakes his head. There are great depths of compassion in his eyes. They sit, the two of them, mirroring stillness.

When we arrive in Knaresborough and they see the castle there is great excitement.

'Oh yes, it's got a portcullis,' shouts Robbie triumphantly as if ticking it off on an invisible list, 'and I can see the drawbridge. Cool!'

Wayne appears at my side, 'Miss, can I carry your bag?'

'Oh Wayne, that's very kind of you,' I say and pass him my haversack. For some reason he sticks out his tongue at Christopher. I decide to ignore it.

We spread our blankets on the grass and make our encampment and after biscuits and juice the festivities begin. It's rather nice not being in charge for once and I'm happy for John and Meg to take the lead. The boys happily don their knight costumes and play a number of team games involving small rubber balls which John insists are cannon balls which have to be passed from one to the other as fast as possible. When John shouts 'fire' they have to aim them at a series of skittles which are, apparently, the enemy. The boys join in with gusto and Peter and Meg act as fielders. I record the results. There are lots of cheers and running and rolling in the grass and it's great fun.

Wayne's helping me keep score. 'Wayne, what's the total?' I ask.

'The total, Miss?'

'Yes, what's the total?' He looks at me blankly.

'The total?' he looks mystified then at last his face clears. 'Oh I know, it's like a tortoise but it swims.' Meg cracks up and I shake my head.

'It's a good job I came here today,' I say to the other three, 'or I would never have known that all my work on mathematical terms has not born fruit, turtle indeed.'

After a couple more rowdy games we settle down for our picnic. John fetches tea in plastic cups from a nearby cafe and we munch our sandwiches in the sunshine. Robbie appears to only have jam, but he swaps Christopher, successfully, for a ham and cheese. I look around to check that everyone is eating. Raymond is as usual, on the edge of the group; huddled in his coat, staring at his feet, there is no sign of any lunch. I get up, taking my sandwiches with me and go sit beside him.

'Have you got any lunch, Raymond?' He shrugs his shoulders; I take that as a 'no'. 'Would you like a salmon and cucumber sandwich, I've made far too many?' He draws his coat together, crosses his arms across his chest and peers up at me beneath his hood. He nods. A nail bitten hand reaches out and takes my offering. We eat in silence. Peter crouches down in front of us and I move over so he can sit between us. He takes two more sandwiches and hands one to Raymond. We hear a mutter which could possibly be, 'thank you' but we're not quite sure.

Wayne, who's never far away from me, crawls over to us. 'Have you seen all them midges Miss, there's loads of them, I expect it's cos we're near the river. Eh Miss, what do you call a midge in a tin suit?'

'Peter answers for me, I don't know what *do* you call a midge in a tin suit?'

Wayne starts to laugh and can hardly speak the answer. '*A midge bite*. Do you get it; our armour is like a tin suit isn't it?' We laugh obediently.

Robbie comes to join us, 'I've got one as well, Miss. What did the dragon say when he saw St. George?' I pretend to think. 'Do you give in?'

'Yes, I give in.'

'Oh no! Not more tinned food!' We laugh heartily and I catch a ghost of a smile on Raymond's face.

'Do you know any jokes, Raymond?' The hood nods.

'Why don't you tell us some, but don't let the others know, then we can catch them out,' says Peter. Raymond appears to be considering. After a while Raymond pulls his hood to the back of his head and says, 'What did the big chimney say to the little chimney?'

'Oh that's a good one, I don't know.'

Raymond giggles then says, 'You're too young to smoke.'

Maybe we are making some headway.

It is jousting next and the boys who are knights on 'horseback' go to John to get ready. Two hoops have been given jewel bright skirts to which have been fixed, horses heads made from cardboard. The boys are each given a newspaper tube to wield like a pike. The aim is to gallop towards each another and to engage in battle. It is hilarious and there is a great deal of cheering and shouting. I'm really happy to see Raymond, minus his hood, his face emanating joy.

At two o'clock we make ready to enter the castle. Our guide comes out to meet us; he is a jovial chap with a red face, a bulbous nose and a wild mass of white fluffy hair, rather like cotton wool fuzz. I hear Jonathan whisper that he looks like a mad professor. However, he has the most welcoming smile and a vast store of information.

As we enter the great hall he asks, 'Now who is going to be the first person to show me the television?' The boys gaze round eagerly, each hoping to be the first to find it.

After some careful searching Wayne says, 'I don't think there is one, Sir.'

'You are quite right young man, and why do you think that is?'

'It was the olden days, Sir, there was no electricity,' says Christopher.

'Absolutely, so what else didn't they have?'

'Oh, Sir, telephones, electric kettles, radios, tape recorders, electric lights and just about everything,' says Robbie. 'In fact it must have been dead awful.'

'You're quite correct, young man, it must have been awful. But that is how people lived for hundreds of years. They relied on candles and oil lamps for light, animals for transport and one another for entertainment.'

'Oh yes, I know what they had, they had court jesters.'

'That's right, and they would juggle and perform amazing tumbling tricks and tell jokes and stories. People loved to listen to stories.'

'Sir, I know why the early days of history were called the dark ages,' says Robbie then, before anyone can answer, he says, 'it was because there were so many knights.' We all laugh and continue our journey around the castle. Our guide points out the tapestries.

'Just look at these huge pictures, they are very heavy like carpets and they were hung on the walls to keep out the draughts, castles are very cold places. It took many, many people to make a tapestry like this because they were all done by thread.'

'Excuse me Sir, Fred who?' asks Wayne. Peter puts his arm around me and gives me a squeeze and we laugh and shake our heads. The particular tapestry we're looking at is entitled, 'John the Baptist in the desert'. The figure of John is wild-eyed and pointing into the distance.

'Eh up, I know what he's saying,' quips Robbie.

'What?' asks Wayne.

He's shouting, 'Ey up Missis tha's left thee baby on the bus.'

At this point our guide appears to be speechless and quickly leads us up a winding stone staircase to the castle toilet.

'Right everyone; gather round, we are now standing by a medieval toilet. As you can see this consists of a hole in the stone work and quite simply, it is a hole which discharges hundreds of feet into the moat. Now you can take it in turns to look down. This is called the *garderobe.'* Christopher is the first to look down.

'Gosh it's an awful long way down. It doesn't stink though does it, why's that?'

'Well I don't think it's been used for a couple of hundred years.'

The boys all take it in turns and are fascinated. I smile as I think that this part of the visit will probably be the most memorable and wonder how long it'll be before someone suggests putting a garderobe in our classroom castle.

Before we leave we ask all the children to walk around and look carefully for any litter, we want to make sure that we leave the area clean and tidy. Jonathan shouts, 'Eh Miss, come and look at this, I've found a cucumber tree.' Peter looks at me and shrugs, the dimple beside his mouth like moving laughter. Stuck in the ground, just behind where Raymond was sitting, a dead branch is stuck in the ground and hanging on the bare twigs, like Christmas decorations, are several slices of cucumber and the crusts from at least 3 slices of bread.

Peter shrugs again, 'You win some you lose some, at least he liked the salmon.'

Church Parade and Planning

We're doubtful whether the new cubs will turn up for church parade, so are pleasantly surprised when they do. Several church people have sponsored their uniforms and the boys wore them for the first time on Thursday when they were invested. Meg told me that they were really chuffed to be so smart and wearing a uniform. They arrive unaccompanied but have walked from the estate together.

'Aye up Miss, do you like my unicorn?'

It's a *uniform*, Robbie, and I like it very much, you look very smart.'

'Aye well, we have inspection tha knows at Cubs, behind us ears and everything. I've scrubbed me 'ands three times this morning.' Then he flaps his ears with his fingers. 'What do yer think, are they ok?'

'Your ears are immaculate, Robbie, you've done very well.'

'Aye well, yer get points for being clean, you should try it at school, some of them kids are dead scruffy.' Meg, standing beside me grins widely and all her fine lines join in.

'Oh my goodness,' says Elsie Bottomley raising her hands in mock amazement. 'Who on earth are all this smart young men?'

'We're Cubs, Missus,' answers Wayne, 'we know how to salute and everything.' She gives them an army salute.

'Do you mean like this?'

'No it's just three fingers to remind us of the three parts of our promise.'

'Oh I *see*, and can you say your promise for me now?'

The boys look embarrassed.

'We would but we'd better be getting on else we'll be late for the service,' says Wayne. The others nod their heads in agreement, all except Raymond, who is still wearing his anorak with the hood firmly fastened. He goes up to her and touches her arm, timidly. She bends her white curly head towards him, 'What is it, pet?'

'*I* can do it for you,' then he removes his hood, stands tall and recites,

> '*I promise to do my best to do my duty to God and the Queen*
> *To help other people and to keep the Cub Scout law.*'

Elsie puts her hands gently on his shoulders and looks him straight in the eye. 'That's brilliant, young man, absolutely brilliant, well done.'

He gives her a heartrending smile and beckons for her to come closer, then he whispers, 'I will an all, I'll do *all* that promise cos when you make a promise you've allus got to keep it.' Then he crosses his arms over his chest, pulls his coat tightly around him and disappears once more into the depths of his hood.

The service is aimed at all ages and is lively and interesting. The boys join in with gusto, manage the hymn books with a bit of help and listen well to the talk. Tom and Peter lead it together and involve all the young people in finding lost sheep hidden around the church. The sheep, of course, are not real, but rather nice knitted ones and precious nevertheless. Peter goes on to tell the Bible story about the lost sheep and how everyone is precious to God. I love watching the faces of the boys and seeing them so enthralled. Unfortunately I can't see Raymond as, yet again, he's buried inside his hood, There is one sticky moment when the collection basket comes round and Robbie takes money out, instead of putting it in, saying, 'Oh thanks very much,' but Meg quickly explains and the money is replaced. After the service we all enjoy coffee and biscuits or orange juice and the boys do take rather more than is expected, but who cares. Just to see Wayne carrying the flag, flanked on either side by Robbie and Christopher all so straight and tall with faces filled with pride is worth more than any number of biscuits.

*

When Raymond got home Billy was very angry. He hadn't told anyone where he was going; he'd just slipped out while they were all asleep. He didn't think they would notice, they usually slept till dinnertime anyway. But Billy was in a bad mood and Mum's head was bleeding.

'Where've you been, you little sod, where the hell have you been? Sneaking out like that in the middle of the night. You little piece of shit.'

Raymond pulled his hood more tightly over his face and tried to shrink inside the coat but Billy grabbed hold of the hood and pulled it backwards, the top of the zip poked into his neck and he felt the cold air on his shaven head.

'Don't you look away when I'm speaking,' growled Billy and then his big hand came down on the side of his face, SLAP! SLAP! SLAP!

His mum started to scream and she tried to jump on Billy's back.

'Leave him alone, you bastard. Don't hurt him, leave him alone!'

'Leave him alone? I'll bloody kill him!'

Billy started to walk away, pulling the hood, dragging Raymond around the room, all the time yelling at him, kicking out at him with his great booted feet.

'Just look at him,' he jeered, 'skinny little runt. Who was his dad then? Some randy piece of shit?' Every insult speared Raymond's heart. Cut into his brain like a knife. The words were sometimes worse than the pain. Raymond put both hands over his head and tried to curl into a ball but Billy was pulling and pulling on his hood, dragging him. KICK! Another dull thump at the bottom of his back, so violent his body jerked. He yelped. Suddenly Billy opened the cellar door, bellowed once more and with one almighty kick sent him hurtling down the cellar steps. Raymond lay still. It was best to be still. He could hear his mum crying. His sister, Sharon, was screaming. Then he didn't remember anything else.

When Raymond woke up it was very dark. And quiet. His tongue felt huge in his mouth. His face was hurting. He touched it with his hand. It felt bigger than before. His arm wouldn't move properly, the pain was really, really bad. It was quiet. Why? Why was it so quiet? There were no footsteps overhead. No shouting. No screaming.

He had to find his mum! Inch by inch he wriggled his way across the floor and then he began the long pull up the cellar steps. Pain shot through him like a great burning. He had to find his mum. His right arm wouldn't work. His head was thumping. Left arm up and pull. Pull upwards, upwards. He was on the top step. Please don't let him have locked the door. He stretched up higher for the handle, it hurt when he breathed. He pushed. The door opened and he fell forwards. He lay on the kitchen floor trying to get his breath. Where was his mum? He dare not shout in case Billy was still here. He tried to pull himself up with a chair. Yes. He took a step, one step forward. He could walk but his back hurt. He looked out of the window. It was dark; He must have been in the cellar a long time. He looked all around the kitchen. No-one there. He went slowly into the living room, holding onto the furniture. Absolutely quiet.

'Where is everyone?' he whispered. Suddenly there was a whimper. It came from under the table. Raymond lifted the cloth, it was Sharon. She was curled up in a ball, her face streaked with tears.

'*Come here, little love,*' *he said gently. She crawled out and they clung together.*

He cuddled his sister and stroked her hair. She was only five.

'*Don't cry, love. I'll look after you. Where's me mam?*'

'*They went out.*'

'*Right, we've got to get out too, before they come back.*'

'*But it's dark!*'

'*I know but we've got to get out.*' *Thoughts raced around his brain like ants.* '*Find a carrier bag and put yer stuff in it.*'

'*What stuff?*'

'*Er, flannel, towel, toothbrush, toys, jumpers and...pyjamas...and...yer reading book for school.*'

They moved around the house, painfully in Raymond's case. They packed their world into two carrier bags and went out into the darkness.

*

I arrive at school early that day; I haven't slept well and am looking forward to getting everything ready before most people arrive. Reg is standing in the corridor looking lost. As I draw nearer I see that he is red-eyed and tears are marching down his cheeks.

'Reg, are you all right, what's wrong?'

'I thought I'd seen everything at this place, but this takes the biscuit, it really does.' He turns his face to the wall and begins to sob. I feel helpless, I touch his arm.

'Reg, tell me, whatever's the matter?'

His thin, angular face is white, his hair, normally neatly combed, is sticking up and all awry. His hands are shaking.

'I found them in the boiler house when I got here at six. Fast asleep they were, all bruised and battered, poor little mites.' He pushes open the head's office door to reveal Raymond and Sharon clinging together huddled in a blanket.

'I've given them a hot drink and I made them some toast. God knows the last time they ate.'

I kneel in front of them. Sharon is flushed with sleep, her thumb in her mouth her fair curls matted and tangled. Raymond, as usual, is hiding inside his hood.

'Raymond, darling, can you take off your hood for me and tell me what's happened?' He shakes his head. 'Come on sweetheart, I want to help you, please, tell me what's happened.' Silence, I stay there kneeling, patiently waiting. Sharon climbs off the chair and nestles into my arms. Between sobs she says, 'It were Billy, he hit him.' Raymond straightens up and pulls his hood to the back of his head. I stifle a gasp. Both cheeks are blue and swollen; he has a burst lip and is cradling his right arm protectively.

Miss Heaton arrives, I whisper what I know. She immediately rings the duty officer at Social Services and an ambulance.

'The social worker will go with them but they need someone they know. Can you go? Don can take your class.'

Soon we're on our way to hospital, Jennie Bowen the social worker, myself, two small, battered children and two carrier bags containing all their worldly goods.

*

Stella Brooks, Raymond's mum, was found unconscious in a ginnel behind Bismark Street. I see her at the hospital later that day. I'm able to comfort her with the news that the children are being well cared for.

'They're going to take us to a women's refuge when we're better. It's time; I've stood it for long enough. I've been a fool. It were bad enough him hitting me but when he started on them. Oh my God! I thought he were going to kill our Raymond. Well I thought he had, when he kicked him down the cellar steps. Is he ok, is he really?'

What can I say? Will he ever get over it? He's obviously been emotionally mangled for a long time.

'Well, his arm's in plaster and he's very bruised. It will take a while, but he's being looked after.' I want to say, he's not wearing his anorak, he's not hiding in his hood, he's hiding under a blanket instead.

*

I ring Peter from the hospital and then make my way back to school. Don is in his element in my classroom. There are some complicated mathematical equations on the blackboard complete with pictures of little knights, shields and swords. The children are busy writing stories and illustrating them with beautiful cartoon type pictures.

Don twinkles at me and says, 'Where did knights learn to kill dragons?'

I sigh, 'Go on then, where did knights learn to kill dragons?'

'At knight school!' chorus the children and suddenly I'm smiling again. Don loves these kids, though nearing retirement he's given over

178

thirty years to this school. Not only has he taught some of their parents, but grandparents too. He is totally dedicated, always has a smile and everyone loves him. I have to remind myself that there are lots of good people in this world.

Plans, Parties and Policemen

Meg and I are in a bridal department once again, this time joined by John's daughter, Alison, and his beautiful granddaughter, Rebecca, who's four. Alison is a well built, glowing, young woman with her father's square, smiley face and dimpled chin but with long red hair as curled and copious as in a Pre-Raphaelite painting. Matthew, who is eleven months, is being cared for by his dad and loving granddad. I immediately fall in love with Rebecca, she has huge brown eyes, apparently just like her grandmother, and blonde curls. She's like a rubber ball, bouncing all around and chattering like a baby monkey.

'Hello, that wind isn't half blowing, it's blowed my hair all over the place and just when I'm learning to be a bridesmaid.' She holds out her arms, palms facing upwards, like a parody of a Jewish mama.

'Oh dear,' says Meg, 'it's blown all mine too and I'm supposed to be learning how to be a bride.'

'We'll have to get ribbons in. I've got a hair slide and it's purple. Mummy sprays hers with glue but I don't like it.'

Meg laughs. 'Well, my wedding dress is a lovely turquoise blue, so I wonder what colour we should choose for you.'

'Not orange cos I don't like that, don't like oranges either.' She pulls a squishy face.

'All right, we won't choose orange then. What colour *do* you like?'

'Pink, I like pink, flamingoes are pink and pigs, they're pink too, except when they roll in the mud.'

Alison laughs and suggests that we go to look at the rack where the bridesmaids' dresses are hung. Rebecca skips and bounces, holding tight to Meg's hand and Meg looks rapturous. She may have lost her chance of motherhood but she has no intention of missing out on being a grandma. I think of what she was like with the Cubs on Sunday and rejoice again in her new found happiness. Meg bends down to point out the many different colours and fabrics.

'Look Rebecca, there are silky ones like this, and floaty ones like this pink one or long ones like this blue one. Which kind do you like?'

'I'd like...I'd like one with spots on,' says Rebecca decisively.

'Oh!' say all the grown-ups in unison. There don't appear to be any spotty ones.

The shop assistant smiles cheerfully. 'Well let me think, we don't have any *spotty* ones but we do have a lovely *stripy* one.' She unlocks a glass-fronted cupboard and searches along the rack. 'Ah, here we are, a turquoise candy stripe, what do you think of that, little Madam?'

Rebecca is suddenly shy, holding Meg's hand and swinging from side to side whilst looking at her shoes.

'Oh it's beautiful,' I say, 'do you have it in my size, a twelve?'

'Indeed we do, would you like to try it?'

'Yes please.'

'Yes please,' says Rebecca and we all breathe a sigh of relief. Minutes later there are two bridesmaids wearing turquoise, candy striped dresses staring into a large mirror, holding hands and smiling happily.

'Are you happy?' I ask the bride softly.

'Happy, I'm ecstatic.' She turns towards her daughter-in-law to be, 'I hope you're happy too.'

Alison faces Meg, puts her hands on her shoulders and whispers, 'I couldn't be happier.' Suddenly they're in each others arms, hugging as if they'll never let go.

I look down at Rebecca, 'What about you, Rebecca, are you happy?'

'I'm static,' she says.

*

Meg goes home with Alison and Rebecca and I make my way back to the car park. There is an ominous roll of thunder and I stare up at gunmetal clouds and quicken my pace, I'm not dressed for rain. A slash of lightning wounds the sky and suddenly great drops smack down on the pavement bouncing up again like marbles. I struggle to find my car keys whilst the water plasters my hair to my head. At last, I'm safely inside and on my way home.

The rain pummels on the roof and even when they are on at speed, the wipers can't clear the screen quick enough to make driving possible. I inch along slowly, peering at the road and eventually I'm forced to a stop. I wait until the rain eases a little then make my way back towards Becklefield. Huge puddles are everywhere and when large vehicles pass, great flumes of water make driving difficult. My nerves are on edge and my head aches with tension. Suddenly there's the whine of a siren, I see flashing blue lights and pull into the side to let the vehicle pass. The police car pulls in behind me. Oh no, what have I done! My heart races. I wind down my window and wait, and then my eye is level with the officer's belt.

'What's wrong?' I ask tremulously and then gaze upwards to meet his eyes. Dark mocking eyes meet mine. It's Mike. 'What on earth do you think you're doing?' I shout 'You frightened me to death and in this weather too. I could have had an accident.'

'I saw it was you and thought it would be a bit of a laugh.'

''Well it isn't!'

'Oh deary, deary me. Have we lost our sense of humour along with our virginity? He won't make you happy, you know. That little pansy of a vicar, call that a man!'

'How dare you? He's worth ten of you and that's for sure. Can I go now or do I have to report you?' He starts to examine my tyres kicking them for good measure.

'Your rear offside tyre, the treads are wearing thin, you ought to get it looked at.' He bends down, thrusts his head through the window and says menacingly, 'I'll get you for something, sometime.' With those words he climbs into the patrol car and drives off. I am shaking.

*

That night there is a family party at church, these are purely social occasions for families to spend time together, play games, dance and eat. This is our third and I'm looking forward to it, especially as all John's family is coming. Alison looks gorgeous in a flowery dress worn with a royal blue jacket, her lush curly hair flowing down her back. Her husband, Colin, is wearing a brown check shirt open at the neck, his sleeves rolled back to reveal muscular arms and large, capable hands. On his shoulders sits Rebecca, obviously enjoying her vantage point.

'I can see granddad carrying three chairs. He's a very strong man, isn't he daddy, just like Pop-eye.'

'He is, nearly as strong as me carrying you, you're heavy as an elephant.'

Rebecca giggles, 'Don't be silly, no person can be as heavy as that.'

'Only if they've eaten two sausages, a mountain of chips *and* baked beans.'

He lifts her off his shoulders and flies her to the ground. She covers her mouth with her hands, laughs then whispers conspiratorially, 'That's what I had for my dinner and do you know what?'

'What,' I ask obediently.

'Beans make you fart.' She giggles again and I say, 'Well, we'd better not have any on the wedding day.' She claps both her hands to her mouth and splutters.

Just then Elvis, Jennie and Linda appear, accompanied by Wayne and Robbie, both in their Cub uniforms.

'Is it all right for us to come?' asks Jennie. 'The boys said we didn't need tickets or anything.'

'Er, no that's fine,' I say, not sure whether it is or not, 'just find yourself a table and sit down.' I go off in search of Reverend Tom. I explain the position, he chuckles.

'Oh it'll be reet, we always have extra food, it's a faith supper so it always goes round. It's grand to have more of the estate folk coming.'

I go off to find them some jugs of squash, hardly what the adults are used to, but never mind. Elvis is in full regalia, white silk shirt with black fringing and white wide-legged trousers. His hair is thick and shining, and the gold medallion is, well, dangling. The boys, for once, are immaculate. As I cross the room, carrying a tray, they run towards me.

'Will there be an inspection, Miss?'

'I shouldn't think so, not tonight.'

'But we've washed us neckerchiefs, Miss.'

'Yes, I bought some Persil and we both washed them then we went round to Linda's and borrowed Jennie's iron.'

'You *have* been working hard.'

'That's cos we're Cubs, Miss, that's what we do.'

I deposit the tray with Elvis and go in search of John. I explain the situation regarding Persil, neckerchiefs and irons and he agrees to sort it out. Then through the door come Christopher and Jonathan with their respective families. A quick glance tells me that they're also wearing Cub uniforms. Reverend Tom sends out for more food, John and Meg do a very impressive inspection and all the boys are awarded gold stars, which will be added to the chart on Cub night. Everyone appears satisfied.

Peter leads the games, some just for children and some in which whole families can join. Then there's dancing. Elvis demonstrates the proper way of doing the Birdie dance; he discovers the Gay Gordons and is amazed by the Veleta. Then he offers to sing. The company bops to 'Rock around the Clock' and 'Jailhouse Rock' and he really is quite good. Then it's time for tea. Rebecca polishes off six sausages on sticks, a small pork pie and strawberries and cream and has us in fits of laughter as only a young child can.

'Kathy, do you know how old I am?'

'Are you four?'

'Yes, you've got it, and in just a few more days I'll be five and *then, I'll be just as old as you.*'

'*Wow!*'

'And you know my daddy,' I answer in the affirmative, 'well; *he's* got a really sore willie.' Colin goes bright red and nearly chokes on his pork pie. 'And do you know why?' This time I'm speechless. 'It's because he doesn't want any more babies. It's because of our Matthew, he cries nearly all night.' Poor Colin he does not know where to put himself.

'You think that's bad,' says Alison, 'she told everyone in Sainsbury's last night. It was all, be careful with your trolley, don't bump my daddy he's got a sore willie. We couldn't get out of there quick enough.'

Matthew is crawling around on the floor and suddenly pulls himself up via my skirt. I hook my hands under his arms and lift him onto my knee. He smells of peaches and his skin is like satin. I rub my cheek against his and plant a kiss on his dimpled hand.

'Be careful, you'll get smittled,' says Meg with a grin and Peter and I share a smile.

Then Mike arrives. He's wearing a smug, self satisfied expression. He's not in uniform. Tom goes to meet him, his face as always, warm and welcoming.

'Good evening, young man, this is a nice surprise.'

'Nice surprise my arse, you don't really care about me, it's all a game, this church lark. There's people suffering all around you and you don't *really* care a damn. Bloody church!'

Concern is written all over Tom's face. It's obvious to everyone that Mike, our special community constable, is very drunk. He weaves around, searching.

'I've come for my girl; I've come to get her. She belongs to me!' Peter stiffens and stands. Tom reaches out an arm and touches Mikes shoulder. Mike's arm swings back as he prepares to land a heavy punch at Tom. Quick as a flash Robbie stretches out his legs and, *thwack* Mike lands face down on the floor. Robbie a picture of angelic concern shouts.

'Oh *dear*, he's fallen on the floor!'

John shakes his head, great sadness in his eyes. 'I think this is the point where I ring the police.' They arrive quite quickly and the drunken community constable is removed from the building.

Apart from that the evening is a tremendous success and we end the night standing in a circle, old and young together singing 'You'll never walk alone' and as I look around and see everyone with linked arms, swaying to the music, a lump comes to my throat. Peter smiles.

Knight Mares

'Miss, when a knight got killed in battle, what did they write on his gravestone?'

'Go on, tell me,' I say wearily.

'Rust in Peace.' The children fall about laughing.

I've had three weeks now of castle jokes and they're beginning to wear a bit thin. Some good news, though, Raymond's mum and the children are in a local Women's Refuge and Billy has a restraining order to stop him from contacting them. Sharon and Raymond are brought to school each day by taxi, though Raymond will still not be separated from his hooded coat.

At break time I'm surprised to see him standing outside Miss Heaton's door.

'Raymond, what are you doing here? Are you in trouble?' He starts to cry.

'Yes Miss.' More crying, two 'candles' from a runny nose. I rummage in my bag and hand him a tissue.

'What have you done, Raymond?' More sobs and tissue flapping.

Then, 'Well somebody hit this boy, see, and he was wearing the same coat as me.'

'Well did you tell Miss Rayworth that?' More crying, but this time he wipes his sleeve across the nasal area.

'Yes but he had the same face as me and the same shoes and everythink.'

'So it *was* you, then?' He nods and cries some more. I start to think about the coffee I'm missing.

'Raymond, why did you hit this boy?' A great paroxysm of sobs.

'I've forgotten, Miss.' I head for the staffroom reflecting sadly that his emotions will take a long time to heal, if ever.

*

I arrive home at six thirty after a very long staff meeting to find a white faced Meg on my doorstep.

'Meg! What on earth is wrong?' Tears well in her eyes and she shakes her head. I unlock the door, and help her into the house. She turns her face to the wall and howls, rocking back and forth. I turn her round and she falls into my arms.'

'Meg?'

'It's Rebecca!' My whole being freezes. 'What's happened? Oh Meg, what's wrong?'

'She started to be ill during the night, high temperature, rash. The doctor came this morning but she got worse as the day progressed so they called an ambulance. She's in Leeds Infirmary. They think...they think it's meningitis.' I sit down abruptly. 'Will you...take me there...Kathy?' Her words permeate the suffocating blanket of my thoughts.

'Yes, of course I will.' I try to think of anything that we'll need, but my mind is blank. We climb numbly into the car and I drive like an automaton. At the hospital we race down the corridor. John is sitting, alone, in the waiting room.

'Where are they?' whispers Meg. He nods towards a door.

'They're in there, with her.' His lips press together as if he's holding back a hurricane of pain. Then he says, 'Pray...I just keep praying.'

We sit in silence holding hands and praying for all we're worth. After what seems hours, I stand stiffly and scrabble in my bag for coins.

'I'll go get some tea.' Tea, always tea. So strange how we cling to its comforting liquid warmth. I return with three plastic cups of hot liquid on a tray.

John takes one, his fingers tremble as he steers it to his mouth. Meg leans back against the padded bench and sips slowly, her eyes staring into space.

'Any news?' I ask, knowing that there won't be, but having to ask anyway.

'No.' John seems to have shrunk in the moments I've been away. His skin is white and waxy, his eyes washed of colour. Suddenly the door opens revealing Colin and Alison as one entity, clinging together. We stand as if pulled by a string.

'She's still delirious, very hot; they're just going to do more tests. She's had a massive dose of antibiotics.' Colin sinks into a seat; this simple speech has leaked all his strength.

'I'll go get more tea, do you want tea?' I gabble. They nod. When I return we just sit, clinging to our cups for dear life. Every footstep is like a heartbeat, every breath, a prayer. Reverend Tom arrives, empathy streams from every pore.

'I've alerted the prayer chain, there are many people praying.'

We have a team of people who are prepared to drop everything and pray in times of emergency. A year ago I would have laughed at the idea but a lot has happened since then. We wait. At ten past nine the door opens and a distinguished looking, white-haired doctor comes towards us.

'Mr and Mrs Simpson? Would you like to come with me please?' Colin leaps to his feet and Alison follows saying, 'Could you speak to us here please. We're all one family.'

'Of course. As you know Rebecca is very ill, very ill indeed and we're not out of the woods yet. But there are signs that her temperature is coming down and she is certainly more peaceful. So, there is hope. Now it's important that all close family members take some strong antibiotics so I have here a prescription. If you could take it to pharmacy and swallow the tablets as soon as possible I'm sure there will be no ill effects. It's just a precautionary measure.'

I take the prescription and find my way to the hospital pharmacy. I'm grateful to have something to do. I collect the tablets and I'm given a message to relay to the recipients.

'The chemist says that you're not to worry if your pee goes red, it's just a side effect of the tablets.'

Alison smiles wanly and says, 'That's a small price to pay. I wouldn't care if my eyes turned red if it meant my daughter was well.'

'Actually love,' says Colin, 'your eyes *are* pretty red and your nose is a lovely shade of scarlet.'

At ten Peter arrives and Tom departs to inform those on the prayer hot line of Rebecca's condition. We drink yet more tea but Peter has brought sandwiches so we are able to keep our strength up even if everything does taste like cardboard.

There is a sudden scream, then, 'Mummy! I want my mummy!' Alison doesn't wait to be given permission; she's through that door in an instant, closely followed by Colin. The rest of us sit and hold hands. The nurse comes out and smiles warmly.

'You can go in now, but only for a minute or two.'

Rebecca is lying propped up on the pillows. There is a drip in her arm and her face is flushed but otherwise she looks fine.

'Is everybody here?' she asks.

'What do you mean by everybody?' asks her dad.

'Everybody I know,' her speech is slurred, 'cos when I was asleep I could see them all inside my head.'

'No darling, there's just us,' says John quietly, 'will that do?'

She declines to answer, closes her eyes for a while then has another question, 'Why, when my head was hurting did they put something in my arm? It's my head that's the problem, now they've made more sore places,' she weeps softly.

'Just be thankful you're feeling better, young lady,' says the nurse, 'you've given everyone a real fright.'

'Yes but I didn't know I was frightening them. I didn't mean to,' she wails.

'Of course you didn't darling. Now all you have to worry about is getting better so you can be my bridesmaid,' whispers Meg.

'Oh I will.' Her eyes close again, then she says sleepily, 'I'll be the best bridesmaid you've ever had at any of your weddings.'

We laugh and leave, sending up a silent prayer of thanks. As we walk to the car I say, 'Anyway, how many bridesmaids have you had?'

'I never had any at my last wedding,' she smiles, 'there has to be a first time for everything.'

Grandmas

Alison practically lives at the hospital for the next couple of weeks. Although Rebecca continues to improve, progress is slow and she's still very weak. Colin, of course, has to work, but is at the hospital every moment that he can be. So Meg's wedding preparations take second place to a lively baby who is just learning to take his first steps. It seems that she's also having a 'baptism of fire' as a Grandma.

Meanwhile, at this late stage of the year I have a new pupil in my class, Thomas Bullin. His mother has evidently just moved into the area after a marriage break-up.

Thomas is a delightful character, chubby, with blond curls, blue eyes and a soft pink and white complexion. He has a ready smile and a trusting nature and I worry about him and his ability to hold his own with some of the very street wise children in my class. He is also very anxious to please and almost every sentence addressed to me begins, 'Miss, are we allowed'…to sharpen our own pencils, to rub out, to go to the toilet without asking, and many other such questions, which I try to answer with patience and reassurance. But some questions worry me, those like, 'Are we allowed to write on this paper?' when given a fresh, clean sheet and 'This is not wallpaper, is it?' starts alarm bells ringing.

When I'm on playground duty, I notice that though he plays happily with other children he stays always in the same place. When I ask if he would like to play football with some of the other boys he seems surprised and asks, 'Am I allowed?'

After break I have a quiet chat with Wayne, who sits next to him in the classroom.

'Wayne, love, I wonder if you could help me?' He smiles broadly, 'Course I will, Miss.'

'Would you to look after Thomas at playtime, just for these first few days? You know the kind of thing, help him to join in the football game, or the races or playing tag, just until he gets used to things. Do you think you can do that?'

'Course I can, Miss.'

'Thank you very much; I know you are a really sensible boy.' He pulls back his shoulders and grins, and then swaggers back to his place.

During afternoon break I notice a woman standing just outside the playground. She has a hungry look and is smoking hurriedly, her hands fluttering, her eyes fixed in one position. I try to work out what is the focus of her attention. Then I see him, it's Thomas, bouncing like a rubber ball, raising his arms and laughing all at the same time. Wayne is pulling weird faces to make him laugh and the child is well nigh hysterical. To see them both brings a smile to my face, but not to the watching woman. She looks like someone who has lost a prized possession, her shoulders hunched, head bent, hair like ginger fuzz blowing in the wind.

*

'Miss, can we start Robin Hood tomorrow? Can we write stories about him then play them in the castle?' this from Sally who absolutely loves dressing up.

'Yes, Miss, or *we* could play in't castle and *you* could write it down,' quips Robbie.

'No,' says Lisa, 'I think we should write a play with songs and stuff in it to do as our assembly.' I'm surprised at this as she doesn't usually show much enthusiasm for lessons and hates writing.

'Well, as its story time now I thought I would tell you some of the legends of Robin Hood and then tomorrow we can all have a go at writing a play for our assembly. So everyone, sit very still and I'll begin.'

'But you haven't got a book,' says Sally. 'How can you tell the story without a book?'

'Because Robin Hood lived long, long ago and there weren't many books and those that did exist were very precious. Only very rich people could read or write so stories were very important. The people loved them so they would remember what they were about and would tell them to one another. Some people were storytellers and they would go round from town to town and village to village sharing their stories. So, that's what we're going to do in our assembly.'

I tell them some of the legends of Robin Hood exhorting them to try to remember the facts so that they can share them with others. They listen carefully, their faces rapt and I marvel, yet again, at the magic of stories. Then it is time for the end of the school day.

'I don't know about you, children, but I'm really excited about beginning our play.' They all assure me that they are and I explain that when they've gone I will put lots of spellings on the board to help them to remember when we begin tomorrow.

'I'm going to be Maid Marian,' confides Linda, softly.

'So am I,' says Sally. Oh dear, somehow I'm going to have to invent fifteen female characters before morning!

*

After I've seen the children out into the playground I notice the woman with the frizzy red hair, standing alone, staring after Thomas and his mother. This time I'm close enough to see that her eyes are red-rimmed, her cheeks skeletal and white. I walk over and stand beside her.

'Are you all right, love, can I get you anything?' she shakes her head.

'No, there's nothing you can do, nothing anyone can do.'

'You look cold, this wind is raw and it looks like rain. Why don't you come inside? I'll make you a cup of tea.' She sighs, but allows herself to be guided towards the staffroom, too weary to resist. Don is standing by the kettle, I whisper my concerns and he departs to tell Miss Heaton, who collects a cup for herself and 'my guest' and joins us in a corner of the staffroom.

'Hello my dear, I'm Agnes Heaton, headmistress and this is Kathy Johnson one of our teachers. I was wondering, do you have a child at this school? The woman gives a long shuddering sigh and passes a hand over her eyes. Her voice comes out like a croak.

'Grandchild. I'm Thomas Bullen's grandma. I've looked after him since he was born, so his mother could go to work. I love the bones of him.' Miss Heaton's eyes never leave the woman's face, they glisten with compassion.

There is a fleeting frown of puzzlement and then she says, 'Are you *Stuart* Bullen's mum, I used to teach him. Oh he was a lovely boy.'

A glimmer of a smile curves the woman's lips, 'Yes, I remember you; I'm Hetty Bullen, by the way.'

'So what's Stuart doing now? I remember he was *so* good at maths.' Hetty relaxes back into the chair, warming her hands on the teacup.

'Aye, he was always good at maths. He works in a bank now, he's done really well, he's manager of the Morley branch. Bought a lovely house out there, was doing fine until Jean, that's his wife, got this fancy man. We knew nowt about it 'til she up-sticks and goes, taking Thomas with her of course.'

'Oh dear,' says Miss Heaton, 'and how has Stuart taken that?'

'Well, he's devastated, naturally. Doesn't know if he's on this earth or Fullers. Now someone else looks after Thomas and I've been told in no uncertain terms that I'm not wanted.' She starts to cry again, tears galloping down her thin cheeks, chest heaving. 'And I love him, I love him beyond words. I feel like my own child has been scooped right out of my body.'

I reach out and squeeze her arm, but words, well they just won't come. What can anyone say? There's a long silence then Miss Heaton ventures a sentence.

'I know that this won't be any comfort to you, my love, but this is becoming a common problem and everyone involved suffers in some way. Presumably Stuart will have access and then surely you'll be able to share some of that time. I know it's not ideal but I'm *afraid* we just have to make the best of what is available to us.'

'Aye, I suppose we do, but nobody seems to think that grandparents *have* rights.'

'I know, but it will come. There'll be campaigns I'm certain of that. After all grandparents hold a very important place in children's lives,' says Miss Heaton standing slowly to indicate that the interview is at an end. I stand too, feeling helpless and useless.

Plays and Films

The next morning the children work in groups to try to tell the legend of Robin Hood.

The class are noisy and excited and I'm kept very busy going from group to group helping, advising and sorting out quarrels. But, the time proves productive and soon they are ready to perform for one another. Sally, Linda, Robbie, Thomas, Wayne and Lisa are in Red Group and volunteer to start.

Thomas stands proudly on the platform, a brown tunic covering his rotund form, a hood hiding his golden curls.

'My name is Friar Tuck; I am one of the merry men of Robin Hood. We are forced to live as outlaws in Sherwood Forest.'

Robbie marches on wearing a tunic of Lincoln green, 'I am Robin Hood, I was once a great nobleman with a lot of land and a castle but they were constipated by the King.'

I interrupt, 'No sorry you've got the wrong word there, Robbie, they were *confiscated,* that means they were *taken away.'*

'Aw, right. They were consci...confid...*pinched* by Henry the second. England was in a right pickle and people were fighting all over the place.'

Sally comes next, 'I am Maid Marian and I am in love with Robin Hood.' Robbie squirms and pulls a face. The boys make silly noises.

'Well I am, aren't I, Miss?'

'Yes Sally, well, in the play you are.'

Linda interrupts, 'Well if you don't want to Sally, I will.'

Sally grits her teeth and readjusts her cone shaped hat. 'It's ok. I can do my own loving.'

Wayne clambers onto the platform carrying a bow and arrow. 'I am Will Scarlett, I'm an excellent bowman. I can hit any target.'

Robbie comes forward once more, 'And so can I! So there!'

Sally shouts, 'Anyway, Henry the second is now dead. Richard the first is King!'

All the cast shout 'Hurray!' and the rest of the class join in.

'But,' says Robbie, 'he wasn't much good, cos he kept on fighting the Crusades and not looking after England.'

'Yes,' says Wayne, 'and all them with money kept getting more money from the poor and keeping it for themselves. They were *bad.'*

The class is really getting into this now and starts to boo.

Robbie comes to the front once more, 'So me and my merry men are going to stop them. Onward!' he shouts. Friar Tuck blows a pretend horn that has been part of the castle equipment and Steven, from the audience, gives a quick 'Da ☐ad a, daaah'

Wayne finishes with, 'We robbed the rich and gave to the poor!'

The audience applauds enthusiastically. Only another five groups to go.

'Well done everyone,' I say and they go back to perfecting their scripts. I take Lisa to one side, 'Lisa, you didn't have anything to say in your group play, why was that?'

'Oh, I was playing one of them you told us about.'

I frown, puzzled. 'Which were they?'

'You know Miss, them what couldn't read and write in the olden days, I was one of them cos I don't like reading and writing anyway.'

'Good try Lisa, but you will *definitely* have a part, and it *will* be a long one.'

*

Thomas was in the new house. It was bigger than his old one and very smart. It even had two bathrooms. His mum liked it. It had two three piece suites. His new mate, Wayne, said that meant that his new dad was a millionaire. If he was he was a bad tempered one and Thomas thought that rich people should be happy.

His grandma was happy even though she was not rich. His grandma only had a little house but he loved it. When she looked after him they had a lot of fun. Sometimes they would bake cakes and he would lick out the bowl and it tasted lovely and then they waited for it to come out of the oven. Grandma's oven had a glass door so he could sit on the floor and watch the cakes rising up as if by magic, then they would go all golden and Grandma would take them out and the smell would wrap all around him and it was beautiful. They tasted really good. Sometimes he would sit at the kitchen table and paint pictures and Grandma would paint too, that was fun. She was always singing, was Grandma, she would vacuum the carpet and sing, or polish the furniture and sing and he would laugh and sing with her, waving a duster and dancing about.

> *'It's a lovely day today and whatever you've got to do*
> *It's a lovely day to do it in that's true.*
> *So if you've got something that must be done*

And it can only be done by one
Then there's nothing else to say
Except it's a lovely day for saying.
It's a lovely day.'

But now he wasn't allowed *to go to Grandma's. He wasn't even* allowed *to see his dad and his dad was the best one in all the world. They used to have boxing matches together and he was also a very good tickler and made him laugh. When he came through the door each night he would shout 'where's my boy?' and then he would run and his dad would pick him up and swing him round. He liked that. His dad used to let him build his Scalextric all over the living room and his train set and they would have races together with cars and trains and it was great.*

Thomas didn't think that his new dad liked him very much cos when his mum said 'Harry, this is Thomas' he said 'bit on the plump side isn't he, you'll have to put him on a diet,' then later he'd said, 'just look at those curls, he's not a three year old, Jean, it's time he grew up!'

Then when he spilled his Ribena on the carpet Harry jumped up and shouted, 'Oh you stupid little monster. Don't you know drinks aren't allowed *in the lounge?' Toys weren't* allowed *in there either and neither were crayons and felt-tips.*

But then when he was drawing at the kitchen table one of the felt-tips leaked and his mum went mad and said, 'Thomas you know you're not allowed *to draw at the kitchen table.'*

So then he thought it best not to draw anywhere. On Saturday he'd been running through the hall when he knocked over a china ornament of a man on a horse. It broke all over the floor and Harry shouted again, then he told him to sit on the naughty step. At first he didn't know where it was, but then Harry grabbed him by the arm and dragged him to the bottom of the stairs and made him sit there.

'Right, now don't move until I say so, it's time you learned some manners young man. Jean, it's time Thomas learned some discipline. OK?'

His mum said, 'All right Harry, it's his grandma she spoiled him.'

Then his mum and Harry watched a film about the war and he just kept on sitting there, on the bottom step. After a while he got bored and started searching in his trouser pocket. He had some bus tickets, a toffee, a conker, three pieces of Lego and a tiny pencil. He played with the Lego for a bit but you can't do much with only three pieces. The toffee was a bit furry so he couldn't eat it. He rubbed his hands on the carpet, it was very soft. He looked at the wallpaper, it was beautiful, he rubbed it with the palm of his hand, it felt like silk. It had a lovely feathery pattern on it, a bit like a Jack Frost pattern on the windows in winter. He picked up the pencil and began to outline each feather. It was a long film, so he sat there for a long time. Then Harry came, and that's when he smacked him, very hard on his bare legs. Apparently drawing on wallpaper was definitely not allowed.

*

Thomas seems to be settling in at last and has formed a good relationship with Wayne, though he is still very reluctant to write or draw. I wish I could get to the bottom of it. Grandma still haunts the pavement outside school and I try to talk to her whenever I am out there. I don't know if I'm allowed to give her progress reports on Thomas but it seems to help her.

Weddings

''Miss, you know I'm supposed to be Maid Marian?' says Sally.
'Yes.'

'Well, do you think me and Robin should get married?'

'No way,' says Robbie vehemently.

'Well, it says in that legend book that I'm your wife and I don't see as I can be if we never get married.'

I'm unsure about this so I parry with those famous words, 'I'll give it some thought.'

The next day Sally is waiting for my answer. I *have* given it some thought and the wedding idea certainly fits the religious education syllabus. This could be a novel way of covering the Christian ceremonies bit. Peter agrees to come and talk to the children about weddings in the Church of England and one of the television programmes that we watch in school has some footage about weddings and we go ahead.

The children design wedding invitations and this is a very popular activity because they're allowed to write with gold and silver felt tip pens. The girls ask if they can design wedding dresses and then they all learn about speech writing.

'So can we have an actual wedding, Miss, and pretend the church bit and have a reception?' asks Lisa. Cos I could be a bridesmaid, I was once and I've got the dress and everything.'

Upon enquiry in the staffroom and in church I discover that lots of people have access to bridesmaid dresses, wedding hats, and posh ties so I garner these together and we plan to have Robin Hood's wedding on Friday. Sally's mum offers to bake a three tier wedding cake, the children bring in an assortment of goodies to share and I bring my camera. The day begins.

We've been doing division and multiplication in maths so there are lots of questions about sharing cakes and jellies and such like. We read Judith Kerr's lovely book 'When Willie went to the wedding' then we write our own wedding stories. In the afternoon it's time to dress up and get ready for Maid Marian's wedding. Robbie insists that we call it that because he is, 'just going to stand there and let it happen.'

Peter talks about the importance of keeping promises and about what a bride and groom are pledging in the marriage service.

'For instance if I were to perform the service for Marian and Robin this is what I would say, and they would take it in turns to repeat the words after me. Miss Johnson has written the words on the blackboard so that we can all see.

'I Robin Hood, take you, Marian to be my wife, to have and to hold from this day forward, for better or for worse, for richer, for poorer, in sickness and in health, to love and to cherish; from this day forward until death do us part.'

'So what do all these promises mean, do you think?' I ask 'What does it mean when it says "for better, for worse?"'

There's a long silence. Then Lisa asks, 'Is it about when you're in a mood and some days you might be in a better mood and sometimes in a worse one?'

'It could be. What else could it mean?'

Wayne looks very serious and starts threading his fingers and making his hands into a boat shape. After a moment or two he ventures, 'Is it like when you've got no money and that and sometimes you might have a bit more?'

'Yes, marriage is often like that. There are bad times and good times, but in the marriage service you are promising to stick together and help one another through difficult times,' says Peter.

I am amazed by how seriously these seven-year-olds are approaching these concepts and my heart aches for those who know very well, how painful family life can be. As if reading my thoughts Robbie suddenly asks, 'What about if they stop loving and they just hate each other?'

Peter glances over at me and his eyes brim with compassion.

'Sometimes that happens. Men and women are not perfect; often we do bad things, sometimes we find it very hard to love. That's why many people choose to make their promises in church, and ask God to *help* them to get things right.'

Lisa looks disinterested and is busy plaiting her hair but says, 'I don't reckon I'll never do it cos you have to kiss and stuff and I can't stand boys. I might try it for a bit, about five hours, but then I think I'll have had enough.'

Peter tries to stifle a laugh and holds his fist in front of his mouth. His eyes twinkle wickedly.

Linda is busy picking at a scab on her knee and says, 'My mum says it's best to look for a man who's kind, it doesn't matter whether they're 'andsome or not because men get bald and stuff when they're old anyway.'

Sally giggles, 'Mmm I'd like a kind one, kinda rich.' The children laugh.

'Well, let's talk about that bit,' says Peter getting in quickly. 'What does it mean when it says, "for richer or poorer"?'

'That's easy,' says Thomas, 'you have to love them whether they've got a lot of money or a little. Actually, people are sometimes worse when they've got a lot. I *know* that.'

'His new dad's rich, isn't he Thomas?' says Robbie. 'He's even got two three piece suites *and* a colour telly.'

Thomas nods miserably then says, 'But he's not my dad, just because he's with my mum.'

Peter smiles encouragingly at Thomas and says, 'You're quite right Thomas, well done. So what does it mean when people promise to love "in sickness and in health"?'

Wayne is keen to answer this one. 'Well, it's like if you've been out and had a skinful and you get back and you're sick...right?'

'Right,' says Peter obediently, wondering where this is leading.

'Well, you've still got to love 'em even if they look 'orrible!'

'Y...es,' says Peter slowly, 'we all get times when we are not well.'

'I've had chicken pox,' says Lisa, 'and you get these really itchy spots even in your pants, *down below.*' She whispers the last two words, her moon-face resembling a Les Dawson mother-in-law character.

'Yes well...'

'And *I* got mumps and your 'ead all swells up around your neck and you can 'ardly swallow.' That one was Steven. There is now a forest of hands, all their owners anxious to talk about personal experiences with *dread* diseases. I decide to intervene.

'So we all know what it feels like to be ill and when two people are married they can look after one another and that's good. Now there's just one more bit to look at, it says to "love and to cherish", I wonder what that means?'

'My grandma says she's perished when it's really cold,' comments Lisa.

'No, love, it's not *perish* it's *cherish*, can you guess what that means?'

Steven says, 'It sounds a bit like polish, my mum loves her

furniture and she's allus polishing it. Is it a bit like that?'

Peter grins, 'Do you know Steven, it is a bit, we polish furniture because we want to look after it. When we cherish a person we look after them and do *everything* we can to keep them well and happy.'

'So now we come to the wedding bit for Robin Hood and Maid Marian. They're not *really* going to be married so we're not going to ask them to say their vows. But in a minute I'm going to ask you to put on your wedding clothes and then Marian and Friar Tuck will walk to the front and stand by Reverend Peter, the bridesmaid's will stand behind them, Robin will stand here with Little John and then we'll all read the wedding vows from the blackboard. Are you ready?'

'Yes!'

'Set...go!'

There is a noisy flurry as the girls don fancy hats, frilly dresses and the boys, Lincoln green, and then we're ready. I click on the tape machine and the glorious notes of the 'March of The Queen of Sheba' burst into the shabby, crowded classroom. Raymond makes a wonderful Friar Tuck because he can hide in the hood, but from what we can see of his face he is taking this very seriously. Sally's face has a maturity beyond her years, she is radiant, carrying a beautiful bouquet of sweetpeas and walking with all the grace of a queen. They stand before Peter, resplendent in his robes and Sally gives Robbie a heartbreaking smile, he sniffs and wipes his nose on his sleeve.

Peter says, 'In church I would say a few words about why we're here so I'll do that now.' And projecting his rich, chocolate voice he says, 'We are gathered here today to join this man and this woman in Holy Matrimony. So, let us say the vows together.'

And suddenly all these wonderful seven year olds are reading the ancient words that have joined so many men and women through the ages and it feels good that they perhaps understand just a little of their meaning at this early stage of their lives.

'And now,' says Peter, 'it's time for the photographs and then, *the party!*'

The children really enjoy posing for pictures, but of course, the reception has their full attention. Mrs Lambing and Don have come to help serve the food and drink and each child is given a paper plate containing sandwiches, sausages on sticks, one cube of cheese and an iced bun. The furniture is set out in the traditional horseshoe shape with the bride and the groom sitting at the head. After we have all consumed our jelly and fruit Steven stands and bangs the table with his spoon.

'As the best man, Little John, I wish to say a few words about the bride and groom. I have known Robin Hood for many years now and he's a really good mate. No-one can shoot a bow and arrow better and he deserves Marian cos he's always rescuing her and when you're married you have got to keep the girl and can't give her back. So I give you a toast, raise your glasses to the bride and groom.'

'To the bride and groom!' we chorus. Well they've obviously remembered all that we practiced. Now it's Robbie's turn to bang the table. This should be good.

'First I want to thank you for coming to our wedding and the Reverend Peter for doing it. Marian works really good in the forest and sweeps up and everything so I think we'll be all right. Actually, I don't think I'll really get married cos the thought of it gives me a headache, but Marian looks nice and so do the bridesmaids. I raise a toast, to the bride and bridesmaids.' We raise our glasses, most of which are now empty. After this Robin Hood and Maid Marian cut the bottom layer of the wedding cake, (chocolate sponge) and the party begins in earnest.

Peter catches my eye and wiggles his eyebrows, then leans over the table and says, 'Well *we* should be all right now we've seen how it's done.'

'Reverend Peter, can I ask you something?' says Robbie.

'Course you can, go ahead.'

'Do you fancy, Miss?' Peter locks his eyes on mine.

'I think she's very beautiful,' he whispers.

There are great chortles of mirth and a lot of whispering and giggling.

'Then you'll have to ask her for a date. Do you know what one of them is?'

Peter smiles, 'I'm not sure.'

'Well, a date is when you go out and eat steak and chips and wine and when you get to the pudding you talk about love.'

'Oh right,' says Peter, his face creased with laughter, 'I'll have to give it a try.'

Linda looks at me worriedly, 'It's all right, all this love stuff but I know what I think. I think that girls should stay single, boys just need someone to clean up.'

*

It's the beginning of July and John and Meg are to be married on Saturday. Rebecca is home from hospital and their household is getting back to normal. We all meet at the bridal shop for our final fittings and then go to Schofield's for coffee and vanilla slices. Rebecca asks for chocolate cake and manages to get most of it down her front, on her face and in her hair. Alison says; 'Oh Rebecca, just look at the state of you. How on earth did you manage that?'

Rebecca grins through chocolate, 'Oh it was easy! I just kept licking.' Then she glances down at her dress and adds, 'I haven't growed my boobies yet, like grandma, or they would have caught it.'

Of course we all laugh, it seems like a miracle that she is well again and back to her bright, mischievous self and I'm sure I'm not the only one sending up arrow prayers of thanks.

At the rehearsal on Friday night the church is a hive of activity. Eileen and Sue, the church flower ladies, have organised a creative and efficient team and works of art containing cream roses, forget-me-nots and pink peonies adorn every windowsill and there's a stunning arrangement at the front of the church. The kitchen is filled with paper plates, plastic glasses and foil containers and tables are already laid out in the church hall.

Reverend Tom greets us, his eyes twinkling with affection, 'Now then, isn't this a great occasion.' He grasps Meg's hands and gazes into her eyes, 'I can't tell you how happy this makes me, lass, John has got himself a jewel of a woman and after enduring so much heartache and pain he truly deserves you. And you have been to hell and back, I know, and nothing pleases me more than the flowering of hope.' Meg's eyes glisten with tears. John arriving at that moment looks worried, but his fiancée's radiant smile soon reassures him.

'Do you mind,' says Tom gently, 'if we just say a prayer before we begin? I know that Irene and Keith are very much in both your minds at this time and I think it would be good to acknowledge that before the rehearsal. What do you think?'

'Absolutely,' says John, taking Meg's hands in his own and then adds, 'is that all right with you?' She smiles her agreement.

So, Tom prays.

'Oh Lord, we just want to thank you for the loving relationships that these two special people have enjoyed in the past. We remember with joy the many lovely times that each has shared, Meg with Keith and Irene with John. They are not forgotten, or pushed aside, but very much alive in all our hearts today. Now, after all the pain and suffering of loss, those remaining have found new joy in one another. We ask you to bless them both, Lord, as they build a new life together. Amen.'

For a moment, as we stand there in the quiet of the church, it feels as if there are bright spirits all around us. I have a lump in my throat but also feel a great peace. Peter holds my hand tightly and as I gaze up at him I rejoice in his bright, open face and the love evident in his eyes.

A stream of light beams through the east window, creating a kaleidoscope of colour around the three figures standing at the front, Meg, John and Reverend Tom bound together by something much bigger than mere human love.

Reverend Tom leads us through the marriage service, slowly and meaningfully and then we all go back John's house where he will be spending the last night before his marriage. It's the first time I've been and there is evidence of Irene everywhere, her cross-stitch pictures in frames on the walls, handmade cushions and silver-framed photographs. I feel embarrassed when John catches me looking at one of them. He picks it up and smiles, it shows two very young people propped against a drystone wall and laughing.

'Are you worried that I'll fill Meg's house with memorabilia?'

'Sorry John, no, I think I know you much better than that, it's just such a beautiful photograph.'

'Yes, this one will be going with me because Meg has one just like it, of her and Keith leaning against a drystone wall. In fact they were probably taken not many miles apart, so we shall put them together, Meg's already decided where. I thought it was a lovely thing that Tom did for us tonight, because I'm sure we were both thinking about those we've loved before.'

'I agree and John, I'm so pleased, Meg couldn't have found a better person to share her life.' I lean forward then and kiss his cheek.

*

The church is full to bursting. All the usual congregation has come to wish them well and there are friends from every other part of their lives. All the Cubs have been invited and they are resplendent in their uniforms, their parents have been invited too so there is quite a contingent from the estate. Elvis is in full regalia and even has a pink carnation in his buttonhole and Jennie is looking lovely in a pretty, flowered dress. Rebecca is an ebullient bridesmaid and is stunning in her candy-striped frock with a circlet of fresh flowers in her curly hair and carrying a matching posy. She loves the way that her skirt bounces and flares with its many petticoats and can't resist a twirl when she arrives at the front of the church. Matthew looks adorable in a turquoise silk suit.

When Tom asks if anyone knows of any lawful impediment why these two people should not be joined in matrimony, Matthew of course chooses that moment to shout, 'Granddad!' thus causing a ripple of laughter.

As Tom leads them through their vows I catch sight of Robbie listening intently and nodding as Meg and John make their promises. Wayne too is nodding sagely and I wonder what they are thinking

Peter reads about the meaning of love from 1 Corinthians 13 and leads the prayers and then Tom pronounces.

'Well, it's all over bar the shouting...that comes later!' More laughter. 'You may kiss the bride.'

And John does. There is loud applause, the marriage has begun.

End of Term

Thomas's mum is continually late picking him up from school. She works in a smart office with his new dad and often has to work extra hours. Today she was very late and Miss Johnson stayed with him and read a story. Thomas thought that everyone had left him. He never saw his real dad or grandma any more and now his mum wasn't coming back either. He began to cry and then he couldn't stop and his chest hurt and great big sobs made his body all shaky and his face was hot. Then suddenly mum was there saying, 'Oh I'm so sorry to be late, we've been very busy at work and I just couldn't get away!'

Miss said, 'I do understand, Mrs Robson, but you really must make arrangements for someone else to pick up Thomas in an emergency. It's not good for him to be so upset.'

His mum grabbed his hand and walked very fast across the playground.

'Snotty Cow,' she said.

Thomas watched Jackanory and Blue Peter and tried not to make any mess. Then Jeremy came home, he burst through the door all excited, shouting, 'I've got it! We're on our way, sweetie pie. I've got the job. You are now speaking to the assistant chief executive of the Sonarel Bank.' He took hold of Thomas' mum and they danced round and round the living room. Thomas watched with huge blue eyes and open mouth.

'Oh I can't believe it,' said Mum, 'we're going to live in America.' She began to jump up and down singing, 'New York! New York!'

Thomas put his thumb in his mouth and lay back on the cushions. He couldn't understand what was happening.

'Oh Thomas,' shrieked his mum catching sight of his frightened face, 'we're going to live in America!'

Jeremy cleared his throat, 'Er, I don't think it's any place to take a child.'

His mum went very still and stared at him. 'What do you mean?'

'Well we'll be living in a high rise apartment in New York; we'll be working long hours and entertaining rich clients. It just won't work, my darling.'

'It won't work?'

'No, how can it? Can you see that idiot husband of yours agreeing

to let his 'beloved son' live across the Atlantic?'

His mum sat down abruptly, her face very white.

'I have to...leave Thomas?'

'But of course. It'll be a completely fresh start, a new beginning. No baggage, just the two of us.'

'Just the two of us?'

'Oh Yes, just imagine the fun we're going to have.' Jeremy opened a bottle of wine and poured two glasses, they drank some and started to kiss. Then they went upstairs. Thomas watched Magic Roundabout and the News with unseeing eyes.

When they came back downstairs his mum went into the hall and spent a long time on the telephone.

Later there was a loud knocking on the door. When Thomas's mum opened it, Dad burst in sweeping past her. He bent down and placed a kiss on Thomas' forehead whispering, *'Come on laddo let's get you out of this place.'* He swept him up into his arms. His mum gave him some bags with his clothes in and tried to kiss Thomas, he turned away and hid has face in Dad's coat. She said, *'Thomas'* in a sort of cracked, broken voice, but he didn't look at her.

His dad lifted him up and held him close and they went out into the darkness.

*

Stuart Robson brings his son into school the next day and after some discussion with Miss Heaton it is agreed that he can stay at Becklefield. Apparently, his grandma had rented a house in the area so she could look after him if the needs arose. Thankfully that's going to happen as mum and step-dad are going to America. I'm so glad; he's a lovely little boy with a great deal of potential.

There is much to do at the end of term. All the plastic toys have to be washed and disinfected, displays taken down and hundreds of staples removed from display boards. Children's names have to be removed from plastic trays and books sorted, exercise books sent on to new teachers and a million other jobs. And in the midst of all this, teaching and learning continues.

'Don't take the castle down, Miss, will you, because me and Wayne's just made a portcullis.'

'Yes and I've been making a tapestry with Sally and it's nearly done,' says Linda, 'me mum started us off; it's in thread and everything.'

'That sounds really exciting, when are you bringing it into school?'

Linda puts her forefinger on her cheek and her head on one side as she thinks about it, 'Possibly about Friday.'

I laugh, 'Well don't forget we break up on the following Tuesday.'

'Our play was really good, wasn't it Miss,' says Steven. 'I liked the tournament best when Thomas and I were jousting.'

'Aye it's a pity we can't carry on after the holidays. I liked being Robin Hood. What topic will be doing then, Miss?'

'I'm not sure at the moment, Robbie. It will be probably be based on geography. Perhaps we'll learn all about another country.' Well at least they seem to have got used to the idea of having me as their teacher for another year. I'm really looking forward to just carrying on where I left off, instead of having to spend several weeks just getting to know the children. At the end of the day, when the children have gone home I sit at my desk and look through my assessments file.

Stuart, that little wide boy who could supply anything, via the tip, was really motoring ahead before his accident but what on earth will happen to him now? Still no sign of him leaving hospital. Julie's reading age had gone up considerably between September and the new year when she was taken away. I find myself staring into the corner where she used to sit. I see again her bending forward and cradling that beautiful pink azalea. I see her sitting, eyes closed, fingers stroking the delph-blue hyacinths and wallowing in their scent. My eyes blur with tears and my heart crumples.

'Oh Julie, where are you, love?'

I continue studying the reading ages. Jamie made no headway at all. How could he? I remember him, crumpled at his table, grey-faced and empty-eyed, pursued by his nightmares. I have a sudden flashback of Jamie, Julie and Linda at the pantomime, white-faced and terrified, huddled together and I curse myself for not realising sooner the truth of their plight. I bang my fist on the desk and the tears pour down my cheeks.

All those poor kids. The door opens and Karen rushes towards me,

'What's wrong, pet, what on earth has happened?' I rest my head in my hands and push the assessment file towards her. My finger pointing at Jamie' results.

'Oh come on, pet. What can you expect after what he's been through? The rest of them have moved on in leaps and bounds. Just look at Lisa, she's moved on two years three months, that's phenomenal.'

'I know, but what if Jamie *never* recovers? We don't even know where he is, or Julie for that matter. We'll probably never know what happens to them. Their lives have been ruined and we could have stopped it.'

'Now YOU stop it, right now. Look at Linda; she's another who's made amazing progress. She suffered too, didn't she?'

'Yes, but we think it was only the once with Linda.'

'But we don't know, do we, pet?'

'No, there's so much we don't know.'

'And perhaps it's as well, how could we ever sleep at night if we did.'

*

The last day of term arrives and I find myself with arms full of gifts. Bless all those parents who have so little themselves but still go to the trouble of writing a thank you card or sending a small keepsake, it means so much. There are chocolates, notebooks, ornaments, ornate pens and flowers. The card from Linda's mum brings a lump to my throat, 'You are the light of my life,' she has written. Linda presents me with a beautifully wrapped crystal heart and then pulls a posy of marigolds from her pocket.

'Here you are, Miss. These are really from Julie because she once said she'd bring you some in the summer, just in case you were thinking of getting married or owt. Don't know where she is or anythink but she wouldn't have forgotten you.'

'Thank you Linda, that is so thoughtful.'

'Aye well, they were one of her favourites. Have a nice holiday, Miss. I'm glad I'm going to be in your class again.'

'I'm glad, too Linda. Have a lovely holiday.'

Steven is the last to leave the cloakroom. He holds out a brown paper bag.

''Ere, this is for you, Miss. I didn't want anyone else to see.' I open it and find a tape cassette. I look at him questioningly. 'It's me Miss, playing me violin. It's a bit of Mozart from Suzuki Book One. I thought you'd like it.'

'Oh bless you, Steven. I shall love it. Thank you very much.'

'Bye Miss, see you at Cub Camp.'

Cub Camp

Just one week to finish clearing my classroom and sorting the paperwork, one week to rest and then we're taking the Cubs to a pack holiday centre near Whitby. Meg and John have been fundraising and have managed to get enough money together to buy sleeping bags and blankets. Hopefully, most of the boys will bring their own wet weather gear but we have spare boots and kagools.

We travel to the centre in an old army wagon borrowed from another scout group. All the gear is packed into the wooden seating store and off we go. The boys sing;

'Oh you'll never get to heaven in an army car
cos an army car, won't go that far,'

and sing,

'On top of spaghetti all covered in cheese
I lost my poor meatball when somebody sneezed'

In fact we sing all the way there. I look around at all those bright faces, even Raymond has let his hood fall back onto his shoulders and his eyes are lit with hilarity as he sings all this nonsense. Peter notices too and whispers, 'I think we're onto a winner at last, if we can make sure there's no cucumber in his sandwiches, we might even get some unblemished laughter.' I grin my reply.

We arrive at the scout camp, purpose built with three log cabins set in deep woodland, two miles from the coast. Civilisation seems a long way off. We give the boys half an hour to unpack then divide them into two teams for a 'wide' game.

John gives the introduction. 'Now, the boys on my left are the Martians and you people on the right are the Aliens. Raymond chortles excitedly and Peter gives me a thumbs up signal. 'During the game you will be given piece of paper with coded instructions and small pieces of Airfix kit in an envelope. Other bits of Airfix are hidden in the forest. The pieces for Martians are in green envelopes, the Aliens are in blue. Your clues will help you to find them. Do you understand?'

'Yes Akela!' they shout excitedly. Raymond and Wayne are jumping up and down and Steven is mimicking a Dalek, 'Exterminate! Exterminate!'

Meg continues the instructions. 'When you have found five envelopes, go to the picnic table where you had lunch and start to put them together to make a spaceship. The winning team will be the first one to be standing in line, at alert, and ready, with their spaceship. Do you all understand?'

'What do we do if we find the wrong colour envelope?' asks Robbie laughing. 'Can we exterminate it?'

'If you're following your clues properly you won't.'

'Yes but if we do?'

'Trust me Robbie, you won't. Now remember, you have to keep coming back to Akela if you are Martians, and to me, Baloo, if you are Aliens to collect all your clues. Right, are you ready?'

'Yes, Baloo!'

'Right, when Akela blows his whistle you can go. Ready, set...' John blows the whistle and twelve excited little lads huddle to decipher their code and then thunder off into the woodland. We patrol the area, alert for any problems.

I remind some of the boys not to open the envelopes, so that all the pieces will be kept safe, but otherwise see little of them. They are all too excited not to be on task and are cooperating well. I watch Steven and Wayne cogitating as they read their clues, Steven chewing the inside of his cheek, Wayne pointing at the paper, the other hand on his face stroking his chin like a wise old man. Raymond comes running out of the trees, face flushed, hair tousled and joins them, reading the clue again and confidently adding his own suggestions. Robbie, boisterous as ever, careers about and is pulled to one side by Christopher and they mull over their clue quietly and then gallop off to delve in the woodland. By three o'clock both spaceships are complete and twelve little boys are standing alert at their tables. John and Peter inspect the spaceships carefully, getting rather glued up in the process, and pronounce them well made and ready for action. But, because Martians have lost a nose cone, the Aliens are declared the winners.

After juice and biscuits, Peter and John take the boys off for a game of football and Meg and I prepare a chicken stew for the evening meal.

'Have you heard the news about Mike?' asks Meg as she chops the onions.

I grimace, 'No, what's he done now?'

'Apparently he's been given a formal warning and moved to another area. I don't think we'll be seeing any more of him.' I feel immense relief.

'So will Beckinfield be getting another community constable, then?'

'No, that's the sad part; they say that there just isn't any more money to fund them which is a shame.'

'Absolutely, in spite of many things that he did, it was so good to have a police presence in school on occasions and I'm sure that having him about on the estate inhibited crime.'

'Well, it's like a lot of things, they just begin to bear fruit and politicians interfere and you're back to square one.'

'Well, having a community constable didn't deter Mr Coggs and his vile cronies. I wonder where they are now. I wish I knew that he was locked up and unable to hurt any more children.' When I think of the harm he's done my stomach plummets and although my head doesn't believe in the death penalty my heart craves it. 'I hate that man so much!'

'I'm with you there,' declares Meg as she decapitates a swede with unnecessary violence and makes short work of a carrot.

The boys return all hot and sweaty and devour large slabs of cake and more fruit juice. We leave the stew to simmer and Meg and I lead a games session that involves lots of running about and tagging and sometimes ball throwing. Then John sets a task for each group to design and make some useful article using tree branches, a penknife and string. Prizes will be presented at the campfire and Peter and John demonstrate *all* the necessary skills to avid listeners. We prepare the room for the evening banquet for which we've brought candelabras, tablecloths and fancy table napkins and chatter happily.

*

The boys are awestruck by the candles and the beautifully set out room and behave accordingly with exaggerated table manners and 'posh' accents.

'And now,' pronounces John at the end of the meal, 'it's time for the presentation of the award for the best designed object.' They wait, saucer-eyed.

'Here we have a beautifully designed shoe rack by the *Alien* group, as you can see there is ample room for four and a half pairs of shoes,' we all laugh, 'the other one and a half boys obviously have to keep their shoes elsewhere! However, it is strong and sturdy and perfectly adequate for its use.' He demonstrates by pulling it about and it does indeed stand firm.

'On the other hand we have a mug rack designed by the *Martian* group.' He stands it up and it falls to one side, being rather top heavy. 'Which when you hang the mugs upon it,' he demonstrates and it crashes to the ground, complete with tin mugs. 'It is not fit for purpose.' There is a lot of laughter, pushing and joshing and the *Aliens* are presented with their prize, a giant bar of chocolate.

The campfire is probably the most exciting time for the boys and when John and Peter arrive complete with guitars they are really impressed. We learn even more silly songs, usually about worms and ants or rabbits being chased by guns. We sing in silly voices pretending to be brownies and ask endless riddles and tell jokes. Earlier in the evening we were plagued by midges which the lads insisted were mosquitoes and consequently they featured a lot. Robbie is first as usual.

'Akela, what is a mosquito's favourite sport?'

'I don't know.'

'Skin diving!' shout a chorus of laughing voices. Wayne is next.

'What do you get if you cross the Lone Ranger with an insect?'

'I know, I know, I know,' giggles Raymond, 'it's a masked-quito!'

'Well done Raymond,' we shout, cock-a-hoop that he is at last joining in with the others.

'Akela?' asks Robbie, suddenly timid, 'how do you go to the toilet without a light?'

'Same way as you do with one,' laughs Peter, handing him a torch.

'Oh just look at that beautiful full moon,' says Meg. We all gaze in wonder at the navy blue bowl above us, spattered with stars, until Wayne asks, 'When is the moon not hungry?' All the boys shake their heads until Raymond shouts, 'When it's a full one!' and then falls about hysterically.

Later, when we've sung some more, had a story and handed round the cocoa I wish that I had a camera to capture these moments with all these flushed, happy, sparkling boys, many who have known such fear and pain in their short, little lives. We still have four days to go what more miracles can simple pleasures bring?'

Schools Out

At last Peter and I have some time to ourselves and set off to visit his family and then on to Robin Hood's Bay where we have booked an idyllic-looking cottage for two whole weeks. The welcome from Harry and Hannah is as warm as ever though we are both rather shocked at how frail Ada is becoming. She struggles from her chair by the Aga and wraps her arms around Peter's waist and snuggles her head into his chest.

'Hello little bird,' he says, planting a kiss in her flossy hair, 'how are you?' He bends down to look into her eyes,

'Oh just hanging on, you know, just hanging on. What about you, have you grown any more?'

'Not upwards anyway, now come on we want to know *all* the gossip?'

'Well, Fred Diggle's got one of them there electric motorcade things-'

'Scooter, Mother, I keep telling you it's an electric scooter,' interrupts Hannah.

'Aye well, whatever. He's lethal in it, he bombs down the road like there's no tomorrow. It's disgusting at his age.'

'She's jealous,' pipes up Harry, 'she wants one herself.'

'You bet I do, it beats sitting here talking to the dogs, any road. I'd be off to Silverstone me, I allus wanted to be a racing driver.'

After lunch Harry gives Peter a wink and says, 'Do you fancy taking the hairy hounds off for a walk, lad, we could go via Black-Moss.'

'Yes, that sounds really good, Dad,' says Peter winking back knowing that they're set for several hours at the dog friendly, Blacksmith's Arms.

Hannah and I retire to the garden while Ada goes off for her afternoon snooze. Blowsy red oriental poppies blaze in clumps on the slope down to the orchard gate, a row of sunflowers glow against the garage wall whilst fat, rich spikes of blue delphiniums make a bold statement underplanted with purple and yellow pansies, lilies and leopard's bane. I walk down the narrow paths my skirt brushing against plump mounds of lavender releasing scent and gaze at sumptuous yellow roses tumbling over trellises entwined with purple clematis.

'Oh Hannah, I thought the garden was beautiful in the spring but this is...well, magnificent. I love it.'

'Well I have to say it's my pride and joy. I love nothing better than whiling away the hours out here. Now, let's sit down and you can bring me up to date on Beckinfield. Peter mentioned something about a methane explosion...'

So I tell her all about Stuart and Trevor and the horror of it all, about the new Cub Pack and about Raymond and Thomas and all their idiosyncrasies. She listens as she always does, with her head on one side and her bright eyes concerned and intent and I think again of how much I've grown to love this woman and how lucky I am to have her in my life. She tells me about how much she enjoyed Meg and John's wedding and I recount the tale of our class wedding and we laugh together.

'And what about you, my love, are you feeling better now? It's been a right old school year for you, hasn't it?'

'It has, but a very special one, they really are fantastic children. I find it hard to understand sometimes how so much good can come from such awful beginnings.'

'Well that's the thing about love isn't it, you spread it around and it grows, like this lot...' She indicates her flowering oasis. 'Who would believe that such beauty could come from a few little brown seeds? Oh, that reminds me, I must tell you, there's a new little girl that Brad and Jennie are fostering, she's a right little gardener, Jennie says she just can't get her out of it, she's forever planting stuff, always asking to visit the plant nursery.'

I leap to me feet, 'It's her! It must be! Oh please can we go there, now!'

'Who love? Who are you talking about?'

'It's Julie, that little girl who was in my class. She's been taken away from her family and fostered. She's mad about plants. Oh please can we go, now?'

Hannah struggles to her feet, I pull her up and then, laughing, we hold one another until she's steady.

'Don't get your hopes up too much, love, you're clutching at straws here, there are thousands of children in care.'

'I know, but it's possible, everything is possible.'

'You're an eternal optimist, I'll give you that. Hang on; I'll just go give Jennie a ring.'

We walk arm in arm down the village street. Wild foxgloves and marigolds have embedded themselves by the walls and under hedges smattering the pinging green with pink and gold. Roses tumble over drystone walls in vibrant shades and a glorious golden robinia tree is the centrepiece of the vicarage garden. Brad and Jennie live in a small stone cottage overlooking the village green with its ancient sweet chestnut tree. Their roof is of red pantiles, typical of the area, and blue tits can be seen flying to and from the eves and a blackbird flutes liquid notes from the apple tree. The front of the cottage is swathed in Albertine roses thick with bloom and the bright green leaves of Agapanthus stand in pots their flowers cool-blue globes against the massed marigolds and nasturtiums.

Jennie emerges through a side gate, plump and smiling with curly brown hair shot through with silver. Hannah performs the introductions and Jennie clasps my hands firmly, and then whispers, 'If it is your Julie, it will be better if you don't use that name; she is adamant that she's called Mary. This little girl has said nothing at all about her past. It seems that she wants to obliterate everything that's gone before and we're playing along with that until she's ready to talk.'

We round the corner of the cottage and I see her and my stomach lurches because it's *not* my Julie. This child is tall and rather chubby with gleaming brown hair tied up in bunches with blue ribbons, there is no trace of squinty eyes and when she smiles there's a definite dimple in her right cheek. She's smiling now, a huge, glorious, welcoming smile.

'Miss! Oh Miss! Hewwo! I'm still wearning to be a gardener. I'll pick some marigolds, they can be fow you. Come and see my wittle garden.' She grabs my hand and starts to run across the grass. I follow on feet that fly.

*

I can't wait to tell Peter my news. Hannah peers out of the window and sees them walking down the lane and I'm off like a rabbit from its run racing to meet them. I fling my arms around Peter's waist and he holds me like a big bear.

'I've found them, I've found them, I can't believe it!'

He holds me at arm's length, 'What? Who?'

'Julie and Jamie.'

'Really, where? How?'

'Here. They're Brad and Jennie's new foster children. Isn't it wonderful, I can't think of a nicer place for them to be and they look really different. Oh Peter, I'm so pleased.'

'Oh that's amazing news, what a God-incidence! Is that an answer to prayer or what?' He places his hands upon my shoulders and bends down to kiss me gently on the lips.

'Oh I do love you, Kathy Johnson.' Then he ruffles my hair and says, 'Come on then, race you home,' and we run, like two teenagers on the last day of school, arriving back at the cottage flushed, untidy and out of breath.

'Come on you lot, the meal's all ready, it's pork and peaches, that'll set you up good and proper and wait 'til you see what's for afters. Harry can you get the glasses for me, I've forgotten to get them out.'

'Where are they?'

'On the whatnot.'

'Which whatnot?'

'Grr! The one by the thingummy,' she says impatiently.

Gran shakes her head; her hair like white candy floss seems to float around her.

'Sometimes you need a translator in this house, I'm not kidding, they've lived together that long they've evolved their own language.'

When we're all served and enjoying this gorgeous fodder Hannah makes an announcement.

'Well, I rang Brad and Jennie when I got back and they're all coming to lunch tomorrow. They'll be over for one o'clock, then after lunch I thought we could play some games, have a bit of a sing-song and a general how-do-you-do, what do you think?'

'I think you've been plotting, planning and scheming as you always do you old rascal but a bit of a how-do-you-do sounds great to me,' says Harry.

'And to me. Thank you so much.'

'It's a pleasure, my love,' Hannah whispers, before popping a kiss on my forehead.

*

We had a big surprise yesterday, I was planting out the asters I've grown from seeds when a lady came through the gate, the sun was in my eyes and I couldn't see properwy at first. Jamie was in the corner playing with marbles. He's always in the corner, especially when there are people around, he still gets scared. We both do sometimes.

Anyway the lady came forward and it were our Miss from school. She was the first one to give me flowers. She brought me an azalea once and it was so fat and bushy with all those pink buds, I loved it. That's when things started to get better; it was just Christmas that was very, very bad.

Anyway, it was lovely when she came in the garden and I showed her my very own bit. I have raked it a lot and the soil is very fine and what I like is to just sit and get great big handfuls and rub it between my hands. It makes them very mucky, but the soil goes fine as sand and that's what I plant my seeds in. I get pocket money now from Auntie Jennie, I don't have to do owt for it she just gives me it and then we walk to the post office. There's only one shop but it sells everything in the world. Well, not tellies or freezers or chairs but all the little stuff what we need in life. Anyway I buy packets of seeds there, just one each week. I've grown marigolds, petunias, clarkia, pansies, poppies and night scented stock, that's under my bedroom window cos auntie says it smells extra lovely at night. I've planted some under Jamie's window too because he needs a lot of nice smelling things and it might stop him curling up like a hedgehog and hiding in cupboards. Sometimes I buy Maltesers or Chocolate Buttons and we share them together. Jamie doesn't buy anything; he doesn't know what he needs yet. I wish I could buy something to stop him wetting the bed cos it makes the sores on his legs worse and it'll look silly when he's a man if he keeps wetting his wife. But he says he won't have one, but he might get a dog...one day.

Auntie says that we're going to see Miss and her boyfriend tomorrow and that I can make her a fwower posy and put it in a doily to make it look pretty. I'm going to take her marigowds to remind her about weddings. I'd wove to be a bwidesmaid. One day.

*

That night I stand in my moonlit bedroom and reflect on how different my life has become over the last few months and of all the people who have been part of it, each one like a shaft of sunlight blazing through. I have focused so much on the bad times in the past, but now I'm moving forward in confidence, grasping each positive thread and weaving them all in.

The sheets on my bed are cool and Arctic white and through the open window I can hear the tumble of water as it leaps and gurgles in the river below. I breathe the scents of new mown grass and lavender and feel at peace. Beside me is a jug of marigolds.

Thank you for buying and reading

A Fistful

of

Marigolds

We hope you enjoyed it.

If so,
We would be honored if you leave a review on the
Facebook page

https://www.facebook.com/fistfulofmarigolds

Or at

www.amazon.co.uk

Fishcake Publications

Have you written a book?
Would you like to see it on this screen?

Fishcake Publications is looking for writers to publish onto eBooks right now.
We are especially keen to hear from new, unpublished writers who are trying to get their work out there.
If you've taken the time to write it, it deserves to be read.
For further information, visit our website at
www.fishcakepublications.com

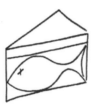

The Independent Publisher with the Author in Mind

**Other Books are available from Fishcake Publications
See our website and our webstore at
www.fishcakepublications.com
for information on where to find them.**

**The following pages are some of latest releases
available as paperback and eBook...**

Murgatroyd's Christmas Club by Steven Bailey

Skint! Broke! Pennyless! Hard-up!
Willie Arkenthwaite, an ignorant, rude and terribly crude dyehouse worker
in Murgatroyd's Mill is feeling a bit poor after his Christmas break and
returns to work a troubled man. Not only does he have to put with the nagging
mother-in-law at home, but he has a family (and pigeons) to look after and he
fears next Christmas will be just as tight.
Until one day this normally docile and inarticulate man does something
he's never done before – he has an idea. Willie wants to start a Christmas
savings club.
So what does he know about running a club? Nothing.
What does he know about setting up a committee? Nothing.
Has he ever saved before? Definitely not.
Luckily his best friend, Arthur Baxter, who has visions of grandeur, is a
little bit more organised and is able to help Willie along and before he knows
it, he's the Treasurer.
What does he know about being a Treasurer? Nothing.
So how on earth will this man be able to collect his wits about him and
make next Christmas better for everyone? Well, with the help of his
whimsical friends and workmates, a kind and generous mill boss and a
eclectic local Yorkshire village community (and not forgetting his tolerant
wife), he might just be able to pull it off although you can guarantee, where
Willie's concerned, there's bound to be some mishaps on the way.

Nonagenarians by Frank & Jessie Littlewood

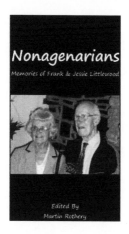

My Grandparents, Frank and Jessie Littlewood, were always
an inspiration to me. As you will see, Frank and Jessie (and some
of their friends) had a way of capturing the spirit of their
generation in a charming prose that can't help but raise a smile.
This is but a small selection of pieces put together from works
that were actually found written down, not only demonstrating
the true entertainers they were, but also showing how much they
loved one another and their many friends.

Free to download at Smashwords.com